Moon Glamour

Samhain Shifters, Volume 1

Aimee Easterling

Published by Wetknee Books, 2020.

MOON GLAMOUR

Large print edition. November 12, 2020.

ISBN: 978-1-7353183-8-7

Written by Aimee Easterling.

Chapter 1

I showed up at the job interview with salt packets in my pocket and a grease stain on my right knee. Scanning the museum steps for a woman with a rose pinned to her blouse, I came up empty. *Good.* I was early enough to nip inside and wash up.

Unfortunately, I didn't quite make it to the ladies' room before words a human wouldn't have been able to decipher percolated into my lupine-enhanced ears.

"I'd hit that."

"Mm mm, me too!"

I turned just a little so the glass case I was walking past reflected the faces of the girls behind me. They were around my sister's age. Sixteen, fueled by raging hormones, and currently proving that men weren't the only ones who objectified members of the opposite sex.

"I mean look at that *butt*."

"Can't. Too busy with his *biceps*."

They sounded like they wanted to lick the object of their admiration. And even though I was on a deadline, I swiveled all the way around so I could follow their gaze.

No wonder the girls were excited. The man leaning forward to peer at the brush strokes of a Renoir measured over six feet of rope-thick muscles. His shoulders were so wide I wouldn't have been surprised if he had to turn sideways to fit through doorways.

He also moved with the grace of a werewolf. I flared my nostrils then coughed as my throat flooded with the wildness that only another shifter could exude.

My fists clenched. Coming face to face with a male werewolf was bad news, even if both of us were currently playing human. If I was lucky, this stranger would acknowledge my right to pass through a territory I didn't rightfully belong in after he saw the rectangle of paper in my pocket. But my get-out-of-jail-free card wasn't likely to hold up to many testings.

Better to fly under the radar....

Leave. Now, my inner wolf whispered. Our heart rate sped up. Human feet were pointing toward the exit with wolf speed hurrying their motion when the girls hissed out disappointment.

"Ew. What a face."

"I'd still do him...if he tied a bag over his head."

Their words descended into giggles and curiosity stole my momentum. This time, I turned all the way around to see what grotesqueness had squashed their juvenile infatuation.

I was too late to catch more than a glimpse before the man angled his body away from us. I'd seen enough, however, to note the relevant facts.

Skin a middling brown that I suspected spoke to a Latin American heritage. Bushy eyebrows. A nose that had been broken and reset without medical attention. Scars, multiple scars.

But that wasn't the reason the girls had reacted so negatively. The charisma of an alpha—and he *was* an alpha; I could smell that on him—should have attracted human women as thoroughly as it intrigued female werewolves. Only, something was off about this particular specimen. Something related to the scars streaking through what might otherwise have been appealing features.

I cocked my head, trying to understand the girls' repulsion. This was an unexpected twist in the well-worn path of werewolf charisma. The strength of an alpha, apparently, could either attract or repel.

And as I squinted, I could almost see what had turned the teenagers off about Mr. Broad Shoulders. More than the scars. Something deeper....

Then I blinked and my face blindness kicked back in.

Well, my face blindness plus his evasive action. Instead of responding with the rage I would have expected, the alpha turned even further so we couldn't catch even a glimpse of his supposed ugliness. Maybe that's why I broke my cardinal rule—never draw attention to yourself.

"The perfect male body," I mused

aloud. "A rare art form. I believe I saw two specimens on the fourth floor, third gallery over from the stairs."

I had, too. Last Sunday when I wandered through the Roman marbles. The men in question, let me be clear, were statues. Naked, though. Muscular. Perfectly featured. The girls would appreciate their chiseled physiques.

I was tempted to add a zinger. Something about the cold harshness that often went hand in hand with perfect masculine beauty. The warmth of spirit that was far more important outside museums.

But these girls were kids. Too young to know better.

So I let their giggling recede without

dousing them in the cold water of adult wisdom. Then I turned my own feet toward the exit, already thinking ahead to my upcoming meeting...

...and ran into a wall of hot, living werewolf chest.

***

"That was sweet, chica." His voice was deep, gravelly. Before I could retreat, he took a single step sideways. Now he was toeing the line of appropriate personal space while also opening my path to the exit in case I needed to make a run for it.

And I *did* need to make a run for it. I'd wasted my hand-washing minute educating teenagers. If I didn't leave now, I'd be late to the job interview. Which, in turn, was likely to cascade into making me late visiting my sister. Late preventing family drama from a stepfather who reveled in inserting monkey wrenches into my well-laid plans.

But my feet merely swiveled so I could stare upward into the face of the stranger. He was taller than I'd thought from a distance. Maybe because he'd been striving at the time not to scare gawking teenagers? Had his shoulders been hunched earlier? His spine bent?

Whatever the reason, I was the scared one now. Or maybe *scared* wasn't the proper word. Some heavy emotion I couldn't quite fathom struck me in the chest area. It was abruptly hard to breathe.

"But unnecessary," the man continued, and for a moment I forgot what he was talking about. "I know what I look like."

Oh, right. Human standards of external beauty.

"We have such a strange obsession with facial symmetry," I observed, forgetting for a moment that I was talking to a male werewolf who could likely freeze me in my steps and force me to do his bidding. "Presumably based on the evolutionary advantage of choosing the healthiest mate. Infections during childhood...."

"These scars didn't come from

childhood infection." His head cocked and he smiled, a slow display of sharp teeth that—I'll admit—sent a tremor down my spine. I flinched and his mouth snapped shut, lips going instantly flat.

"I apologize." His eyes struck the floor, as if *he* was afraid of *me*.

I wanted to stay and tell him he had nothing to apologize for. Because even as the tremor flew through me, I understood it for what it was—instinct no more rational than that which had disgusted the teenagers.

But I was late. My sister needed the cash this job would offer.

And this man was a werewolf. Dangerous to me in ways I couldn't afford to handle. A threat to my tenuous understanding with another alpha, one that allowed me to see my sister while she lived far too close to the heart of his territory.

"Keep your chin up," I told the stranger as I spun toward the open door. And why, when distance eased the tightness in my chest, was I left feeling heavy rather than light?

Chapter 2

I recognized my employer-to-be by the rose on her blouse, just like she'd promised. Unfortunately, my handshake wasn't up to her standards.

"What *have* you been handling, Athena?" Marina offered in lieu of a greeting. Pulling a dainty, lace-edged handkerchief out of her handbag, she dabbed at her fingers as if we were attending a tea party rather than hovering at the edge of a roiling crowd.

Oops. I'd lost track of the grease

from my sister's fries in the midst of my werewolf sighting. Still, I wasn't the only one who'd overshot societal cues.

"I replied to your message telling you this was a bad time," I countered, "but your account had been closed."

As I spoke, my gaze dropped to my cell phone. Harper's weekly visiting window started in two hours. And while I'd been willing to be late to this job interview, if I didn't show up in a timely manner at my sister's boarding school afterwards, her dad would sneak in and "visit" instead....

"Do you have somewhere more important to be?" Marina's voice was steely as she interrupted my contemplation of time and sisterhood.

I was losing whatever chance at this job I'd once had. Still, I answered honestly: "Yes."

The word hovered between us for several seconds before Marina shrugged. "Then we might as well get on with it."

As she spoke, she gestured up at the pseudo-Grecian facade of the museum behind us. Surely she didn't mean...? I'd assumed this was a neutral public meeting place, not....

"I don't steal from museums." That clinched it. Marina was too much trouble and....

The check materialized out of nowhere. One moment my right hand was empty. The next moment, my fingers clasped a crisp rectangle of paper sporting more zeroes than I'd ever seen in my life.

I blinked. Magic? Or just my tired eyes playing tricks on me?

Either way, my free hand slipped into my pocket, feeling for the salt packet that went with my sister's weekly fast-food treat. Harper liked her fries double-salted. She'd be sad if I lost her favorite seasoning.

Still, I found myself worrying one corner until it frayed open. Then I let a few grains dribble out onto the pavement. Better safe than sorry, right?

And...Marina took a single step backwards. Coincidence, I was sure of it. After all, magic didn't exist. Well, I mean, magic other than *werewolves.*

Shaking off my uncertainty, I stuck to the tangible. "What's this?" I asked, waving the check between us.

"The first half of your payment." Marina leaned in closer than was really appropriate by human personal-space standards. She didn't, however, step over the line of salt.

Still, she was close enough now for me to count her pores...or would have been if she'd had any. Instead, her skin was so smooth she might as well have been airbrushed. My nose, though, didn't report any metallic hint of makeup.

Instead, Marina reeked of rose petals. Not from the flower at her lapel, which appeared to be a simple, unscented supermarket offering. But if the rose aroma emanated from a perfume, why couldn't I distinguish an oil or alcohol base?

Curious. Still, it was the zeroes that prevented me from taking my own step backward, that prevented me from hightailing it away to my more important engagement. "What do you want in exchange for another check like this one?" I asked finally.

Marina's lips didn't turn upward, but I scented her smugness. I'd been the first to cave. She'd won that round.

"Follow me," she promised, "and you'll find out."

***

She turned away, heading up the stairs without waiting to see if I'd follow. I flared my nostrils...and something furry and wild impinged.

Wolf. Not from Marina. Not from the ugly-fascinating man I'd met inside either. Instead, the scent rose from behind me, the variety of sub-odors suggesting multiple shifters were present amid the chattering humans entering and exiting the museum.

I itched to swivel and hunt for trouble. Instead, I kept my eyes on Marina. After all, she was the more immediate danger and I'd run out of salt.

"The museum doesn't own the object in question," she called back, heels clicking as she strode up the marble steps away from my stationary figure. "It's on loan from a rich, white dude. And isn't your sister's tuition due soon?"

Her knowledge of my preferred thieving target—complete with slang that sounded awkward on her lips—plus my familial weakness was chilling. More dangerous than shifters because it was more focused. I dismissed the wolf scent and jogged to catch up with my maybe-boss.

"I chose you for this job because of your special abilities," Marina continued as we wended our way past the recommended donation box. She ignored it while I dropped in a ten-dollar bill.

"Special abilities?"

"Furry abilities."

My feet froze on the stairs I'd been following her up. My nostrils flared again.

But there was no wolf scent about Marina. No fur. No wildness. She shouldn't have known what I was capable of.

Still, I disabused her of that notion. "I don't use any furry abilities on the job."

Not since making a deal with the local alpha, that is. Not since Harper had begun attending boarding school so close to the heart of Rowan McCallister's pack.

"What, never? Well, no matter." Marina's voice was perfectly museum appropriate as she dismissed my refusal to use my wolf and returned to the object of her fixation. "Before the current owner took possession, the item had been in my family for generations." She paused long enough to spear me with eyes bluer than the sky. "I'm not asking you to steal, Athena. I'm asking you to return what's already been stolen."

Again, she turned away, this time leading me into a well-lit gallery. We didn't speak as she made a beeline for a glass case housing a metal bracer.

It was a decorative arm cuff, meant to be worn at the wrist. Three inches wide, made of pounded gold and silver.

The pattern portrayed a running wolf.

I shivered. A wolf...like me? Like the scent outside? Like the world I did my best to steer clear of?

Ignoring what felt like more than a coincidence, I focused on the sign beside the artifact. What I saw there made me shake my head in disappointment.

Of course Marina had lied. All of my employers lied sooner or later.

"This is over a thousand years old," I noted, raising my eyebrows. "It was dug up last month somewhere in England. You couldn't even bother dreaming up a story that matches the obvious facts?"

"It was stolen from a cemetery," Marina countered. "A cemetery in which my ancestors were buried. Do your research. Then cash the check if you want the job."

The sweetness of rose petals wafted past my nose as Marina turned away. She was leaving. Walking out on me.

Which was good. Safe. And yet....

All those zeroes prompted me to call after her. "What's to prevent me from cashing the check then disappearing?"

At first, I thought she wasn't going to answer. But Marina spun in a cloud of flowing fabric when she reached the arch separating the gallery from the hallway. Her hair looked more blue than black there. Her teeth appeared werewolf sharp.

"I wouldn't recommend it. Harper would regret anything that prevented me from receiving my prize."

Her use of my sister's name chilled me down to my marrow. My breathing didn't slow until the scent of rose petals had faded to nothing on my tongue.

Chapter 3

I hadn't decided whether to take the job, but I did my due diligence anyway. Wasted precious minutes pretending I was interested in other items in the gallery beyond the bracer so the security footage wouldn't look so suspicious if this turned into a crime scene.

In fact, I was snapping photos of a Viking's helmet when the scent of wolf once again surrounded me. This time it was closer. Stronger.

I whirled...then relaxed as I took in the same ugly shifter I'd met downstairs.

"You're very recognizable," I greeted him.

I'd intended my words as a compliment, my face blindness meaning that I often couldn't pick out people I'd met only once or twice or, let's be honest, seven times before. The stranger didn't take it that way.

Instead, he sidestepped as if once again opening up my escape routes. His face tilted away from me so I could only see the unscarred left side, and his voice was apologetic as he rumbled, "I didn't intend to startle you."

"I wasn't startled," I began. But my nostrils flared and proved me wrong.

Because I didn't smell wolf now. I smelled *wolves,* plural. More than this single gentleman in a shifter's malleable skin.

I spun, not quite comfortable with having the wolf I knew at my back but even less comfortable with being unable to see the wolves I didn't know. There were two of them. Both just as tall as the one behind me but totally different in every other way.

The one on the left was white, tattooed, and decked out in studded leather. A biker or biker wannabe. Definitely someone I'd cross the street to avoid passing alone at night.

The one on the right was black, clad in a suit that could only be tailored. As perfectly featured as Marina while still exuding virile masculinity. This one the chatty girls would have eaten up.

Still, something about his eyes suggested his gentility lay only skin deep. His wolf scent was overwhelming. The hairs on my arms stood on end.

So I was relieved that the biker spoke instead of the more dangerous man beside him. "What's this?" he asked, his eyes skimming over me then rising to meet those of Mr. Ugly. "Tank?"

Tank's answer confirmed his identity. "She was here when I arrived."

For half a second, I relaxed into the already familiar rumble. Scary men stood between me and escape, but Tank wasn't scary. He was gentle beneath his massive exterior. The kind of man who forced himself into a small box for the sake of skittish teenagers.

And...his breath was hot against the back of my neck.

Maybe not so safe then. Tank had advanced without me realizing, sandwiching me between himself and the other two shifters. His earlier sidestep now seemed less like politeness and more like baiting a trap.

A trap I'd blithely strolled into.

I swallowed. Tried to talk my way out of a situation that would have been better avoided. "Look, I have a card in my pocket from the local alpha. He's granted me permission to hunt here...."

"Does it look," Scary Suit asked, "like

we're interested in cards?"

Adrenaline consumed me. Fight or flight. Unfortunately, neither was an option at the present moment. Not when I was penned in by shifters, each of whom boasted double my mass....

Reprieve came from an unexpected source.

"Are these men bothering you?"

The interruption materialized into an ordinary human. Museum security guard, if his uniform was any indication. Late fifties, chubby around the middle. Nowhere near a match for one of these werewolves, let alone all three.

Still, his official tone and the gun at his hip promised an authority that might just get me out of this mess. I grasped at the offered straw.

"Yes," I answered, tarring all three shifters with the same brush. Never mind that Tank had been nothing but polite to me. I tried to ignore the bitter disappointment wafting from him as I continued, "They were."

The guard lifted his walkie talkie, calling in backup. I slid out from between the trio of werewolves, expecting at any moment for a hand to slam down and pin me in place.

None did. No one stopped me. Not even the security guard as I slid past him, through the arch, and hurried down the hall.

Four museum patrons seemed to be too much for one security guard to juggle.

So I didn't have to use my backup plan—begging for a bathroom break then using the ladies' room as a staging ground for escape. Didn't have to give my name and address. Just slid away from the werewolves and the human authority figure like the burglar I was.

I did spare a hint of remorse for Tank. But I doubted he'd be held up for long. After all, security cameras would confirm the men had only spoken to me, never even touched me. The guard would have no reason not to let them go.

Which meant I needed to make tracks before they were released. My tennis shoes snicked softly against marble as I plummeted back down the main stairwell. The front entrance drew me, but a stray thought changed my trajectory. *Scent trails.* It had been a year since my last run-in with other werewolves, so I'd almost forgotten. I needed to think less like a human and more like a wolf.

I wasted thirty seconds spinning through the smelliest aisle of the gift shop. Scented candles were always good for overwhelming a lupine nose....

They certainly overwhelmed mine. I had to pinch my nostrils shut to prevent a sneezing fit as I inserted myself amid a large family exiting the museum. These humans were just as stinky as the space I'd rushed out of. Fruity shampoos and manly body washes. Helpfully foul. I let their forward momentum carry me two blocks in the wrong direction before peeling away to strike off on my own.

That should be enough. Or at least I hoped so. The benefit of a city—there were too many people passing to make it easy to trace a single scent trail for very long. Add on my evasions and any followers wouldn't stand a chance....

Not that I really expected the trio to track me. They had no reason to. Yes, I was a female shifter, but I didn't possess the enticing chocolate aroma of a pack princess. My half-blood heritage had provided that much for me at least.

And my wending route away from the museum had turned up an unexpected side benefit. A fleeting glance down an alley caught golden arches on the next street over. *Perfect.* I'd pick up another salt packet for Harper before heading back to my car....

I was halfway down the alley when the scent of wolves rose around me. Halfway down the alley when something leapt from above, landing on my back and bearing me all the way to the ground.

Chapter 4

I rolled while jabbing upward with my elbow. Someone grunted. The grasp on my shoulders relaxed just enough for me to wriggle free.

But whoever had leapt off the dumpster wasn't my only problem. Out of the corner of my eye, I caught a glimpse of wolf fur that matched a warning growl. Meanwhile, the thud of boots on pavement promised there was at least one undamaged two-legger backing up the one swearing on the ground.

Then the wolf was upon me. Gray around her muzzle suggested age but her speed rivaled that of a teenager. She snarled. Snapped. Stopped one inch away from my skin.

I was on my hands and knees, lacking the leeway I needed to scramble upright. The wolf was providing just enough breathing room so I could scuttle backward. An attempt to herd me toward whoever I'd elbowed? I couldn't see him, but I could hear him griping, the expletives loud and harsh.

He was the least of my worries, however. So was the wolf.

Or, at least, *that* wolf. My own inner animal was alert, angry, powerful. She grabbed at our shared body, doing her best to burst free of my skin and clothing....

And her instincts were good. Going wolf *would* help us escape this ambush. But I couldn't afford to break the rules I'd agreed to when I accepted the card in my pocket.

Not now, I told my inner animal. *Harper needs us.*

Without the card, we couldn't see our sister. Would be forced to leave this territory and beg for refuge in another. Or, more likely than begging, would be forced to make a deal we didn't want to make.

My inner wolf was driven less by rational thought and more by instinct. But even she could see the juice wasn't worth the squeeze in this instance. So she subsided...for a moment, until the gray-muzzled wolf snapped another offensive, her teeth cutting through my shirt and into my wrist.

Great. Just great. Wolves always responded so very rationally to physical challenges.

Not.

The growl rising out of my throat didn't originate with my human self. Fur slid from the skin of my arms....

And I held my breath while scrabbling atop the greasy pavement in search of a weapon. If I could prove to my wolf that I wasn't defenseless, she'd subside. Or at least I very much hoped so.

Fingertips turned up a bottle cap. A

flattened piece of metal. Nothing useful. Couldn't the litterbugs be bothered to drop a knife now and then?

"We're not going to hurt you." The voice twenty feet down the alley was deep, soothing. *Tank.* Why did his presence here make me so disappointed?

Still, he'd been helpful. My inner wolf stopped struggling the instant he spoke.

"Of course you aren't," I agreed just as my hand closed around something sharp and pointy. *Aha.* The litterbugs had come through after all.

The shard of glass bit into my palm as I fisted the found weapon. It wasn't much. But perhaps enough to get out of this mess without going lupine? I hoped so.

"That's why you're attacking me in an alley," I continued.

As I spoke, I eyed my route to safety. I'd only have one go at it. Slash the wolf's face with the shard of glass, kick out a second time at whoever had initially leapt on top of me, then vault on top of the dumpster and from there onto the fire escape.

The shaky vertical staircase would keep the wolf from following until she could shift back to human form. I hoped Tank's distance and my original attacker's nosebleed would similarly slow them down.

It was a sliver of a chance, but I'd take it. Better than going full-on fur and wearing out my welcome in the city closest to Harper's boarding school.

So I feinted with my empty fist. The wolf swerved just the way I knew she would. The glass shard bit into my skin as I teased it out behind my fingers...

...then something hard and unyielding clenched around my middle. Air wheezed out of me. My chin sunk to my chest as I peered down at tattooed arms cocooning me in an unaffectionate bear hug.

Meanwhile, the wolf shimmered upward into a woman. Mid-forties if I had to guess, with short black hair and dark eyes that seemed to see all the way through to my inner wolf.

Her voice was dry as she turned our

recent fracas into a minor misunderstanding. "We just want to talk to you," she said, walking away to pick up a pile of clothes from behind a dumpster.

Not only clothes. There was a gun there and a shoulder holster. The woman donned the combination so easily I had a sinking suspicion her profession lay in the field of law enforcement.

My past, it appeared, had caught up to me. Now I wished this had been a mere mugging carried out by an unruly group of male werewolves.

"I have the right to remain silent," I informed her, trying and failing to hold my body away from the biker's.

Because, of course, that's who had disarmed me in the most embarrassing way possible. Or I assumed so, despite the way faces tended to slither out of my memory. How many other tattooed, leather-clad werewolves were likely to be hanging out downtown?

Meanwhile, Nose Bleed rose from the ground and materialized into a beautiful black man. The third member of the museum trio, presumably. *Great. Just great.*

This time, there was no security guard to rush to my aid. Instead, I bristled, not wanting my assailants to realize how intimidated I was by the odds, the gun, the *badge* the woman surely had in her pocket.

But one of them noticed. "Will you feel safer in a public space?" Tank murmured.

One minute ago, he'd been on the far side of the alley. Now he was so close his heat warmed me. Tank's huge hand closed around my right wrist, then he jerked his chin upwards. "Ryder. I've got her. You can let her go."

The tattooed biker snorted. The arm around my waist tightened. "Finders keepers."

Tank growled and I got the absurd impression I was being fought over like a bag of Halloween candy. The air sharpened with alpha electricity and....

"Boys." To my surprise, the woman's voice stopped the incipient battle before it had time to begin.

Ryder released me. Tank took a step

away from his former opponent, even though his hand remained clenched around my wrist.

Without meaning to, I'd followed Tank sideways. Now, I peered up at him, trying to assess his intentions. But his face twisted sideways. Not away from Ryder's glare. Away from my searching glance.

"Should we take this somewhere more public?" he rumbled, repeating his question. The uncomfortable bend to his neck seemed habitual. A way to see me out of the corner of his eyes, I guessed, while hiding most of his own face from view.

His grip, meanwhile, was firm but not painful. I expected my wolf to rise onto the offensive. Instead, she sighed and settled down for a nap.

Traitor. Perhaps that's why my voice came out curter than I intended.

"I'd feel safer if strange men stopped manhandling me."

Tank's lips—what I could see of them—thinned. But he didn't release me.

And the woman, once again, took the lead. "I have handcuffs if you'd prefer. Can't risk you doing another runner."

Her eyes promised she was far scarier than Scary Suit. Whatever she wanted to talk about mattered to her as much as bringing fries to my kid sister mattered to me.

I swallowed down aggression and accepted reality. The faster I gave them what they wanted, the sooner I could see

Harper. "A public space it is."

Chapter 5

We walked right past the McDonald's. Breezed into a fancy coffee shop where the only item on the menu that appeared to contain sugar was a so-called Super Shake...which came out green and seedy and thoroughly disgusting.

I gave up on my beverage after one abortive sip then focused on Tank's fingers curled into my fingers. Because he'd slid his grip down to my hand while walking. As if we were lovers instead of captor and prisoner. Even now, our intertwined fingers rested atop his knee.

I hated how aware I was of the flesh separated from mine by one thin layer of fabric. Of the muscles that slid beneath our joined hands when he leaned over to draw the sugar dispenser down the table toward us. Of the care he took tearing open sweetener packets to pour into my drink.

Thus doctored, the Super Shake became marginally less vile. The fact Tank had noticed my disgust and made an effort to remedy it was far more enticing.

There's nothing sexy about being kidnapped, I reminded myself. Inside my belly, my wolf hummed disagreement. I clenched my free fist and told her to shut up.

Thief, I reminded myself. *Cop. Bad combination.*

"What do you want from me?" I asked Lupe—the woman, who appeared to be these werewolves' leader. We'd faked amiability while ordering, sharing introductions. First names only. I wasn't about to offer identifying information to someone who had attacked me in an alley and Lupe didn't press the point.

Now she smiled before answering, as if she was well aware of my lupine half's interest in Tank's proximity. "The Samhain Shifters...."

Shifter I understood. But—"Saw Win what?"

"Samhain," she said again, slower. "Sunset on October thirty-first through dawn on November first. The Samhain Shifters are a group assembled to keep the most dangerous night of the year safe."

She eyed me, as if expecting instant understanding. And, yes, I could do calendars. "Halloween," I confirmed. Then, unable to help myself, I glanced around at the guys who were silent observers of our conversation. "They don't even need costumes. Posh Spice. Biker Spice...."

"And Ugly Spice," Ryder—the tattooed biker—suggested when I couldn't come up with a name for Tank.

"No, he's...."

Lupe spoke over me before I could finish my sentence, which was probably a good thing since my rebuttal had originated with my wolf and involved the word *tasty*. "This isn't about trick-or-treating," the gun-wielding female told me. "Nodes pop up every Samhain. I'm one of several full-timers who assemble a crew of shifters two weeks beforehand, a member of which is drawn from each nearby pack. Our teams start out as strangers and train just long enough to learn to work together without building pack bonds. After that, we keep the fae in check for a very critical fourteen hours."

I was nodding along until the last sentence, at which point my eyebrows scrunched up in confusion. "Are we talking bad fairies? Like Tinkerbell with an attitude?"

Lupe shook her head, humorless. "More like full-size beings who use glamour to look and smell like your best friend then suck your pack bonds dry to fuel their depredations. Thus the short-term team."

Pack bonds. My lips thinned. Based on a bad encounter as an orphaned teenager, I'd sworn off werewolf packs for the duration. I certainly had none of those much-touted connections with other shifters to be threatened by these hypothetical fae.

Still, I'd heard how pack bonds worked. They let mates communicate telepathically, allowed an alpha to locate his underlings, and could even be used to heal. So I guessed I could see why others found them so important. Regardless, they had nothing to do with me.

"Our job is essential," Tank told me, sliding into the silence my lack of a response offered. "I met a pack once that was impacted by fae. They self-destructed. Tore each other to pieces. The few survivors told me they didn't even understand what was happening for months after it started. They just thought long-time friends had turned into enemies. Family members became backstabbers...."

His cheek twitched. The pack, I could tell, had mattered to him. Despite myself, my left hand slid toward the one Tank had rested on the table. I stilled the pesky appendage before it could get me into more trouble than I was already in.

Lupe watched us both with eyes dark and hard. "The fae aren't always that overt," she told me. "The subtle ones are even more dangerous."

"Dangerous enough to make it kosher to assault total strangers in an alley?"

In response, Lupe speared me with one of those alpha glares that made underlings shiver. "If we think she can help us, then yes."

And maybe I *could* help. Marina's rose-petal aroma shimmered in my memory. The way the check with all those zeroes had materialized out of thin air. "I might have met one." I hadn't realized I was speaking aloud until Lupe's eyes narrowed. "A fae," I elaborated. "Fairy. What's the singular?"

"No." Lupe shook her head. "The fae —singular and plural the same—only cross over during Samhain, although they can talk mortals into working for them in the interim. We call those helpers Sleepers. They're trouble, but not our primary objective."

A burst of masculine annoyance: "Why are you telling her this?"

I blinked. I'd forgotten there were others present beyond me, Tank, and Lupe. Now, I shifted my focus to the black man I'd punched in the nose. Butch, his friends had called him, even though the name made no sense for someone blessed with such sublime physical perfection. Despite my punching, his face remained as perfectly formed as before.

"We tracked Athena down," he continued, voice melodious and at the same time grating, "because Ryder had a hunch she was a Sleeper. She could be taking notes right now, intending to sell us out to the enemy."

"She's not a Sleeper," Lupe interrupted, still pinning me with her gaze. "Are you?"

About that, at least, I could be honest. "This has nothing to do with me. I appreciate the invitation and the drink...."

Ryder snickered. He was the one

who'd recommended my so-called treat. He'd known, I now realized, that the Super Shake was full of kale and chia seeds.

My punishment for leaving him to the mercy of the security guard? Or a jab at Tank, who'd been ready to fight Ryder over who got the pleasure of restraining me?

Whatever the reason, Ryder's childish means of retaliation reminded me to glance at my watch. And what I saw there made me wince.

I needed to leave *now* if I wasn't going to be late to Harper's visiting hour. Sixty minutes once a week. Stepfather aside, I wasn't willing to lose one second of sisterly bonding time.

"As delightful as it was to meet you all..." I rose, or tried to. Unfortunately, Tank's loose grip on my fingers had hardened to the implacability of iron.

"This is important," he told me. "My alpha's territory is close to the node this year. We have pack mates there overcoming trauma. Pups who require a safe haven. Their fate depends upon Samhain Shifters. On *us*."

His point made, he turned his attention to Lupe. "Athena has skills our team lacks."

I hadn't thought Lupe was particularly impressed with me, but she nodded. "Our team could use another woman. Consider it your civic duty to participate. Like voting, but more intense."

To save the world...or at least werewolf pack bonds? For half a second, I wavered. This was what I'd dreamed about when I was a child. Making a difference, not stealing baubles from and for the rich.

But childish dreams didn't last into adulthood. "Does the job pay?" I countered, knowing it didn't.

Only, I was wrong. "I could squeeze a little out of the budget," Lupe answered, ignoring the way Butch's face wrinkled in disgust that, on him, still appeared beautiful.

So that's what this was? Another job interview? "I'm flattered," I answered, "but no."

After all, squeezing out a little cash didn't sound like it was going to pay Harper's tuition. I couldn't afford to save the world pro bono.

Saying no to werewolves, however, was a bad idea. I tensed, fully expecting the kid gloves to come off.

Instead, Tank released me. Released me...and pressed a business card into my hand before I could retreat.

"At least think about it." His words and his touch made it hard to swallow.

Still, I managed to rise this time without being yanked backwards. Took a step away from the table...and no one leapt up to stop me.

"Sure, I'll think about it," I said, knowing every one of these werewolves could smell my lie.

Chapter 6

Which is how I came to be both saltless and late when I rolled into the parking lot of Harper's prestigious boarding school. Despite the buzz of voices elsewhere, the picnic table where my sister and I always sat was empty. But the scent of middle-aged alcoholic led away from the table along with an aroma that matched my sister's shampoo.

Unlike most werewolves, I couldn't latch onto signature aromas. A symptom of my face blindness, likely. But the combination of coconuts and stale beer could be none other than Harper and Nick.

So I followed. Hurried down a tree-lined path, out onto a grassy field...and stopped in my tracks.

There in front of me was the slender and ever-moving body I'd recognize from a mile away as Harper. But she didn't have her feet on the ground. Instead, she was perched atop a horse that could likely trace its ancestors back to the Mayflower. Its neck curved proudly, hair shining in the sun.

In contrast, my sister appeared a little shaky—after all, this was only her third term at Highlands and most of her time had been spent catching up on the academic and the social. Still, she was riding. My kid sister, an equestrian. My cheeks stretched into a doting grin.

Harper was too engrossed in her task to notice me, but Nick did from atop his own horse. His greeting was fake-jovial. "Athena. Pull up a horse."

So...my stepfather wanted something. Still, I strode forward. "You look good, Harper," I called to my sister.

She swiveled in her saddle to wave, loosening the reins as she did so. Which is the moment disaster struck.

I can't say whether all horses dislike all werewolves. But I can say that equines have never been my biggest fans. Still, I was too far away for the horse to have been bothered by me. Or at least so I thought.

Still, a haze of floral scent curved around me in a mini-tornado. Fallen leaves whipped up, flashing across the field in a burst of color. One second later, Harper's purebred steed flinched as the wind and debris slapped it in the face.

Maybe it was the leaves or my own wolf scent flowing in the same direction. Whatever the reason, Harper's horse rolled its eyes to show white as it flared its nostrils. Then, whipping its head sideways, it yanked the reins out of Harper's hands and broke into a run.

***

This was Marina's fault. I somehow knew it. A warning? A test?

Didn't matter. My sister was atop a runaway horse.

Her feet had already slid out of the stirrups. She grabbed for reins that whipped wildly. Came up with only a few tendrils of mane.

And Nick, who was a mere six feet away, watched impassively. Or maybe he was frozen with terror. I'd give him the benefit of the doubt.

I wasn't frozen. Even though my inner wolf might have been what set the horse off in the first place, I sprinted toward disaster rather than away from it. Hooves slammed down inches from my sneakers, but I dove beneath the massive beast's neck anyway. Slid my fingers between polished leather and hot flesh...

...And hung on as the horse reared up, up, up. I didn't weigh enough to keep the beast from rearing. Didn't know enough about horses to prompt it to stop.

Harper shrieked. I could just imagine her sliding straight off the animal's back. If she hit the ground wrong, she'd break her spine....

And there was nothing I could do about it. Not until the ride reversed.

Down, down, down. My feet struck just before the horse's did. Then Harper was beside me, alive, whole, grabbing the reins and jerking them sideways to force the horse to walk rather than rear again.

"I think maybe your wolf spooked her," she told me, voice solid even though her chin quivered. "I'll walk her away from you...."

Suiting actions to words, she turned the massive beast and started it moving. Pride and fear made my eyes stay on her even as I strode in the opposite direction. Harper was nothing like her father. She felt fear and pushed through it. He felt fear and...

"I need a drink," Nick muttered, right on cue.

Then hooves were pounding toward us from the direction of the barn. A student slid down off her mount. "Whoa. That looked gnarly. Are you okay?"

"Hey, Clara," Harper greeted her roommate, her voice staying carefully level. *Right, I should have realized that was Clara, with her long, tangled hair and unfashionable glasses. I likely would have if my sister hadn't been pressed up against a horse whose eyes were still rolling back in its head.*

But the thousand-pound animal only twitched an ear and kept walking as Harper relayed what had happened in an animal-friendly sing-song. "I'm fine. Athena is fine. Cloudburst is fine. We're all just fine."

The skin on the horse's neck stopped twitching midway through Harper's litany. Or maybe the animal was responding to the fact that I'd finally found a downwind spot where it could neither see nor smell me.

I took advantage of the momentary respite to spin in a circle, hunting Marina. But there was no one else present. And the floral scent, now that my sister was no longer at risk, materialized into late-blooming honeysuckle on the fencepost beside me. No rose petals. No magic. Just a plant out of sync with the season.

Plus, Lupe had told me there would be no fae present until Samhain. I shook away the conspiracy theory, focusing on my sister instead.

Harper's cheeks were still red, but her breathing had slowed. Meanwhile, now that his daughter had everything under control, Nick finally decided it was safe enough to approach. Sliding off his horse, he held his mount's reins so laxly I half expected it to bolt also. "Here, take the horses back to their stalls, why don't you?"

Clara snatched his reins one moment before they dropped. And even though Nick had been the one to screw up, Harper was the one whose shoulders slumped.

"Sorry, Dad. I know you were looking forward to riding."

"No problem, kiddo." He shrugged, but his tone of voice didn't entirely let her off the hook. He never did. An anxious child was far more eager to please him. "Run along and meet us back at your picnic table."

I wanted to punch the guy, but Nick was Harper's father and legal guardian. The line I walked here was a precarious one.

A fact that Nick knew as well as I did. His gaze turned to me and his eyes went predatory. "I have something to discuss with Athena."

Chapter 7

The girls and horses walked one way. Nick and I ambled in the other. Silence hovered over us until Nick reached out to finger the hem of my leather jacket.

Despite myself, I jerked away. This jacket was the only item of my mother's I still owned. The rest of her possessions had long since been sold...by Nick, without my permission. This one thing I intended to keep.

"How much do you need?" I

demanded. Only after I spoke did I realize my voice had been louder than intended. If Harper possessed wolf ears, she would have heard my opening.

Harper didn't possess wolf ears, though. All she had was a no-good, alcoholic father and me.

Speaking of the no-good alcoholic, Nick stepped closer until his fumes enveloped me. "A couple of grand. No, make that ten grand."

"Ten thousand dollars?" Breath hiccuped out of me.

"You make it sound like a few bucks is an imposition. We're family, aren't we? Family gives and family takes."

I knew better, but I let myself get drawn into the argument anyway. "Family gives and family takes? The taking part I get, but what have you given lately?"

Nick waited a solid second, as if he knew he possessed the trump card and wanted to relish his moment of victory. When he spoke, I realized he was right.

"Harper." His eyes narrowed. "I give you Harper. I sign the papers and let her attend a hoity-toity boarding school, don't I? I stay out of your way for weekly visits. I ignore the fact you're an *animal*, a threat to her safety. Seems like I give a lot."

He was right and I had no rebuttal. Instead, I picked up my pace, heading toward the picnic tables. Nick would follow. He always did.

Sure enough, the reek of cheap liquor caught up with me before the rest of the visiting families came into view. Nick's taller form cast a shadow across my face as we stepped out of the trees side by side.

"I could yank her out of school today you know." His words were ice picks in my spine. "Take her home with me."

Home to the beer cans, the late nights, the gambling debts piling up. Harper worked hard at Highlands. She didn't deserve being forced into unpaid maid service.

"How about I pay whoever you owe?" I suggested. Because that was when Nick came to me for extra beyond his usual weekly stipend. When he gambled too much and IOUs were called in all at once.

I'd learned the hard way that it was safer to deal with his creditors directly. Then the debt was sure to be cancelled. Otherwise, my hard-earned money slid down the black hole of another binge.

Unfortunately, Nick's scent morphed into bitter anger. "I'm not a child. I won't be treated like one."

I'd pushed it too far. And we'd spent too long discussing the issue too, because Harper was now entering the picnic area from the opposite direction.

Boarding schools must have staff members to take care of horses for the students. Whatever the reason, my sister was unencumbered as she waved at us. She'd be within human earshot within seconds.

Nick didn't budge. "Well?"

"Give me a week," I told him, "and you'll get your cash."

***

The rest of our visit went nearly as badly as the first half. Harper pretended not to be disappointed by the lack of salt packets. "I forgot," I lied when she dug through the sack and came up empty.

"They're salty enough," Ms. Stiff Upper Lip lied back.

Nick, of course, was always good for lowering the mood yet further. He glowered as Clara and Harper competed to see who could stuff more soggy fries in their mouths. But, for once, my kid sister was having too much fun to focus on her parent's moodiness. So, yeah, that part didn't suck.

Since Harper didn't seem bothered, I didn't exert myself to tease Nick into good humor. Instead, I leaned on the picnic table and reveled in the fact that Harper was hanging out with someone who looked more like a friend than a colleague.

This was a major change from her first year at Highlands. For two terms, I'd watched and worried as my sister nurtured acquaintances, ensuring she'd have a warm body to spend vacations with if her father failed to step up to the plate.

But now Harper appeared to

relinquishing thoughts of the future. She was laughing and being silly like a child. That felt unbelievably good.

The thought of vacations, though, reminded me of something I'd meant to discuss with her. "Break is week after next, right?" I asked.

"Next week," Harper countered. Her face shuttered, my fault this time instead of Nick's. "It starts Friday at 5 pm. But, I mean, if you guys are busy, I can stay here. Clara does."

Clara did because her mother was the headmistress. "It's like a mausoleum," the other girl countered. "Dark. Cold. Dinners in the cafeteria with Mum."

Harper's eyes smiled even if her mouth didn't. "I *like* your mother."

"She's a termagant."

Whatever that meant. Highlands students definitely liked their big words.

"She's fair," Harper countered. "And...she's directly behind you."

So, yeah, that was uncomfortable. The headmistress peered down her nose at her daughter before turning to face me. "Your tuition payment is overdue."

I hated discussing this in front of the kids. But the headmistress clung to silence until I muttered, "I'm on the monthly payment plan...."

"And late." Then, turning to Nick, she added, "Meanwhile, you haven't signed the parental agreement for this semester. That, at least, is easily remedied." As she spoke, she whipped out a sheaf of papers, as if she expected Nick to jot down his signature right there at the picnic table.

Which, knowing my stepfather, was probably a good idea. He wasn't the best at follow-through unless it involved accepting a round of drinks....

But Nick didn't seem to be in any hurry to grab the papers. Instead, his eyes slid to me as he spoke to the headmistress. "I forgot my pen."

"I have one." Clara was either deeply oblivious to the mood or very, very good at pretending. Either way, she dug into her backpack and came up with a glittery, sparkly thing that I supposed could have been called a pen.

"Naw." Nick waved away the writing

utensil. "I'll sign it when I bring Harper back from vacation."

"I'll expect full payment of this and *next* month's tuition payment at the exact same time," the headmistress agreed before sweeping away.

The coldness of her reaction seemed to take all of the autumn sunshine with her. No wonder the four of us sat there in stunned silence for a solid minute before Clara dipped back into the insulated bag for another soggy fry. "Don't mind Mum. She has to be a hard-nose or no one would ever pay her."

I nodded, accepting the fact that it was likely just as awkward for Clara to be the daughter of the headmistress as it was for Harper to have an alcoholic father and a sister who had trouble dealing with bills on time. I cleared my throat. "Anyway, about break, I'd love to have you both come stay with me. Girl time. We'll paint our toenails. Binge on ice cream...."

Nick opened his mouth to interrupt and I raised both eyebrows. A reminder of our agreement. He'd get his cash. In exchange, I'd get Harper for spring break.

And...Nick nodded. Closed his mouth without anything vile spewing out of it.

Gradually, the sun emerged from behind the clouds. Clara and Harper regaled us with chemistry-lab mishaps and crushes on actors.

And, on the way home, I stopped by the bank to deposit Marina's check.

Chapter 8

The museum was impenetrable to thieves...well, to *human* thieves. Luckily, I had an ace up my sleeve.

The ability to transform into a wolf.

And, yes, I knew it was a bad idea. I'd never utilized my lupine form during previous heists for three very good reasons—the card in my pocket, the alpha it represented, and the necessity of keeping the existence of werewolves a secret from the larger human world.

If I was found out during this heist, I put my ability to visit Harper in jeopardy. The idea of losing our weekly visits left bitter terror in my mouth.

But two days of scouting showed up no other obvious avenues of entrance. The night guard I brushed past on the sidewalk at the end of his shift had dog hairs on his trousers. And the deadline of Harper and Clara's fall break loomed.

Plus, there was the check I'd already cashed with all those zeroes on it. The carrot that a single job could pay Harper's tuition all the way through to college. And the stick—the memory of smelling flowers that really shouldn't have been blooming at the end of October moments before Harper had an incident with her horse.

"Just this once," I decided. "We can be in and out before anyone notices. Authorities will assume I'm a dog with a human handler...and if they see no signs of the handler there will be no leads to follow up."

Inside my belly, my wolf pranced. She was in total agreement with any opportunity that allowed us to don our fur form and get frisky. She'd been cooped up way too long, other than short shifts inside our apartment. It wasn't smart to take her enthusiasm as evidence I was making the rational choice.

But there were no other avenues open to me, so I took her approval at face value. Started planning a heist that seemed inclined to be easy...as long as the local alpha never heard about it.

I dropped my standards in another way also. After hitting a town I seldom visited to purchase supplies, I drove up to the Highlands campus. "Harper lost her inhaler," I lied in the main office. "She needs a replacement." They pulled her out of class to chat with me as I'd known they would.

"Is everything okay?" My sister was wild-eyed when she met me in the quad. She knew she didn't use an inhaler.

"Fine. Here, take this." I slipped her a shopping bag with everything she'd need in it. Gloves. Burner phone. "I was hoping you could help me out with a job."

"Yes!" Harper sparkled at this evidence of my trust in her. She'd begged for years to be included in the family business. For years, I'd told her it was too dangerous for the underage.

"What do you want me to do?" she continued. "I can sneak out anytime after curfew. Hitchhike to town...."

I held up a hand before my sister could give me a heart attack. "All I need you to do is to take a call for me. Then drop the phone in the culvert at the west end of campus. Fifteen minutes, then you're back in bed. Do we have a deal?"

Harper wanted a larger part in the project, but she could tell that was all I was offering. So she shrugged and quieted while I provided the rest of the details.

Which is how, by 9 pm, I was ready

to put my plan into action. Wrapping the sparkliest collar imaginable around my throat, I shifted at the edge of the park where a muddy morass made it easy to roll soft fur into matted awfulness. My costume was now complete.

At 9:15, a sad, stray version of myself padded up to the guardroom. Security cameras caught every feature in their databanks, but who would recognize me? It's not like facial recognition works on wolves.

Bullet-proof—or technology-proof at least—I ignored the surveillance and scratched the glass door panel. Whined. Peered up into the guard's concerned eyes.

The door opened. The guard was

even more covered with dog hairs than he had been last time. Curly, white. They belonged to a miniature poodle, if I didn't miss my guess.

But the guard wasn't averse to larger canines. Crouching, he held out a hand toward me—the ultimate in dog-greeting politeness. I sniffed his fingers, pretending to hesitate. Then I let him scratch behind my ears.

"You poor thing." The guard's hand was skilled. And in the right position so a twist of my neck tapped him with the tag dangling from my collar.

Just as I'd hoped he would, the guard pinched the metal between thumb and forefinger. Rubbed mud off the digits. "Let's call your owner and get you cleaned up."

So, yeah, it was going to be the easiest heist of my career. Would have been, too, if Tank hadn't shown up.

***

I didn't even realize anyone else was there until the guard sank back onto his heels. "Two strays?"

I craned my neck and took in the wolf who had padded up behind me when neither the guard nor I was looking. Tank hadn't mudded up his fur like I had, but body language made his tremendous size inconsequential. In lupine form, his scarred face was endearing rather than wince-worthy. He whined and pinned his ears, shrinking in on himself.

The posture had worked on the testy teenagers, and it worked just as well on the museum guard. "You poor thing," he repeated.

Invisible to our human companion, I glared at the big, burly wolf who was going to ruin my night, my financial solvency, and my sister's safety. Then I widened my eyes and curled my lips back in silent warning.

This was my turf. Tank needed to move along.

Not that my lupine half wanted him gone. Even as my lips snarled, my body swayed toward him. I sucked up a deep breath of Tank's aroma, strong and furry and deeply male.

And that's what Tank chose to respond to. When I curled my lip, he took a step backward. But then he sank down onto his rump and brushed his plumy tail against the dusty concrete. Cocking his head, he whined a second time, the sound as thready as a pup's.

No wonder the security guard took out his phone and dialed the number from my tag. Tank, of course, lacked both tag and collar.

So that part of my plan was working at least. Together, all three of us listened to ringing on the other end. Then...

"Oh, please tell me you've found Princess!"

I winced. Harper was overplaying it. After all, the guard hadn't even stated his business.

But he was a dog lover. Maybe he believed that someone missing their pet could be as single-minded as my sister, answering every call from a stranger with a heartfelt plea.

"Yes, ma'am," the guard replied. "We're...."

"Oh, thank goodness! Can you believe she jumped a ten-foot fence? I really think she might be in heat...."

Tank's tongue lolled out. I wanted to grab my sister and shake her. The ten-foot fence part wasn't even in the realm of possibility. The heat part was just plain embarrassing.

"Ah, so this big mutt dogging her footsteps is looking for a date?" The guard insinuated himself between me and Tank. One boot shot out to nudge Tank sideways, as if the guard intended to protect my canine virtue. As if a dog in heat would be waiting to have sex rather than pouncing the moment a male came within range.

A pause. I hadn't expected there to be another werewolf present, and Harper wouldn't know what to do with that information. Hopefully she'd realize I always worked solo. Hopefully....

"Oh, no, you don't need to worry. Cutie-Pie is neutered. But he's devoted to Princess. He follows her everywhere. Please, can you lock both of them in then stand on the street so I can find you?"

"It won't be hard to find me, ma'am."

The guard was reaching in his pocket now for a milk bone. He waved the doggie biscuit in front of my nose.

My stomach rumbled. Tank raised one furry eyebrow. So I'd skipped dinner. It wasn't as amusing as Tank's gaping grin suggested. I had a sudden impulse to bite off his tongue.

Or maybe that was an impulse to slide my tongue into his mouth and take what his body language suggested he was offering. I found myself sidling closer. One step, then another, as the guard gave my sister directions she didn't need.

"I'm at the art museum downtown. The building has big columns out front. It's really unmissable...."

"Oh, please." Harper and I had

rehearsed this part of her schtick together. *"Princess takes her sense of direction after me. I'm really afraid I might miss the museum if you're not outside waiting for me. And I do so want to pick up my darlings as soon as possible...."*

One second before my furry flank rubbed up against his, Tank rose, stretched, and trotted up to the closed door of the museum. The milk bone wasn't even in front of his nose now. He was terrible at subterfuge.

And...the security guard didn't notice. Waving his ID against the sensor then pulling the door wide, he continued to soothe my sister. "I understand, ma'am. I'm taking the dogs inside now. How soon can you be here?"

"Five minutes. No, three minutes. I'll stay on the line. Just, please, protect my fur babies!"

The milk bone descended back to nose level. From inside the guard room, Tank's eyes twinkled.

He was in and I was out and this was my one chance to steal Marina's bracer. The only reason not to enter? I didn't trust Tank...and, even more, I didn't trust my own reaction to him.

As if responding to my thoughts, Tank barked, a quick yip of impatience. "Come on, Princess," the guard wheedled.

What could I do? I accepted the treat graciously and trotted inside.

Chapter 9

A glance around the room made this gig seem easier and easier...as long as Tank stayed out of my way. To start with, a bank of screens broadcasting camera data from inside the museum was fully visible without the need for human fingers to scroll through it. My own lupine face stared back at me from one image...but stepping a yard away from the computer terminal shielded me from view.

Well, that will be easily avoided.

Meanwhile, the door leading from the

guard room to the rest of the museum had no swipe plate beside it. So I wouldn't need to pretend to be dying of thirst in order to get through that barrier.

Scene surveyed, I settled myself in a perfect "Stay" position while Harper gave the illusion of prattling while actually following through on phase two of our plan. *"Is Princess okay? I hope she doesn't look agitated?"*

"No, ma'am. Both of your dogs are very well behaved."

That was Harper's cue to get the guard outside as soon as possible. So she did, diving back into her concern about a supposedly faulty direction sense. *"I suppose I should just get a PGS,"* she said, purposefully mangling the acronym. *"But I'm so concerned about the radiation damaging my poor doggies' brains."*

"Don't worry about it." The guard patted me once, did the same for Tank who had sunk down beside me, then turned back to the outside door. "I'll be waiting for you on the front steps. I'm wearing a blue uniform and...."

His voice was cut off by the only real barrier to entrance. I was inside the museum and the guard was outside. It was hard not to be smug.

Still, I waited fifteen seconds just in case the guard remembered something. Then I sidled backwards into the small camera-free zone beside the interior door and shimmered upward into humanity.

My hands were at my throat, pulling items out of the pouch I'd attached to the inside of my collar, when warmth pressed up against my bare back. "What are we doing?"

Ripples of awareness swam through me. Tank was there, behind me. Naked just like I was, our bare skin separated by nothing but air and not much of that. I swallowed.

His voice was irresistible. Even though I knew better, I angled my chin to see what he looked like without any clothes.

Muscles. Shadows. A hint of stubble on his jaw....

He wasn't looking at me, though. Instead, his face was partially averted. As if my nakedness held no appeal.

Annoyed by my own focus on the immaterial—or, rather, the very material—I swiveled to face my un-asked-for companion head on. "*We're* doing nothing," I snapped back. "You're pretending to be a good dog while I visit the museum for a couple of minutes. After that, we're parting ways and will never see each other again."

Tank totally ignored the part of my statement I'd intended to be incendiary. Instead, he straightened his neck until his face came back into view.

I felt the moment his gaze struck my nakedness. Heat flooded my body and I smelled a surge of awareness emanating from him as powerful as my own.

Okay. Not so uninterested then.

Still, his words were flat. "You're stealing art from a museum."

There'd been no overt judgment in his tone, but I responded as if there had been. Fighting was safer than dealing with this *whatever* spinning between our wolves and our bodies.

"I'm stealing art *on loan* to a museum. Art belonging to a rich guy. He won't miss it and neither will the museum." Because, yes, I'd double-checked the ownership issue. Harper's needs aside, I didn't willy-nilly deposit that check.

Tank leaned in a hair closer. His heat pressed up against my chest, my throat, my stomach. We were separated by a millimeter of air space. That distance suddenly felt like far too much.

Until his words slapped me. "When the museum's insurance premiums go up, they'll miss whatever you take."

His business card, I remembered now, had been succinct yet edifying. *Tank Morales. Attorney-at-Law.* The profession explained why he jumped straight to rising insurance rates. But I had an answer for that as well.

"The rich guy has it insured. The museum doesn't. That fact was in the newspaper article. A quote of appreciation from a board member. The museum won't lose out."

As I spoke, I dropped the small block of wood from my collar pouch to the ground, kicking it close to the door and preparing to wedge the space open for easy retreat. Finally, I shook a mini pry bar out of the pouch, letting it fall onto my palm.

No fingerprints on either item. There wouldn't be, even after I was finished. Just wolf saliva. My preparations were complete.

"Are we done with the inquisition?" I demanded, preparing to turn the door knob. I was frustrated by my own reaction to Tank's presence. I needed to focus and the hormone storm inside me was making that difficult.

Taking a deep breath, I ran through the plan one last time. The door knob was the only part I needed human fingers for, and if I smeared as I turned there would be no prints left behind. After that, I would be an unidentifiable wolf. It would work....

"Ready," Tank agreed, reaching around me to yank the door open. Wedging his body into the gap, he used the back of his hand to smudge away any evidence of his grip.

That solved the fingerprint problem, but a question ripped out of me anyway. "What are you doing?"

The faintest smile pulled subtly lopsided lips upward in a gesture that was almost beautiful. "Every thief needs a good lawyer. I'm coming with."

***

There wasn't time to argue. Not when opening this door would make the first warning ping show up on the guard's cell phone.

So I gave in. Shimmered back down to wolf form in tandem with Tank, falling through the doorway even as the door glided shut.

Or, rather, not quite shut. The wooden block stopped the metal barrier one inch shy of its frame just as I'd intended. Meanwhile, my second tool—the iron pry bar—lay cold against my tongue.

Then I was running, counting down the seconds. I had no way of dodging motion sensors, so I didn't try to. Which meant the security guard would be getting a second alert right about now. The question was, would Harper be able to talk him into ignoring the double dose of digital caution? How long did we have before he realized notifications were more than a malfunction and alerted the police?

Despite the countdown, I was exhilarated as my nails clicked against smooth marble. The scents of old paint and new floor cleaner curled around me. Tank, at my shoulder, was a presence that felt strangely right.

Then the ancient British exhibit loomed before us. The plexiglass case that covered the bracer wasn't alarmed or high-tech, its purpose just to shield the art from sticky fingers. My pry bar would do the trick.

I'd practiced this with wolf teeth. Tricky to hold the tool between sharp canines, but doable. Trickier, I found, to try the same while standing up on my hind legs.

The pry bar made my teeth feel brittle. The beveled end should have slid into the crack, but it refused to do so. Instead, the tool bounced off, the other end biting into the soft interior of my cheek.

Despite myself, I whined. This wasn't going to work. Seconds were ticking by faster and faster. I couldn't leave Harper on the phone long enough for cops to be alerted and start tracing the call to

Highlands....

I huffed out frustration. I'd have to abort.

***

Then Tank was above me. His furry body cupped mine far too intimately. As if I really was in heat and he was an animal guided only by the urge for reproduction.

I froze.

He responded by *biting* me. Gently, on my nose. Not an animal bite. A human bite, telling me to hurry up.

To shift. Use human fingers while his body shielded mine from the inevitable cameras.

That required trusting him. Trusting a

male. Worse, a male *werewolf*. Something my past promised was a very bad idea.

But this wasn't depending on a guy to watch my back for the long term. This wasn't signing on the dotted line and giving a drunk access to my bank account. This wasn't agreeing to be part of a pack.

No, this was one moment of accepting assistance from a willing companion. I wasn't so emotionally scarred that I couldn't do that.

So I slid into humanity. Tank's fur brushed against my bare skin, making me shiver. Ignoring the sensation, I spat the pry bar into shaking fingers, forced the narrow end into the gap between plexiglass lid and matte black pedestal, then pounded down on the other end of the lever with my fist.

The hinges snapped. The plexiglass lid toppled off. The bracer before me gleamed in the dim light of the glowing exit sign.

I tensed, waiting for Tank to snatch up the precious artifact. After all, why else had he come along? Did he intend to turn me in or take the prize for himself?

Neither. Tank nipped me again, even gentler than before as if he was well aware of the effect wolf teeth would have on the thin, human skin of my shoulder. He hovered above me, a protective presence, while I thrust the pry bar back into my collar—wouldn't have to leave it behind after all. Then I shifted and plucked up the bracer between lupine teeth.

Only after Tank saw that I had what I'd come for did he leap down and take the lead for our retreat.

We sprinted back through the dark museum together. Retraced our footsteps past the stairs I'd hurried down yesterday in an effort to escape the Samhain Shifters, back through the staff-only hallway, all the way to the door I'd doctored with my wooden door stop.

It was still open. But my conversation with Tank plus my moment frozen by the bracer had added up. Harper must have gotten off the phone just when I told her too...which ended up being one minute too soon.

Because the security guard was coming back through the outside door just as we reached the cracked opening of the inner door. His eyes were trained on the bank of monitors, not noticing that we were mere feet away.

The external door was slowly sliding shut behind him. If we were fast, Tank and I could make it out before it clicked shut and required a shift to humanity to reopen.

But the guard blocked the exit. The room was too small to be sure we could rush past him. And I was wearing the collar I'd used to stash my tools in. A collar that would be easy to grab....

Tank leapt at the guard before I

could decide on the best course of action. His scent was perfectly calm, yet he snapped and snarled like a wild animal. One bite that didn't quite connect. A bone-chilling growl. Then he'd slid past the guard and into the night.

He meant to clear the way for me. I knew that. After all, any normal rent-a-cop would have been traumatized by Tank's behavior. Would have backpedalled and provided me with an easy escape.

But this security guard was a dog person. He wasn't traumatized and his eyes were keen. "What's in your mouth?" he demanded, lunging for me.

I tried to sidestep, but I wasn't quite fast enough. The guard caught my right hind leg just as I made it to the exterior door.

Chapter 10

I wasn't about to drop the bracer, which meant I couldn't bite the hand that held me. But I *could* kick backwards for all I was worth. Maybe my toenails would catch on the guard's skin....

No dice. The foot he wasn't holding skittered off his clothing. The guard swore and clenched down tighter on my other leg.

The door pressed against my shoulder as I was dragged inexorably back into the guard house. A wild glance in the opposite direction proved that Tank was too far away to stop the inevitable. Within seconds, I'd be locked behind a door that required a keycard to open. I'd lose the bracer and be captured in my lupine skin.

No. Wasn't happening.

I twisted, ignoring the pain in my stuck ankle and the strain down my side that felt like the worst sort of power yoga. Lashing out with my right front paw, I scratched at the guard's face, careful to steer clear of his eyeballs.

And this time, he reacted. His hand twisted against my ankle, pain and instinct working against his impulse to be kind to furry critters. A sharp spike of agony ran up my hind leg. Despite myself, I yelped.

The yelp, not the scratch, is what made the guard let go. He was a dog lover at heart and he knew he'd hurt me. His formerly unbendable fingers sprang away as if my leg had turned into a hot poker...

...And I accepted the reprieve. Squirmed out the gap between door and frame, glad that I had four legs so running was feasible despite the throbbing in my right rear appendage....

I was ten feet from the door when something furry brushed past me in the opposite direction. *Tank.* Darting between our pursuer's legs and tangling him up. Or so I assumed from the burst of expletives and the thud behind my back.

Tank hadn't left me. Even when my injury turned me into a liability. My lungs expanded, something fierce and joyful pushing my legs faster.

Unfortunately, the guard was equally tenacious. Tank caught up to me within seconds, but human footsteps weren't far behind us. And unlike Tank, I couldn't outrun our pursuer. Not when I was hobbling on three paws, biting back each jolt of pain when I skipped the fourth.

It was all I could do to follow Tank's tail as he led me to a hole in an old wooden fence. As if he'd scouted out a human-proof escape plan before joining me. My own plan was fuzzy beneath the pain of my ankle. All I could focus on was Tank, waiting solid as a stone.

This time, I didn't even consider distrusting him. Instead, I shimmied through the gap. Followed as Tank once again took the lead and guided me down a path I was unfamiliar with.

Behind parked cars. Down dark alleys. I could neither see nor smell the guard now. We'd left him far behind.

Only then did I realize we were traveling in the wrong direction. Away from the safety of my apartment rather than toward it. Still, I didn't curve toward my original destination as Tank skittered down a steep slope into a pool of pure darkness. Instead, I followed, my paws splashing into slowly moving water. In front of me, Tank had finally stopped.

I did too, panting hard and trying to

ignore the throb of my injured ankle that made my teeth ache. Tentatively, I dropped that paw down to join its fellows. Frigid liquid soaking through dirty fur felt unbelievably good.

As I recovered my equilibrium, I remembered the spot we were in from earlier scouting. The stream where I soaked my sore paws rose to the surface for half a block before being channeled back beneath streets and residences. It wasn't a park. Just a forgotten corner of wild land.

No one came here in daylight. In the dark, it was bound to be empty. Safe enough to risk shifting into humanity.

Safe...other than my lupine companion. Still, ignoring the shiver of bad experiences with other male werewolves, I sucked in courage and shifted up.

***

Cold air struck human skin as fur receded. I shivered. Spat the bracer into one hand, slapped it onto my opposite wrist for safekeeping...then fought for balance as my injured ankle collapsed beneath my weight.

Broad hands caught my shoulders before I fell. For an instant, they burned heady awareness into me. Then exhaustion and pain beat out attraction.

And it was as if Tank could smell my mood. His fingers stayed far from erogenous zones as he growled out an order. "Sit," he demanded, lowering me onto the muddy stream bank.

Then his fingers were prodding my ankle. I hissed, barely able to see the buckling of skin as his jaw tensed.

I didn't want to know, but I asked anyway. "How bad is it?"

Tank's head shook ever so slightly, a flutter of movement in the darkness. "Could be worse. Probably a minor strain."

"Minor?" Despite the cold water, my ankle felt like a train had run over it.

"If you keep the foot elevated, it'll likely heal within twenty-four hours."

Well, that was impossible. Not the healing part—the keeping my foot elevated part.

After all, I needed to collect my car then head up to Highlands to nab Harper's cell phone. She'd promised to remove the battery as soon as she hung up, but I couldn't trust a teenager to dispose of incriminating evidence. The guard had seen me leave the museum with the bracer. This wouldn't be a cold case, unnoticed until the following day....

Tank's hand returned to my shoulder, pressing me backwards. "What do you think you're doing?"

"The job's not complete. I need to...."

My voice trailed off. I wasn't about to spill my guts in front of a stranger. It was oddly difficult to remember that about Tank. That he *was* a stranger.

"Stay here," he ordered, ignoring my abortive explanation. His hand retreated and something in me regretted the loss of contact.

Just because of the cold, of course. Cold air, cold water. A bit of shock in the aftermath of my injury. I was shivering and Tank's hand had provided much-needed warmth.

Now, he loomed above me, more like a tower than a tank. "I'm getting my car. I'll be back in five minutes."

Before I could answer, he was gone.

***

I didn't intend to wait, of course. Not for a man who'd butted his way into my life without explanation or permission.

But it took over a minute to feel around for a stick hefty enough to lean on. And when I struggled my way to standing, there was someone present at the top of the bank.

Not Tank. Not a male of any sort. Instead, the streetlight behind her silhouetted feminine curves. Meanwhile, I inhaled the scent of blackberries so strong I could almost taste summer on my tongue.

Marina's voice had all of the berries' tartness and none of their sweetness. "You look...terrible."

"How did you find me?" I demanded as she picked her way down the slope. Her lack of answer was answer. She'd found me, I knew, because she was more than human. Whatever Lupe thought, Marina was somehow affiliated with the fae.

But that wasn't the most relevant point. She held out her hand in silence, demanding the bracer. Instinctively, I twisted sideways so the thick metal bracelet wasn't within stealing distance. "The check," I countered.

Unlike most of my employers, Marina didn't try to cheat me. "Of course," she murmured. "Must adhere to the formalities."

And...there was a check between her fingers. I was 99% certain there hadn't been one present a second earlier. But the night was dark and my ankle throbbed and Tank would be back any minute.

I took it. Unfolded the paper to ensure my name appeared on the proper line and a scrawled signature on the other. There were quite a lot of zeroes. More, if I was honest, than I'd seen in my bank account in my life.

While I gawked, Marina plucked her own prize from my wrist, raising it to rub against her face. Like a cat scent-marking her favorite armchair. The aroma of blackberries intensified. Out of the corner of my eyes, I thought I caught half a dozen fireflies illuminating a city sidewalk.

"Should I leave you alone to make out with your jewelry?" I asked dryly, sliding the check away into the hidden pouch in my wolf collar. Even though the precious paper would be safe there, my fingers lingered for a second before I managed to force them away.

Marina didn't miss my reluctance to lose skin contact with my payment. Her eyes glinted...which they shouldn't have. Not here in the darkness by the creek.

After all, the moon—if there was one—was hidden behind clouds. The street lights were arranged to illuminate road and sidewalk rather than stream bank.

Her voice, when she spoke, was similarly wrong. Musical, like the peal of bells. "There's more where that came from."

I didn't need more. For once in my

life, I had enough cash. I could finally consider scratching itches that had seemed irrelevant while serving as Harper's secondary guardian. Perhaps I'd sign up for an art class....

And yet, my body disagreed with me. It leaned forward without my permission. My mouth echoed Marina's assertion. "More?"

She smiled, the gesture so beautiful it shouldn't have chilled me. But it did. "If you're interested, I'll be in touch."

She turned away...and my greed popped like a soap bubble. What was I thinking? If there was even a 1% chance that Marina had been involved in the horse incident....

"This is between you and me only," I

called after her. "My sister isn't involved."

But Marina was already gone.

Chapter 11

I wasn't alone for long. By the time I fought my way to the top of the bank, a car idled there. Emerging from behind the wheel was the male werewolf I'd met yesterday, the one whose ugliness scared teenagers and whose refusal to leave me alone raised my blood pressure...and woke other long-sleeping parts of my limbic system.

To my combined relief and disappointment, he was dressed now. Because werewolves tended to keep spare clothes in their vehicle. The contrast to my nakedness made his power even more intimidating when his hand clamped down on my right elbow.

"Where to?" he asked, his words quiet. He hadn't intended to intimidate me, I gathered as he half lifted and half guided me toward the passenger seat. There, he pulled out baggy sweats and steadied me as I wriggled into them. He even knelt to assist my injured ankle through the door.

He stayed down there, too, eyebrows raised while waiting for my answer.

Or at least, I thought his eyebrows were raised during the fleeting glimpse he granted me. After that, something

Tank saw on my face must have reminded him of his supposed ugliness, of the brightness here beneath a street light. Because he curved his neck away from me, twisting so far tendons bulged out of his skin.

That wasn't why I agreed to go with him, of course. I was just reacting to the sure knowledge that my throbbing ankle wouldn't have been able to press the gas and brake pedals of my own vehicle. Urgency pulsed through me, the need to ensure my sister's safety.

That was the only reason I didn't shoot Tank down.

"Head for the highway," I said against my better judgment. "I'll tell you where to turn next."

Directions were our only conversation for the next hour. As if Tank didn't want to scare me out of the decision to trust him. Still, I regretted my choice the instant the tree-lined curve at the furthest corner of Highlands' grounds opened out before us. There was the culvert, an easy hiding place for a misused cell phone. And there was a human shape standing next to it, arms crossed and feet spread hip-width apart.

The car slowed as Tank took in the same view. "You didn't say you were meeting someone."

"I didn't think I was." After all, I'd given Harper strict instructions to ditch the cell phone and go back to bed. Not stand shivering in the cold, dark forest waiting for me.

But that shape *was* my kid sister. I could tell by the way she swiped hair off her face, the way she shielded her eyes against our headlights. She wasn't sure this was me. Perhaps recognized that the shape of the car was wrong the same way I'd recognized the shape of her body was right.

Tank slammed on the brakes a good long trek from the culvert. "Stay here. I'll deal with it."

The car stank of aggression. He thought Harper was, what, a cop? A backstabbing co-conspirator? I guessed I couldn't blame him since I'd turned up the radio and ignored his one attempt at questions during the commute.

But—"No. *You* stay here. That's my...." *Sister.* I snapped my teeth closed around the word. Couldn't imagine why it had almost come out in front of this near stranger in the first place.

After all, the purpose of this trip was to protect Harper from repercussions. Not to throw her under the bus.

Tank waited for me to finish the sentence. When I didn't, he reached behind the seat and came up with yet more spare clothing.

"I'm already wearing more than I need," I reminded him. The clothes he'd lent me didn't fit, but they were functional. Only my feet remained bare.

Tank apparently disagreed. Shaking his head, he continued rolling the sweatshirt up into a bundle. "Padding. For your stick," he rumbled while pressing the fabric down over the jagged wooden end of the object in question.

As if he'd noticed the scratches on my armpit from using the found crutch to pull myself up the stream bank. My skin warmed, then I focused.

Tank's padding meant he wasn't going to raise a stink about me going to speak with my sister solo. This felt too easy.

I cocked my head. "You'll stay here?"

"No."

My fists clenched...then relaxed as he continued.

"I'll drop you off and drive past. Park far enough away to be out of earshot. If you need me, just wave."

It was impossible to be angry with him after that.

***

"Did it work?"

Harper was bouncing with excitement at being part of something grownup and illicit. So I didn't have the heart to chastise her for waiting out where anyone could see her. Didn't have the heart to tell her that she'd taken off her gloves too soon—the plastic bag she'd slipped the phone into would carry prints.

But I'd dispose of everything carefully enough so she wouldn't be implicated. The phone, I noted, had both battery and SIM card removed and dropped into the bag separately. So I leaned in and planted a kiss on her forehead. "You done good, kid."

"I *know*." Harper was dancing around me now, oblivious to the fact I was leaning on a homemade crutch and barely managing to stay upright. But she was fully human. Unlike me, she couldn't see in the dark. "That guy on the phone totally believed that I was a crazy dog lady. He recommended a trainer and a groomer. You *could* use a haircut, especially if you're working with other 'dogs' now. Do I get to meet him? Is he cute?"

Harper pranced in closer as she

spoke, arm extended as if she intended to grab my hair to illustrate her point. But her eyes weren't good enough to see where she was going, and I was too tired to take evasive action. Whatever the reason, Harper's heel came down on the unshod toe of my injured foot.

I hissed. I didn't mean to, but breath escaped along with a word I tried not to say in Harper's presence.

"Athena?" She froze. "What's wrong?"

Then hands were on my shoulder. Big hands. Hot hands.

Tank. I blinked, trying to figure out how he'd materialized out of nowhere.

He hadn't, obviously. Instead, he'd done exactly what he said he would—

parked beyond the reach of wolf ears. Then he'd used the hum of the idling car engine to cover up the sound of his approach.

"Who are you?" Harper demanded. Her fists were clenched. She was going to punch him. This was why I kept my sister far away from werewolves, myself excluded.

I tensed when Tank stepped sideways, one arm slipping down to cradle my waist. The gesture felt far more intimate than I suspect he intended. As if he was doing more than holding me up.

But the important part was how he responded to my sister's show of aggression. "Tank Morales," he answered, extending his free arm for a handshake.

I exhaled, tension I hadn't even realized existed flowing out of me. Tank was being a gentleman. Harper, after a moment of consideration, accepted the peace gesture. "Harper D'Argent," she replied.

"Good grip," Tank observed. Which likely meant my sister had tried to squeeze his fingers off.

"Ditto," Harper answered. Her eyes, when they met mine, were full of questions.

Well, there was no point in pretending we weren't sisters at this point. "I'll pick you up tomorrow at five," I told Harper. "We can talk then."

And, to my surprise, she accepted

the brush off. "Okay," she agreed. "Nice meeting you, Tank."

She slid me a glance that was full of mischief. Her eyebrows wiggled. Then she took off, heading back to her simple human life.

Together, Tank and I stood watch until my kid sister made it safely back across the lawn and into her dormitory. My foot and ankle both throbbed, but my waist was warm where Tank's arm encircled it.

The contact felt strangely right.

***

It was so late that even the highway was empty by the time we made it back to the exit closest to my apartment. Which meant no nosy neighbors noticed when Tank pulled into an empty parking space and helped me pry myself out of the car.

By this point, one of my toenails had turned purple from where Harper had stepped on it. My ankle had swollen to the size of a cantaloupe. My muscles felt like they'd been attached to lead weights.

For the first time, I sincerely regretted choosing an apartment on the seventh floor.

But even though stairs felt insurmountable at the present moment, I wasn't about to lead Tank into my ramshackle building. Not that I was ashamed of the books spread across my couch and the dirty dishes in the sink...much. The real issue was who he was and who I was. No way I was inviting a strange werewolf into my den.

"Thanks for the ride," I dismissed him.

Rather than leaving, Tank waited, head turned slightly away. Silent. Immovable.

I sighed and unlocked the downstairs door.

"Look, you don't need to come up with me. I'll be fine," I told him at the bottom of the dark stairwell. It seemed to rise up into eternity, as if I lived at the top of a lighthouse rather than in an ordinary, if run-down, apartment building.

Tank's response was diffident. "I

don't have anything better to do."

I blinked and his arm was around my waist again. I was leaning into him...for no reason other than the fact that each stair loomed approximately ten feet tall. When had they expanded from their original size?

"Step up," he murmured, and I did. Again and again and again. Time and space tunneled. I lost a few minutes to a strange combination of pleasure and pain.

Then we were on my landing. Tank's hand rose in front of me, palm up. "Key?"

My growl was half-hearted. "I can open my own door."

After I fumbled at the lock for ten long seconds, however, me swaying and

Tank as solid as his namesake, it became apparent Tank had won that round. Who knew silence could be so effective? He turned the key in the lock, opened my door...and froze.

Adrenaline woke me out of my haze as I took a step forward. "What?"

My nose provided an answer. The air, which should have stunk of carpet that refused to release its dirt plus the musty hint of ceiling mold, was filled with the wildness of wolf. Someone had been in my apartment since I was here last. Had shifted and, if I wasn't mistaken, had *peed* on the door jamb.

I'd hoped to have at least until morning before anyone heard about a pair of wolves robbing the local museum.

But word, apparently, travelled fast.

"Keep an eye on the stairs," Tank demanded before pushing me back out the door and closing it in my face.

I rattled the knob. Blinked. Had he seriously just locked me out of my own apartment?

Endless minutes later, the door I was leaning against opened. Tank's grip on my arm was firm as he pulled me into the overwhelming brightness of my own living room. "There's no one here. I tried calling Lupe, but my phone doesn't have service."

"The office building across the way blocks it." I waved vaguely. "You'll get three bars down on the corner."

Tank lowered me onto the couch,

propped my injured leg up on a pillow, then crouched down to my level. His head was averted as he spoke to the wall. "I'm going to lock the door behind me. Stay here. I'll be back once I've made a call."

The raised hairs on his arms and neck were too long to be human so I didn't bother arguing with him. Tank was acting like an alpha werewolf, which meant he wouldn't listen to reason. I'd learned that the hard way. Didn't need to beat my head against that particular wall ever again.

Instead, I watched him leave. Waited as my own key turned in the lock to protect me from danger that wouldn't come from that direction.

Then I wrestled my way back to my feet. Hunted down my wallet. Opened the sliding glass doors across from the metal one Tank had locked behind him....

The instant I stepped out onto the seemingly empty balcony, a werewolf dropped down from above.

Chapter 12

"Rowan," I greeted the alpha I'd known would be lying in wait for me. The one who'd given me the card in my pocket. The one I'd hoped never to see again.

"Ace's daughter."

As if I had no name other than a relationship to an absent father. My face twisted but I didn't argue. After all, I was the one in the wrong.

Instead, I dug in my wallet for the card that had granted me safe passage through this alpha's domain for the last year and change. I'd known what I was risking when I took the furry shortcut at the museum. Had hoped it wouldn't come to this, but had accepted that it might.

Losing access to Harper's visiting hours was a gut punch, but it would be worth the loss now that I could afford to pay for the rest of her high-school career and part of college. Our relationship would survive the hiatus. I could always call my sister and bug her with endless emails and texts.

Swallowing down bitter regret, I held out the card representing an in-person relationship with my sister. "You want this back."

Rowan didn't snatch it out of my

hands the way I'd expected him to. Instead, he stepped in closer. The musk of alpha werewolf made me choke on my own inhale.

"That's not enough, Ace's daughter. You fucked up. You really fucked up this time."

"Did I?" I straightened despite the fact my ankle was trying to tell me how much it missed the couch and pillow. "If you already know about my mistake, then you've had plenty of time to cover up any leaks. Admit it. You have the police in your pocket. The story won't even show up on social media let alone in the evening news."

Rowan's head shook slowly. "No." His eyes glinted in the darkness. "You stole from a *museum.* They filed a report with a national alert network at the same time they contacted the police."

Goosebumps rose on my arms. I'd sent Tank away so he wouldn't do something stupid while I accepted the knocks I had coming. But...this was bad. Rowan wasn't taking my card and tossing me out of his territory the way he'd threatened to. The story of my furriness had escaped his control.

I swallowed. "What do you want then?"

Rather than answering, Rowan peered down over the railing into the darkness beneath us. When the apartment complex had been built, I suspect there'd been a rather nice view from each balcony. Since then, more buildings had sprung up cheek to jowl. By the time I moved in, the only view was of a dirty alley, now barely lit by a couple of lights above back doors.

Still, I could make out two lupine forms down there, moving toward the center from each end of the alley. Of course Rowan hadn't come alone. He was the alpha. He travelled with lackeys for appearances' sake. Plus, he wouldn't want to be the one huffing and puffing after me if I thought running was a good idea.

I shifted my weight, well aware that I had no ability to run tonight.

"Alpha?" I prodded when the silence stretched longer than I'd expected it to.

But Rowan didn't answer. Just kept peering downward, brow wrinkled as if he wasn't just staring off into space.

Of course. Pack-bond communication from alpha to underling was common among werewolves. But the effort didn't usually last this long or cause so much facial contortion.

I sidled away from Rowan's overwhelming presence to give myself a little breathing space then leaned over the railing, pulling on a little wolfishness of my own. Vision enhanced, I finally saw what Rowan was reacting to.

There was a cat down there—Mr. Fletcher's tabby, I was guessing—being stalked by Rowan's lupine underlings. They had the feline cornered in an indented stairwell and seemed an inch away from progressing from tease to torture.

They were going to tear the poor thing apart. Or would have if their alpha hadn't stopped them.

Rowan's frustration was bitter on my tongue. His words, when he gave up on the pack bond and went audible, came out as a bark.

"Leave the damn cat alone and get up here!"

The wolves ignored him. One slammed his paw down on the cat's back. The other widened his jaws as if to swallow the hissing feline whole. And....

"Now!"

The cold blast of alpha compulsion

froze both me and the shifters in the alley. As the effects faded, I stumbled back onto the cheap plastic folding chair that had come with the apartment. What happened to the wolves in the alley I could no longer tell.

I could, however, see Rowan turning away from the railing. He had no interest in the cat's survival. He'd only snapped at his crew because a wolf-mauled pet threatened shifters' ability to slide beneath the radar.

After all, Rowan was alpha. His priorities revolved around the future of his pack.

Which was bad news for me. My theft in wolf form was ten times as dangerous in that regard as tearing apart a house cat would have been.

***

When I opened my eyes, Rowan stood above me. Barely restrained fury pinned me in place the way it had a decade ago when I tracked him down in his office to beg for help.

"You're not my father," I'd said then, bamboozled by the fact that the name on my child-support checks had materialized into someone only a few years older than me.

"You figure?" Rowan leaned forward, sniffing as if he was in wolf rather than human form. Just like today, I'd backpedalled until I fell onto my butt.

I had no weapon other than words, so I used them. *"I want to speak with my father."*

"About what, exactly?"

"My mother's dead."

Rowan nodded and strode to his desk, giving me a second to pull myself together. By the time I scrambled to my feet, he'd drawn a checkbook out of a drawer, uncapped a fancy fountain pen, and raised one eyebrow. *"How much extra do you need?"*

"My little sister...."

Both eyebrows pulled down into a V over his nose. *"Harper stinks of humans. She's not my problem."*

Rowan had been close enough to smell my sister? *"I don't want your* money!"* I exploded, the four feet between us enough to unleash my teenage temper. *"And I don't want you close to my sister either!"*

If I'd taken the time to think about it, I would have expected to be slapped down. After all, Mom had warned me so many times about male werewolves, alphas especially. She might have only spent one night with my father, but she'd made other connections—and later severed them—when I turned old enough to shift.

But Rowan didn't live up to her warnings. Instead, he merely cocked his head. *"What do you want then?"*

So I told him. The whole sad story in three short sentences. *"My stepdad is a drunk. I can take care of my little sister on my own, but I need someone over eighteen to be in charge on paper. All I'm asking is my father's signature on a few forms...."*

As I spoke, Rowan came out from behind his desk. He advanced on me, step by step, something sharp and interested in his eyes.

"I could, perhaps, make your life easier if you had something to offer." His voice was low and lupine. *"Something that would make the effort worth my while...."*

The air stank of an aroma both pungent and wild. I couldn't pull in enough breath to deny him. Could only frantically shake my head.

And Rowan shrugged. Clicked the cap back on the pen he held, as if nothing had happened between us. *"In that case, your sister isn't worth the hassle."*

The only reprieve I'd been able to dream up was disappearing like the shreds of my own childhood. And while I couldn't accept what Rowan had offered, I wasn't too proud to beg. *"Just let me talk to my father. Tell me his name...."*

Rowan breathed out through his nose, not quite a snort but more than an ordinary exhale. *"You don't get it, do you, pup? I'm the alpha. I say no and your father won't speak with you. Now, how much extra money do you need?"*

He twirled the pen around his

fingers, the motion captivating my attention. This was a leash and I knew it. If I took his money, I'd also be accepting the barely concealed deal his wolf was offering.

So I swallowed back terror. Ground out: *"None. I need none."*

It was a lie, of course. Without Mom's steady paycheck, our family was floundering. But I could get a job. I could fend for myself and my sister....

And I could find my father. It wasn't really all that hard. The day after slamming out of Rowan's office, I paid for a copy of my birth certificate at the county courthouse. Memorized my father's name from the appropriate line and used that information to track Ace to his lair.

There...my father had refused to so much as speak to me without his alpha's permission. Pack wolves. They had no concept of self will. No interest in family outside the alpha-approved clan.

And, despite all that, my child-support checks kept coming. They doubled, in fact. Started being made out to me instead of to my mother.

I cashed them. Had to when my employment prospects as a sixteen-year-old high-school dropout became obvious. I cashed the checks and waited for the other shoe to drop.

But the shoe just hung there above me for a decade. Checks arrived every month like clockwork. Long past the point where I needed the cash.

Which is what gave me the idea, a bit over a year ago, to make a new deal with Rowan. At that point, Harper was starting school much closer to the center of the pack's territory than I'd dared travel after my sixteen-year-old slap down. I needed to be able to visit Highlands without being hassled by Rowan's pack mates more than I needed additional money.

So I'd traded in my chips for the card in my hand. The card Rowan now said wasn't enough to make up for my museum lapse.

Thirteen months ago, Rowan had made me another offer. A more overt one. But he'd let me walk away when I refused.

Unfortunately, I had a bad feeling I wouldn't be able to walk away this time. I swallowed down bile as I stared up at the alpha who had grown older and more powerful since I first met him. He took a single step forward and my wolf bowed down my head.

Sure enough, the scent emanating from Rowan now wasn't the sour scent of annoyance he'd exuded earlier. Instead, his aroma had morphed into something sweeter that was even less appealing.

"You've grown into an appealing woman. So I'll deal with your mistakes." Rowan's murmur should have been heartening, but it wasn't. Instead, my blood chilled as he continued to let me off the hook. "I'll stand up for you when other packs call for your blood. It's an alpha's prerogative."

I felt sixteen years old again. My reply came out as a squeak. "And in exchange?"

"In exchange, you'll take your proper place in my pack." He leaned in closer. "Assuming, that is, you want access to the territory your sister calls home."

Chapter 13

There was no answer on the tip of my tongue, so it's a good thing the door behind me slammed open. I hadn't heard the scratch of a key in the lock first. Still, I had to hope this was rescue....

I spun to see who had kicked my door down. A mistake, I realized, the instant Rowan's hand clamped down on the back of my neck.

His gesture wasn't reassuring. Instead, it screamed ownership. Threat. Fingers squeezed my spine as if my bones were sticks ready for cracking....

And the person who'd kicked open my door materialized into...not Tank. Instead, it was a woman who ignored me while speaking to Rowan over my head.

"Chief McCallister. I thought we had a deal. We protect your pack from the node. You provide every requested assistance. Which, primarily, means staying out of our way."

The woman's hand slid toward the bulge holstered under her arm, and I recognized her at last. *Lupe.* Tank's temporary boss. The one who'd tried to hire me.

The one who, I was pretty sure, had a day job as a cop.

"I've left your affairs alone," Rowan

growled. "I recommend you return the favor."

I wasn't sure what he was talking about—other than me—until my ears popped. Then I heard it. The snarls of wolves in the stairwell were quiet enough not to wake the neighbors. But scritches of fast-moving toenails were more ominous for the muted nature of the resultant thuds.

No wonder Rowan's fingers pinched down harder. It was all I could do to prevent my shoulders from hunching upwards. This, I'd learned, was a fact of life around alpha werewolves. They took out their aggressions on those under their thumbs.

Literally in my case.

Lupe took a step closer, which didn't help matters. She was goading him, whether she meant to or not. Rowan's body twisted behind me, and now there were two hands around my throat. Two hands squeezing, cutting off my oxygen....

And instinct took over. My head morphed before my body. Wolf teeth bit into Rowan's forearm even as the rest of me became a dead weight dangling from his grip.

"Shit!"

He flung me against the wall, the electricity of his impending shift prickling against my nostrils. I scrambled to four feet, trying to work my way out of the baggy sweats Tank had lent me. My wounded ankle throbbed.

Okay, that wasn't working. Giving up on shedding clothes, I gathered my haunches under me anyway even though my right hind leg felt like I'd slammed it in a door.

Then Lupe was between me and Rowan. She hadn't drawn her gun and her body was still fully human, but the air oozed with near-shift tension. "Athena is one of *mine* for the next week and a half."

Rowan, to my surprise, reined in his feral impulses. There was fur on the outside of his throat, but his speech was fully human. "Is this true, Athena? You're a Samhain Shifter? You chose to give up your lone-wolf status to someone other than me?"

He'd smell a lie. It was one of many downsides of hanging out with werewolves.

So I made my answer truthful. Accepted Lupe's offer, belatedly and in my head only.

Then I nodded. Barked out a soft yet audible reply.

Rowan's cheek twitched. He was annoyed but holding onto his anger.

"Alright then." He spoke to Lupe, not to me. "She's your problem until Samhain. Come November, though, Athena will be mine to command."

***

That was bad...but a problem for the

future. Because Rowan left, muted growls from the stairwell cutting off the moment he passed out of sight beyond my shattered door frame. Seconds later, two wolves entered my apartment, shimmering upward into Tank and—I assumed based on his tattoos—Ryder. Both were naked, but I had eyes for only one.

Tall. Broad. Magnificent. I took a step forward without meaning to and....

"Pack your stuff," Lupe demanded, drawing me away from my perusal of masculine perfection even as she tossed Ryder and Tank clothes I hadn't noticed her carrying. "Bring whatever you need for the next five days."

Her words slapped me with the need

to obey. An alpha imperative, even if she wasn't an official pack leader. I winced, realizing that my stint as a Samhain Shifter was going to suck.

Because it wasn't any more palatable having my legs forced into motion by a female alpha than by a male alpha. Muscles struggled against themselves. Behind Lupe, Ryder smirked as he yanked up his jeans.

He clearly wasn't impressed by my addition as team mate. And, having survived middle school, I knew what it meant when one of the cool kids had it in for you.

The solution was to prove you were stronger than they were. Browbeat the bullies until they left you alone.

Among werewolves, power equated to alpha commands like the ones Lupe and Rowan tossed around—something I was incapable of. Instead, I aimed for the next best thing. A snappy shift.

Unfortunately, exhaustion dragged me down like glue on my paws. I scrabbled my way to humanity rather than bursting out of my fur.

A show of weakness. Ryder rolled his eyes and turned his back.

Not because I was naked either. Because I wasn't, not really. My human tongue untangled itself while I struggled to get my arms back into the top that had twisted around my neck.

"I took the job, but that doesn't mean I have to leave my apartment." My voice,

I was glad to hear, was firm. "My sister and her friend are coming here tomorrow for fall break. I won't let them down."

Although I'd be letting Harper down for sure in a week, unless something miraculous happened. Rowan wanted me in his pack, and I intended to refuse him. Which meant I'd be explaining to Harper why I couldn't come see her. Why the alpha whose territory encompassed her boarding school was refusing me access.

Our impending separation made spending her upcoming vacation together even more important. So I stood firm, even in the face of an alpha unlikely to appreciate that stance.

Annoyance rolled off Lupe, but she wasn't the one who answered. "Bring them along." Tank's face was hidden as he tapped into his cell phone. His clothes were rumpled, as if he'd spent more time focusing on the device in his hand than on dressing. "Kira's close to their age. She said she'd keep your girls company and out of trouble."

Lupe huffed deep and low in her throat, then turned her reaction into words. "Kira isn't the one who makes that decision. You'll have to wait until morning to see what Mai has to say about that."

Another round of thumb typing. Another answer without glancing in my direction. "Mai's awake too. She says it's not a problem. She wouldn't mind a brief vacation from parenting a teen."

Mai? Kira? Mate and daughter? My

clothing mishap was now sorted so I shouldn't have felt so cold.

Ryder's annoyed interjection was almost welcome. "We're babysitting?" He turned back around, arms crossed. "I thought we had a single goal until Samhain. Fae. Not puppies. This is bullshit."

Lupe pressed a finger to her lips and Ryder's complaint petered off. Not a pack leader, huh? She certainly acted like one.

Whatever Lupe's role, all three of us waited out her silence as she considered the two males, then me swathed in Tank's baggy clothing. She hummed noncommittally then addressed Tank.

"You'll deal with it?"

It, I gathered, was me. Harper. Clara.

Babysitting duty.

Any attraction I'd felt toward Tank vanished as he nodded. "I'll deal with it," he agreed, as if I was twelve bags of groceries waiting to be unloaded out of the car.

Chapter 14

Tank's way of dealing with logistics was heavy-handed. "Athena will spend the night here. I'll watch her."

"*Watch* her?" Ryder's eyebrows waggled. "Is that what the kids are calling it these days?"

"Go home," Tank growled. And I must have been tireder than I thought because when my eyes blinked back open, he and I were alone.

Alright then. I hadn't invited Tank into my home, but this was better than packing up and leaving while my ankle throbbed like the pounding of a heavy-metal drummer. I would make the best of the cards I'd been dealt.

"There's an air mattress in the closet." I sucked in a deep breath and started hobbling in that direction, but Tank was in front of me. Immovable. He didn't bring his hands down on my shoulders this time, but he *did* sidestep to prevent me from walking around him.

"The couch," he rumbled, "will be fine."

"It's ratty. I mean, not actually ratty. No vermin. But this isn't the cabin in the woods I always wanted." I tended to run at the mouth when tired, and now was no exception.

Arms swept me up as Tank asked, "What would your dream cabin look like?"

One of his hands was beneath my knees as if I was a child; the other cradled my back. I was airborne. Tingling everywhere his fingers touched. And, at the same time, relaxing in a way I hadn't since my mother died.

Perhaps that's why I answered his nosy question. "There'd be light. Lots of light for painting."

Tank hummed as he carried me toward my bedroom without asking for instructions. He'd already scouted it out while I was locked in the hallway, I gathered. Plus, it wasn't as if there were many doors to choose between.

"What else?" Tank rumbled.

I tried to squash my lips shut, but they kept flapping. "A potbelly stove. The roar of a waterfall rather than traffic outside."

Tank was silent as he lowered me onto the bed, mattress so soft it almost made up for my ankle throbbing. I blinked. How exactly had Tank managed to pull the sheets and blankets down while holding me? Everything was turning fuzzy, the weight of the day and my choices falling down on my head.

"Do you need both of these pillows?" Tank demanded.

"What?" I pried my eyes open with an effort. I couldn't believe I'd fallen asleep with Tank looming over me. I needed to wait until he was out in the living room then push my dresser under the door knob. The effort wouldn't keep me safe, but it might slow Tank down in case his animal nature came to the fore in the night....

"Do you," Tank repeated more slowly, "need both of these pillows?"

There was no animal in his eyes. Or what I could see of his eyes before he twisted his head away from me. That habitual gesture drove me crazy. I might have growled, just a little bit.

"Athena?"

Right. The pillow. I fumbled for the spare I'd bought so Harper would stop bugging me. *"If you only own one pillow, you're telling the world you want to sleep alone for the rest of your life."*

"Here," I said, handing my sister-silencing pillow over to the first man I'd willingly allowed to visit my apartment since moving here. Of course he wouldn't want to bed down with only couch cushions to support him. "There are sheets in the closet...."

My jaw cracked as I lost words to a yawn so intense it brought tears to my eyes. And when I wiped them away, Tank was gone.

No, not gone. His fingers settled on my injured ankle. Gentle as butterflies, they lifted my foot and slipped the sister-silencing pillow beneath it.

When exhausted, I lost my filter. That's the only explanation I can give for the words that slipped out of my lips. "Mai is one lucky woman."

"Mai?" I smelled Tank's confusion one second before a huge hand settled on my forehead as gently as a cloud kissing a mountaintop. "You mean my alpha's mate?"

Absurd as it was, his answer softened the mattress yet further. I'd forgotten, for a second, that Lupe wasn't Tank's alpha. That he answered to another shifter somewhere in a nearby territory.

But that wasn't what my tired brain fixated on. Instead, it drew other connections.

Mai wasn't Tank's mate. Kira wasn't his daughter.

A feather of breath fluttered against

my forehead. "Dream about your cabin," Tank murmured. "You'll have it someday. You deserve it."

I forgot about the dresser and the doorknob and let myself drift into the healing silence of sleep.

***

Hours later, I woke to an empty apartment. Crutches leaned against my bedside, which should have chilled me. After all, it meant Tank had entered my room while I was sleeping and I hadn't noticed. Instead, I leveraged myself to my feet, tested my ankle, then winced as swollen muscles twinged beneath my weight.

"Tank?" I called, sliding the crutches beneath my armpits.

No one answered. When I limped my way out into the combined kitchen/dining/living room, the only sign that he'd ever been there was a nearly invisible dent in the couch cushions.

Well, that's not quite true. There were other signs when I widened my search perimeter.

For example, the reek of wolf urine in the entranceway had been replaced by the cheap chemical aroma of my dish soap. When I opened the repaired door, I discovered a metal plate on the inside of the door jamb, presumably to make it harder to kick in. And....

"Are you ready to go?"

The voice just out of sight in the hallway wasn't Tank's. I jumped, a bad idea with crutches. Especially when no helpful hands were there to catch me when I fell.

Luckily, the door was once again solid. I clung to the knob and got one crutch back under me while holding the other out like a weapon. "Who are you?"

Because the speaker was now visible. A well-dressed man stood just outside my door, close enough so I could smell the fur of wolf about him. He cocked his head. "You really don't remember me? We met less than a week ago."

I noted the elegance of the man's posture. The darkness of his skin.

His face, like everyone's, told me nothing. But, yeah, this probably was the fourth member of the Samhain Shifters. The one I'd spent the least time around. The one whose name didn't match him at all.

"Butch," I acknowledged. "What are you doing here?"

Keys twirled around his pointer finger. "I'm here to take you to camp."

"Come back later then. I have places to be." The list in my head was long enough to use up most of the remaining daylight hours. I needed to hit the bank to deposit Marina's second check and figure out how much longer it would be before the first registered in my balance. A bit of shopping after that would make sure the kids thought spring break was an adventure rather than forced boredom. Then off to Highlands to gather up my sister and Clara while (bank willing) paying ahead for the rest of the school year.

Plus, I needed a bit of time to figure out whether this really was Butch. Face blindness didn't usually cramp my style, but I wasn't about to invite a stranger into my apartment without being utterly certain of his identity.

"Anywhere you have to go, I'll drive you," Maybe-Butch said, just as I'd suspected he would. He didn't seem the type to let small matters sidetrack him from his chosen destination. Which raised the stakes—now I'd be risking my sister's safety on my faulty ID skills.

Meanwhile, as Maybe-Butch spoke, the keys snagged on his fingers and stopped spinning. No, not on his fingers. They'd caught on the seam of the soft leather gloves that fit his hands' shape and color so well that I hadn't at first realized his fingers weren't bare.

But why wear gloves inside a heated hallway? Without a coat or a hat to suggest the weather had chilled down outside?

Phantom fingers squeezed my throat, a memory of last night's altercation. Gloves would prevent leaving fingerprints. And Rowan might not mind sending an underling to break his word to Lupe, not if it meant regaining the upper hand....

I took a step backward into my apartment...and the stranger caught the door before I could slam it in his face.

Chapter 15

"What are you doing?" Maybe-Butch had appeared deceptively slender from a distance. Up close, I could see the strength of his arms. The cat-like grace of his movements.

Whoever this was, I'd recognize him if I ever met him again.

"Packing," I answered, turning the excuse into truth before I spoke it. If this really was Butch, I'd need to gather up my clothes and toothbrush before moving in with his boss for the foreseeable future. "It might take awhile."

"I'll wait inside, if you don't mind."

He brushed past me. I can't explain how exactly. It's not as if I was a slave to politeness. But one moment I was blocking the way into my apartment, the next moment Maybe-Butch was settling down cross-legged on my couch.

Now I was the one to ask: "What are you doing?"

"What does it look like I'm doing?" He was in full-on lotus position, middle fingers touching thumbs while hands rested atop his knees. His eyes were closed.

"Meditating?"

"Very astute."

Dismissing me, he began to hum

softly. If this was Rowan's choice of enforcer, he was a very strange one.

Still, I did my due diligence. Turning my back on Maybe-Butch raised hairs on my neck, but soon I was alone in my bedroom. There, I dug through dirty laundry until I found the business card Tank had given me. Then I keyed his digits into my phone.

I didn't call, though. Instead, I snuck back out to snap a surreptitious shot of the man meditating on my sofa. Maybe-Butch's eyebrows rose even though he couldn't have seen me through his closed eyelids. My inner wolf whispered: *Run.*

Instead, I shut the bedroom door, attached the photo, and texted Tank. *"This is Athena. Is the photo Butch?"*

Tank's answer came quickly. As if he'd been waiting by his phone to hear from me...or was hiding his face in the screen so someone wouldn't wince at his features. *"He's your ride for the day."* A pause then, as if he'd reread my text. *"Yes, that's Butch. Why do you ask?"*

"Long story," I typed. Then, despite myself: *"I'm a bit face blind. Makes recognizing people difficult."*

And why did I tell him that? Face blindness was a weakness. I'd be working alongside Tank for the next five days. I needed to keep my guard up.

But Tank's answer had no crow of victory about it. Instead, the text came slowly, as if he'd taken a moment to google before typing out his reply.

"Noted. Thank you for trusting me. Please let me know if I can lend a hand."

Trust. I blinked. Did I trust Tank?

I crept back out into the hall and glanced at the meditating stranger that another near-stranger had vouched for. Then I accepted the inevitable.

"Five minutes," I told Butch, "and I'll be ready to go."

***

Butch was endlessly patient as we worked through my long list of responsibilities. He didn't, however, put the top up on his convertible despite the cold wind that made me snuggle deeper into my sweater. So maybe that explained the gloves?

I had enough oddities of my own that I chose not to remark upon Butch's. And within a few hours, thoughts of his affinity for gloves faded into the background.

What didn't fade into the background was Nick, immediately apparent as we pulled into the visitor lot at Highlands. My stepfather sat on the stone wall outside Harper's dormitory, licking ice cream out of a triple-decker ice-cream cone as if he was a kid and this was summer instead of nearly the end of October.

I must have breathed funny at the sight because Butch asked, "Someone you know?" He removed the key from the ignition, flicking the metal part into the plastic base by pressing it against the steering wheel.

Fastidious. That was the word I'd use to describe my unasked-for companion. Unfortunately, the related term—*perceptive*—was equally true.

So I didn't try to sidestep my relationship to the ice-cream licker. "My stepfather," I admitted. "If you don't mind giving me a minute...."

I'd used the same phrase all day. While picking out fresh underwear for my sister. While depositing my ill-gotten check and learning that the bank put holds on deposits containing so many zeroes. I kept expecting Butch to make some snarky comment about how many minutes he'd given me already. But he simply did that half-bow thing, the same way he'd done repeatedly throughout the day, then let me limp toward Nick alone.

"Get run over by a truck, kid?" my stepfather greeted me, jerking his chin at my crutches. I didn't really need them, my ankle having loosened up over the course of the day. But Tank had left the crutches for me. And, anyway, it was better to be safe than sorry.

"Yes," I lied. After all, Nick wasn't a werewolf able to smell untruth...and he couldn't care less about my ankle. He was here for one thing only—money. The fact that Harper expected me in five minutes made it certain that he'd get his way.

Before Nick could demand cash, though, a family clattered past us.

Mother, father, daughter. All perfectly dressed. All smiling. "I love the Eiffel Tower at night!" the girl emoted, twirling into a pirouette. "Chocolate croissants! Picnics by the Seine!"

"Try not to sound so posh," the mother chided, tucking a strand of hair behind her daughter's ear while reining in her exuberance. "There are scholarship students here. Not everyone can enjoy fall break in Europe."

I flinched, knowing that Harper was one of those scholarship students. But, thanks to Marina, I'd no longer struggle to pay the tuition portion we *were* responsible for. Maybe one day I'd take my sister to Paris....

Nick had no such regrets about his

child-rearing abilities. Instead, he licked furiously at his ice cream to prevent it from melting onto his fingers. Only after that disaster was averted did he acknowledge me again.

"I hear you paid for the rest of Harper's school year."

"How could you know that?" I'd been in the bursar's office only half an hour ago. Although, technically, Nick was wrong about my payment. I'd asked the clerk not to deposit my check until Monday, which is when the bank had suggested Marina's initial payment should clear.

"Went to pick these up," Nick answered, pulling a sheaf of familiar papers out from under his butt.

My stepfather had been sitting on Harper's permission forms to keep his butt dry on the damp stone. Worse, there was no signature at the bottom of the page. My teeth clenched so tight my jaw ached.

So we were being overt about the quid pro quo. I shook off my fury and started negotiating. "I'll have your money Monday. Plus an extra hundred if you sign the papers now."

"Do I look like an idiot?" Nick flung his hands wide, the gesture dislodging the remainder of his ice cream. The semi-solid lump flew through the air and landed at the feet of a woman whose handbag, I was pretty sure, cost as much as Butch's car.

Nick smirked and I realized the gesture hadn't been accidental. He was going to make a scene. Right here, in front of Harper's schoolmates and their parents.

So I pulled out my wallet. Removed every bill I had—which wasn't very many. "Will this tide you over for the weekend?" I asked, keeping my voice low and hoping he'd get the message.

Rather than answering, Nick counted, muttering numbers under his breath as if he couldn't manage the simple arithmetic silently. My cheeks heated. I could only hope no one linked us to Harper....

Then hope faded as my sister and Clara pushed out the dormitory's front door.

***

"Dad?" Harper shifted her weight from foot to foot, face uncertain. She'd been expecting me, but given our relative positions, Nick was the more obvious sight.

I swung my crutches around so I could clomp sideways into full view. "Harper. Your dad and I were visiting, but he's got to go..."

"...Get you girls some ice cream." Nick was all smiles as he rose off the wall, dropping his empty cone onto the sidewalk as if Highlands' grounds were a dump rather than a spotless showplace.

"I've come into a small windfall. Shall we hit up the truck in the quad?"

For some reason, I half expected a werewolf to show up and get rid of Nick before he could cause any further damage to Harper's vacation. But a glance toward the parking lot showed that Butch was in the back seat meditating. His eyes were closed. Unless I called out to him, he wouldn't know I needed assistance.

Which was fine. I was used to dealing with Nick solo. "We're on a schedule...." I started, only to be interrupted by the person I least expected to find on campus.

"Harper, a moment." Marina's melodic voice was instantly recognizable.

But that didn't make any sense....

I turned to face the approaching woman. It really was Marina, even though she was dressed completely differently in a pencil skirt and fitted jacket. Still, I recognized the grace of her steps as she insinuated her way into our little cluster, the way the air sweetened as she came near.

"Ms. Rothschild." Harper's eyes dropped to the pavement. "I've got my history textbook with me. I'm going to study over break, I promise."

Marina/Ms. Rothschild's gaze met mine even though her words were directed at my sister. "Perhaps I could speak to your guardian for a moment."

Harper's face twisted. "Dad? Do you

mind?"

Feeding his daughter ice cream was about as much parenting as Nick was up for. No wonder he slid out from under the responsibility like a cat bowing away from an unwanted pat. "I promised these girls a treat. Athena can handle school details."

And then they were gone. My hodgepodge of family walking away in a disjointed cluster, nothing like the perfect Parisian vacationers. Clara winced as she hopped over the melting ice cream my stepfather had dropped moments earlier. Nick veered sideways to shake the hand of a Congressman who I was pretty sure he hadn't been previously introduced to. And Harper bowed her head and scuffed her feet, uncomfortable as the linchpin that held their trio together.

I wanted to help, but Ms. Rothchild—Marina—drew my attention back to the immediate problem. "As requested, I found another job for you," she purred. "We'll discuss it at the museum. Tonight. 7:30 sharp."

So shaming Harper about her grades had been an excuse to speak with me. I tamped down a burst of protective rage and focused. "I'm not so sure..."

"About returning to a crime scene?" Marina took a step closer. "No one will recognize you."

That wasn't what I'd been about to say. Instead, I'd had time to realize I didn't need more money, that Harper would be safer if I severed this connection. The things I truly craved—independence from Rowan, for example—were beyond Marina's ability to provide.

But parents and students swirled around us. This wasn't the time or the place to say no to someone who, I suspected, wouldn't be pleased by rejection.

"I'll come to you then," Marina continued, taking a step closer. Today, she smelled like wedding cake, frothy with undertones of sugar and vanilla. In stark contrast, her words were as predatory as a hunting hawk. "Where exactly are you staying now that you've moved out of your apartment?"

She knew I'd moved out of my apartment? This was a mistake. Such a mistake.

"I don't think...." I started, my lips numb as if I'd just left the dentist. Why was it so hard to speak?

"Don't fear me, child. I'm here to help you." Marina's scent enfolded me, gentle and supportive. "I hear you're having a problem with your alpha. Is that what's put you so on edge?"

I had a nearly overwhelming urge to spill my guts. To tell her everything.

Instead, I pressed all my weight onto my injured ankle, using the pain to keep me focused. My words, I was glad to hear, came out clearly: "You promised not to bother my sister."

"Did I?" Marina cocked her head. "I don't recall making such a promise. But I could. When we meet tonight to discuss your job."

Harper was already on her way back from the ice-cream truck. I refused to discuss this in front of her, especially now that I knew Marina was her teacher.

I'd been boxed in and we both knew it. So I nodded. "The museum. 7:30. I'll see you in a couple of hours."

Chapter 16

The ice-cream visit must have gone better than expected because Harper was cheerful during the ride to our new, albeit temporary, residence. Cheerful...and curious.

"You're sure Butch isn't your boyfriend?" Her fingers clung to the back of my seat as she pulled herself far enough forward to be heard over the rush of wind against our faces. I glanced at Harper's waist to make sure she was wearing a seat belt before answering the nosy question.

"Positive."

"You should reconsider," Harper told me. "This car is pretty awesome."

For the first time since I'd met him, I thought Butch might have sported a faint hint of a smile. But when I turned to look at him directly, all expression was gone.

"So Tank's the one who has you all hot and bothered?" my sister continued, blithely ignoring the way her words heated my cheeks.

"I'm not hot and bothered," I lied, smelling Butch's amusement this time.

"Maybe she's looking for a girlfriend, not a boyfriend," Clara suggested as if the "she" in question wasn't right in front of them. "Is Athena straight?"

"Not sure," my sister answered. "I feel like I should know that...."

"I'm not looking for anyone," I rebutted as the convertible pulled through a gate and stopped in front of what appeared to be a private campground. Meanwhile, my eyes proved me a liar when they flew directly to Tank.

He was manning a grill, shirt off to reveal muscles that were more mouthwatering than the meat he was tending. The latter, though, demanded all of his attention. Perhaps that's why he didn't bother to shield his face as Butch and I wrestled the girls' extra-large suitcases out of the car.

Harper and Clara weren't as intent upon their tasks as the rest of us. No wonder their eyes widened as they took in the shirtless male. No wonder they flinched as their gazes rose up to take in his face.

I tensed, remembering the shallowness of the museum teenagers. Harper opened her mouth and I closed my eyes...

...Only to reopen them as an unfamiliar female voice intruded on the scene. "Tank's the best griller ever."

The girl who'd spoken was a teenager—Kira? Yes, I decided. This had to be Tank's pack mate. And, even though she wasn't his daughter as I'd initially suspected, she was standing up for him against two other girls nearly her own age.

Not only standing up for him, literally standing between the other girls and Tank. Kira's arms were so full of tupperware containers I could only see her from the nose up, but her eyes flashed with the intensity of a shifter protecting her pack.

So this was why Tank thought joining the Samhain Shifters was so important. This was the positive side of pack bonds. I took a step forward. "Do you need a hand with those containers?"

Kira shook her head, gaze not touching mine. Instead, she continued to stare down Harper and Clara until my sister gulped and muttered, "I'm sorry."

"Yeah," Clara echoed.

"Nothing to be sorry about," Tank

answered before either girl could elaborate. His hand touched Kira's shoulder, one quick tap. In response, her face scrunched up in annoyance. But then she nodded and pasted a welcoming smile on her face.

"Either of you vegetarian?"

"I am," Clara said tentatively. She was unaware of the shifter byplay that had chastened me and my sister, but she understood that *something* had just happened.

"Great!" Kira's honest enthusiasm blew away the bad air between them. "We've got veggie kebabs here and soy dogs in the freezer. If none of that sounds good, I think there're some tofu burgers, but they're yuck. For dessert—s'mores!"

And even though Kira had refused my help, she lifted the top bin off the stack now to hand to my sister then passed the next down to Clara. "Should we put them on the grill?" Clara asked.

"The other one." Tank pointed with his tongs at a second grill smoking gently on the other side of the walkway. "No meat-juice contamination." Then, facing Butch, who I'd forgotten about in the midst of teenage drama: "Thanks for your help today. I owe you one."

Butch shook his head. "Don't thank me." The words, sounded oddly formal, not the usual shrug-off of unnecessary appreciation. Without further explanation, he left us alone with the pile of luggage, heading for a cabin at the end of the row.

Awkwardness hung in his wake. The girls were busy, but Tank's face was now averted. Averted from *me*, the only person close enough to pay attention.

Despite my best intentions to ignore this thing between us, I reached up to cup his jaw, pulling his face back front and center. "Don't do that," I ordered. Then, realizing how abrupt I'd sounded: "Please."

Beneath my fingers, Tank's lips quirked ever so slightly. "Alright. If you insist."

***

If Marina's timeline hadn't hung heavy on my mind, the rest of the evening would have been delightful. Ryder built a bonfire out back, which is where we all retreated once dinner was ready. The girls roasted s'mores, getting punchier the more sugar they consumed.

"Watch this!" Kira demanded, grabbing the open bag of marshmallows and spraying a couple of dozen into the air...then catching each one in an athletic feat that only a shifter would have been capable of.

"Ooh, I want to try!" Clara's response, thankfully, was sidetracked by our leader rising and brushing off the seat of her pants.

"Training starts tomorrow at 7. Don't stay up too late."

Then Lupe was gone into the

darkness while Harper's head cocked in question. "Training?" Of the three teens, she was the only one still acting like a guest rather than a hooligan.

"Not for us," Kira answered before I could. "We get to sleep in then laugh at the 'dults in the morning."

"Who you calling a 'dult?" Ryder growled, grabbing Kira around the neck. Butch scooted sideways away from the tussle while I tensed, not liking the idea of the tattooed male manhandling someone halfway between girlhood and womanhood.

Tank didn't like it either. He'd been browning a marshmallow for my sister, but the end of the stick stabbed into the ground so fast I didn't see it leaving his fingers. His demand was barely audible but scarier for the low register.

"Don't touch her."

Abruptly, the air stank of fur.

Just like that, the mood soured. Firelight reflected off of wolves in both Tank's and Ryder's eyes now. We appeared to be seconds away from a lupine explosion.

I considered calling for Lupe but hesitated. Clara was unaware of the existence of werewolves while my sister had only heard about—never seen—our dark side. If I called in reinforcements, were Ryder and Tank more or less likely to go wolf?

"What's your problem?" Ryder's dark eyebrows lowered into a ridge of shadow.

"She's just a kid."

"Yeah." Kira was the one who broke the tension. Scrambling out of Ryder's hold—looser now—she pressed up on tiptoes so she could kiss Tank's cheek. "Use your nose, you big goof."

"Your nose?" Clara asked. She and Harper were both wide-eyed, but for very different reasons. Clara was trying to figure out what was going on. Harper, I suspected, was shell-shocked by memories of Nick.

Not that her father had a wolf inside him. But he liked to fight. Boy did he like to fight.

And...Tank didn't. He inhaled once, long and slow. Then the sharp bite of electricity faded. "My mistake." He dipped his chin, acknowledging his error.

Ryder, to my surprise, didn't push the issue. Instead, he was graceful in victory. "Apology accepted."

"Who wants to learn to juggle?" Kira asked, as if we hadn't barely evaded a wolf fight.

"Ooh, me!" Clara clapped her hands.

And, just like that, danger dissipated into the night.

***

Well, the danger had dissipated, but my sister was still edgy. She reached for her marshmallow then winced as Tank's hand landed in the exact same spot.

"Sorry," my sister began, yanking her

fingers away as if the fire had reached out and burned them.

"Let me tell you something I learned during my first year as a lawyer," Tank murmured, body unmoving as if Harper was a stray dog as likely to bite as to flee from him. "Never apologize when you've done nothing wrong."

"Sor—" my sister started, only to catch herself before she could spit out the word a second time.

Tank shrugged. "And ask for what you want. You want the marshmallow, or you want me to finish roasting it?"

"I—" Harper's eyes slid sideways, seeking escape. But Tank just sat there, still and silent. And eventually she cleared her throat and spat out a complete sentence. "If you want, you can finish browning it for me."

"Is that what *you* want?"

This time, Harper didn't hesitate. "Yes."

So he reached forward slowly, gently, then twirled the roasting stick by infinitesimal fractions between strong fingers. Beside us, Clara and Kira dropped marshmallows onto the ground while trying to juggle, their laughter easy and infectious. Butch suggested they move closer to the firelight. Ryder made snarky comments that managed not to sting.

And Harper engaged, ever so gradually, with the roaster of her marshmallow. "What's it like being a lawyer?" she asked, voice so quiet Tank could have pretended not to hear her.

But he didn't ignore her. Instead, he answered the same way he would have answered an adult. "It's empowering. Knowing the law lets you deal with bullies without resorting to fisticuffs." His lips curled into a self-deprecating smile. "Which isn't to say I always manage to remember to use my words."

Harper glanced in my direction, and I got the distinct impression she didn't want me to hear her next question. So I focused my eyes on the other girls' juggling fiasco while straining shifter ears to their limit to pick out her opening gambit.

"Do you ever deal with custody

cases?”

Tank nodded. “I do. They can be messy if there’s no clear evidence who should be a minor’s guardian.”

“How do you figure that out?”

I hesitated, wanting to be privy to the rest of this conversation. But Harper hadn’t wanted me to listen. All three girls were safe, and I had another engagement calling.

“Will you guys be okay if I catch up on emails?” I asked, rising off the log I’d chosen as my seat. My ankle didn’t twinge once.

“Sure.” Harper was too intent upon smashing hot marshmallows into melting chocolate to look at me, but Tank gave me his full attention. He glanced at the abandoned crutches, at me, then left whatever he'd been about to say silent. Offered a single nod instead.

He'd take care of Harper and Clara. He wasn't hiding his face either.

So I left them there. One big, happy, temporary family.

Left them there and strode to the cabin on the end that Butch had come out of earlier. None of the doors here had locks, and Butch seemed like the sort who'd keep his car keys on a hook where they had no chance of getting misplaced.

I was wrong. A carved wooden shelf sat where I'd expected a hook to be. The shelf looked newer than the faded wall around it, intricate indentations turning what could have been simple braces into two trees holding up a cloud-shaped top.

The keys were right there, though. Easily accessible. Just what I needed since my own car was parked in front of my apartment where I'd left it before the museum gig.

It was stealing, but stealing was what I was good at. I grabbed the keys, borrowed the convertible, and headed back into the city to meet my boss.

Chapter 17

The streets stunk of wolves. I parked four blocks over from the museum but ended up veering out of my way when the first wave of fur hit me. Ducking down behind a hedge, I surveyed the dark and empty street.

Nobody was present, but the strength of the scent suggested werewolves had been here recently. Perhaps they'd passed by repeatedly? Best guess, these were Rowan's henchmen, patrolling the city to ensure no one else made the same faux pas I had. I wasn't so sure the safe-passage card in my wallet would be enough to get me off the hook a second time if I was caught.

So don't get caught. I crept toward the darkened house the hedges surrounded, intending to cut through the backyard and find a less wolfy route leading to my destination. Only problem? The residents had installed motion-activated floodlights. The sudden flare of fluorescence was blinding. I jerked, twisting my injured ankle the tiniest bit and setting off a cascade of pain.

"It's not that bad," I muttered as I retreated. Back to the street and away from the backyard that was now fully illuminated. It was safer to risk Rowan's scouts than it was to set off a burglar alarm and draw in human police.

Stepping back onto the sidewalk, I ignored the prickling of skin that promised I was acting like prey at a watering hole. The streetlight's glow wasn't as intense as that of the security light, but it was more wide-ranging. The open street made it impossible to guard my back and my front at the same time...

A yip made me jump. Wolf, not dog. And close, somewhere between me and the museum....

I hesitated, eying the path ahead where a streetlight had burned out and plunged the street into total darkness. I was going to be late if I didn't keep walking.

But late was better than caught. Late was better than explaining myself to Rowan when Lupe wasn't there to bail me out a second time.

I retreated to Butch's car and eased the vehicle back onto the street.

***

It took two tries to find a wolf-free parking space. Even then, I didn't trust that patrols wouldn't stumble upon my trail as soon as I rounded the first corner.

So I used an old dog trick, finding a patch of fresh excrement and step-smearing awfulness across the bottom of my tennis shoes. Marina was going to turn up her nose even worse than usual when she came within nose range, but shifters sniffing at my trail would think I was just a scent-challenged human. They'd never guess I was another wolf.

By the time I reached the museum, the lights were out and the steps were empty. No wonder—it was closer to 8 than 7:30. Still, I found a shadowed spot behind a Grecian column and settled down to wait.

And wait. And wait. When I'd arrived, I was panting from evasive actions and wincing at each step on my throbbing ankle. Now, the only sensation was chill from the marble beneath my butt.

Well, part of that chill may also have emanated from the questions running through my head. Why was I hanging out in such a dangerous spot when Marina looked to be a no-show? Did I have a death wish? Or—as seemed more likely—an inability to relax into a friendly gathering complete with bonfire and s'mores?

The image of Tank twirling Harper's marshmallow stick over flickering flames warmed me ever so slightly. Warmed me enough that I was able to tamp down my indecision and rise, stuffing cold fingers into not-quite-so-cold pockets.

Whether Marina had stood me up or I'd missed her due to tardiness, we weren't meeting tonight. I might as well ditch my stinky shoes, return Butch's car, and hope he hadn't noticed it was missing.

I took a step...and my phone chirped. As if someone was close enough to see I was about to leave and, only then, chose to contact me.

"You're being paranoid," I muttered.

But when I looked at the screen, the text had come from an unknown number. *"Something came up."*

"Marina?" I typed back, peering out at the street as best I could without raising my head and making it obvious I thought she was watching.

A couple strolled past arm-in-arm. Multiple busy cafes and restaurants boasted full views of the museum. My boss could be anywhere, or nowhere.

Meanwhile, her answer was fast but

vague. *"I'll be in touch."*

I waited a solid minute, expecting further explanation. But nothing else came through after that.

Eventually, I put away my phone, stretching and turning for one more view of my surroundings. There were too many people present to tell whether one was a watcher for Marina. And the longer I hung out here, the more likely I was to run into another werewolf.

You won this round, Marina, I admitted. Still, I'd learned something in the process.

My employer was testing me and I'd passed. I'd passed...even if it was at the expense of my self esteem.

***

The private campground was dark by the time I rolled back up the drive. Giggles from the girls' cabin promised that Harper was fine, but everyone else seemed to have followed Lupe's advice and turned in early.

I did my best to park exactly where I'd found the convertible, then I debated whether to return the keys. Perhaps if I left them on the leather seat, Butch might think he'd made a mistake and forgotten to place them on his tree shelf? The chance of me sneaking into Butch's cabin with him present seemed halfway between zero and zilch.

My ankle wasn't the only reason I

winced as I wavered between the car and Butch's cabin. I hadn't thought this far ahead. Wasn't used to working around people I'd have to eat breakfast with the next morning. Or to having my sister a hundred yards away from the crime scene.

Each step now sent a spike of pain through my ankle. Each thought of Harper sent a similar spike of pain through my gut.

I shouldn't have brought her here. I should have found another way to....

The scent of approaching fur warned me one second before a hand clamped down over my mouth.

Chapter 18

A second hand gripped my arm, hard, unyielding. I was silenced and I was caught.

But I wasn't vanquished. Adrenaline pushed away pain and exhaustion. Raising my good foot, I prepared to slam the heel into my attacker's kneecap. Then I crumpled as my weak ankle rejected being asked to hold my weight.

I was falling...then I wasn't. The hand that had covered my mouth gripped my waist instead. I found myself tucked against Tank's torso while he breathed into my ear.

"What exactly have you been up to?"

Relief made me snarky. "I don't think that's any of your business."

But Tank wasn't listening. Instead, he maneuvered me into the convertible so skillfully my ankle didn't twinge once. Slipping the keys out of my hand and into the ignition, he lowered the top then tilted back my seat so he could elevate my foot.

Fingers skimmed across my ankle bone, their gentle touch devoid of any annoyance. So maybe I'd misunderstood his question? The hand over my mouth, I now realized, was intended to silence any startled emoting. Tank had prevented me from blowing my cover to the nearby werewolves.

"Relax," he murmured, his massaging fingers backing up the suggestion. And I did. Sinking back into the seat leather, I gazed up into the sky.

The expanse was full of stars I couldn't name, just like my body was full of equally unfamiliar sensations. Like Van Gogh's Starry Night. All swirls of color and utter confusion, yet so engrossing I never wanted this moment to stop.

But it did. Tank's fingers released me at the same moment his words brought me back to reality. "Your ankle isn't worse, but it will be if you keep overdoing things." His tone was gruff, growly. "I bought you a brace," he continued.

"Boots with ankle support. I'll go get them. Wait here."

I pushed my torso upright. "I have to bring Butch back his keys...."

"You'll only confuse him." Tank was a dark shape above me, one that should have been menacing but wasn't. He was just far enough away that I could have rolled sideways and evaded his offensive if he lunged for my throat.

Not that Tank had given me any reason to be afraid of him. But that was the whole point. The distance between us now was an entirely unwerewolf-like promise of personal space. So sweet I found myself leaning toward him instead of away.

I barely managed a hum of question,

but that was enough to spur Tank to elaborate. "When I saw you and the convertible were both missing, I asked Butch if I could borrow his car. Take you for a ride."

A ride. His words raised goosebumps on my arms, even though I was pretty sure he hadn't intended the double meaning.

Then I remembered tomorrow. Breakfast with shifters who would sneer at me behind their hands. Tank's quick thinking solved one problem, but opened up a whole 'nother can of worms.

"Thanks," I said, not really meaning it.

And Tank must have understood my tone because he shook his head, something I felt more than saw as a breeze caressed my cheekbone. "Butch keeps his own confidence." A pause, then: "Will you wait here? Three minutes."

What could I do but say yes?

***

I was lost in the stars by the time Tank returned. Was imagining pulling out the markers I rarely had time to play with and creating a night landscape from thousands of colored dots. Like Seurat if he'd discovered astronomy, pointillism turned to feeling instead of science....

I should have jumped when the door squeaked open and a werewolf slid into the seat beside me. Instead, I turned to face Tank, breathing in his proximity like a hit of pure oxygen.

"Do you want to tell me where you went tonight?" he asked.

Ah, there went all the oxygen. My lungs seized up. I shook my head rather than reply.

"Hey." His finger skimmed across my cheek, disappearing as quickly as it had made contact. "It was only a question. No wrong answers."

That wasn't how male werewolves acted. But Tank was more than a male werewolf. He was so close now that his heat lit me on fire, strumming my nerve endings into a sensitized alert.

As of that moment, I could have

given Clara a definitive answer to her question about my sexuality. *Men.* I was definitely attracted to men...or at least, to this specific man.

"I'm going to kiss you now."

Tank's words were a deep breath, almost inaudible. But I felt them all the way down to my toes.

After that, he waited. One, two, three seconds. Giving me time to say no or just to wriggle sideways. When I didn't, his hands thudded down on the seat back on either side of me. His broad chest blocked every one of the stars.

I should have felt caged. Instead, I arched up to meet him.

And, for half a second, I fell into paradise. Lost in the cascade of sensation as if I'd caught a ride on a falling star and plummeted through the atmosphere....

Searing heat. Overwhelming desire. I couldn't quite manage to breathe.

Then I remembered where I was. Who I was with. A werewolf. Someone who would be in my life for five days only.

The deadline struck me like a bucket of ice water. So much like my father, the man I'd seen once. I couldn't even remember the deadbeat's voice.

Tank must have been less lost in the moment than I was, because he responded the instant my brain started churning. Pulling back, he took the starbursts with him as he retreated.

"What went wrong?"

"Nothing. You did nothing wrong."

Tank's head, I noted, was twisted away from me for the first time since I'd asked him to cut out that behavior. It felt like pushing through molasses, but I reached out to bring his chin back front and center. "This has nothing to do with your face."

"What then? Talk to me."

A faintly stubbled cheek sank into my palm, as if I wasn't the only one finding space between us inconceivable. Maybe that's why I said it. "I know nothing about you."

"I'll text over my CV."

His phone was in his hand, and I couldn't help myself. I laughed at him. "You're a geek."

"Geek. Lawyer. Medic. What else do you want to know?"

Each syllable raised a rumble of desire. But there were so many questions in my stomach, most of which couldn't be summed up with words.

Instead, I started with something easy. "Why did you join the Samhain Shifters?"

"Do you want the reason I gave on my application or the real reason?"

"Real reason."

"Part of it's simple. You've met Kira. There are dozens in our pack just like her —smart, kind, strong. I can't risk losing them to the fae."

I nodded. "But that's not your only purpose." After all, he'd said there was a reason that wouldn't have fit on his application. I was sure Lupe would love the idea of hiring someone as loyal to his pack as Tank was.

In response, he inhaled deeply. Jaw muscles bunched beneath my fingers. Then he told me:

"I've lived in the same pack all of my life. I'm related to most of them. Anyone I'm not related to, I've considered already."

The word *pack* made me twitch. But that was Tank's life, not mine. I focused instead on what he was saying. "Considered for what?"

I only realized my hand was still on Tank's cheek when the words vibrated through my fingers. "Considered for the role of mate."

Chapter 19

Mate. The word was worse than *pack.* I jerked away as if I'd been burned, thrusting my hand under my thigh so it wouldn't be tempted to reach back out to him. "You think you can choose a mate in five days."

A simple matter for male werewolves. After all, they considered their mates little better than chattel. Keep the home. Churn out babies. Do everything her partner and alpha demanded.

When Rowan had insinuated his interest in me, he hadn't mentioned the M word. But he'd made it clear where my duties would lie. I was endlessly grateful my mother hadn't gotten caught up in the werewolf world of misogyny. Even saddling us with Nick was better than that.

Tank kept talking as if he hadn't just proven he was no better than the other werewolves I'd had the misfortune of knowing. "The timeline was fourteen days when this gig started. And, yes. I think I can choose a mate in that time."

I'd been such an idiot thinking Tank was different. I shook my head as I fumbled in the darkness for the ankle brace he'd slipped onto the console between us. "Thanks for covering for me," I said, giving up on the brace and pushing my door open. Maybe Tank wouldn't notice my lapse in the darkness. Maybe he wouldn't use his gift as an excuse to come after me....

I wasn't so lucky. Air followed as I tried to retreat. A dark shape loomed, not quite far enough away for me to slide past him. "You're angry."

He was right. I was furious. "Angry that you're willing to kiss any female wolf who isn't related to you? Angry that I happened to stumble in front of your lips? No. Why would that make me angry?"

My throat was tight, my words more heated than I'd meant them to be.

"Athena." His hand hovered a

millimeter away from my arm. As if he wanted to grab me but was forcing himself not to. "Hear me out. Please."

The *please* did it. Or perhaps the fact that he could easily have used his superior size and strength to force the issue but didn't. I swallowed cold air, tamping down anger. Nodded and waited while he searched for words.

"I don't think 'mate' means the same thing to you that it means to me," he said finally.

Doing everything I could to look away from his magnetic presence, I focused on the sky behind his head. The view was breathtaking, or more like breath giving. As my chest expanded, the darkness of my anger was pricked by endless points of perfect light.

Calmed by the beauty of the cosmos, I managed a question. "What does 'mate' mean to you then?"

His answer came fast, as if he'd thought it through at length. "A mate is an equal life partner. Someone to stand back-to-back with in the face of adversity. And, yes, there would be sex."

My traitorous body clenched in certain very specific places. Tank's words were as seductive as his kiss had been.

But I wasn't looking for a mate. I wasn't looking for anything other than two more years of good money to get Harper through boarding school. I'd found the cash. Now I just needed to hold the line.

I shook my head. "Look...."

Then Tank's hands were on my shoulders, pushing me behind him. I nearly tripped. Managed to stay upright. Inhaled the overwhelming scent of a wolf riled and aggressive and nothing like Tank.

***

By the time I caught my balance and turned around, they'd faced off. Two huge males, darkened to anonymity by lack of moonlight. Both had fists clenched. Both were leaning into the other's personal space.

"Ryder." Tank's voice sounded like a wolf with ruff raised. "What are you doing here?"

Ryder didn't answer. Instead, he smiled, ready to fight.

I paced along the perimeter of their sight line, ready to throw myself between them at the first hint of danger. After all, I'd seen this sort of posturing far too many times during my childhood from a stepfather who tended to be a mean drunk.

Tank wasn't mean, but I wasn't so sure he was thinking straight either. Our conversation had been intense, and to have it interrupted by another male would set off any werewolf. For some reason, I wasn't willing to let that happen now.

Ryder, in contrast, thought the whole thing was funny. He shook his head, voice syncopated with the faintest hint of a chuckle. "Tank, Tank, Tank. Your wooing skills are rusty. Allow me to show you how it's done."

For a big man, Ryder moved fast. One second, he was four feet away from me, feet pointing toward Tank's feet. The next second, I was bent backwards over his arm while he whispered in my ear.

"Play along. This is going to be a hoot."

Ryder's words reflected the fact that his embrace was entirely impersonal. He wasn't feeling me up the way it likely appeared from the outside. He wasn't going to kiss me either, even though his face slid so close to mine that he easily could have bridged the gap.

Ryder was teasing Tank...and that

pissed me off.

"Get your hands off me," I growled, letting my knees buckle so I could slide down through the loop of his arms. My ankle twinged only slightly as I swept a foot in a long arc, intending to pull Ryders's feet out from under him. But...I didn't manage to connect.

Because Ryder was already falling. The crack of a fist connecting with a face was followed one instant later by Ryder thudding down beside me on his back.

Not that a direct hit kept Ryder down for long. He spat out blood along with a string of expletives, the latter fading into growls as his body morphed into lupine form.

Tank had already shifted. The pair

were perfectly matched, a recipe for a long, bloody battle. They'd wind up broken. Far worst off than me on my gimpy ankle.

And the fae? Our Samhain duties? Apparently the big picture had faded in the face of werewolf instinct.

Whatever they were thinking, the males struck each other like battering rams. Two feet from me, the glint of teeth and flashing eyes promised this fight wouldn't end until someone was hospitalized.

It was hard to make out what was happening, but Ryder must have won the first round because Tank grunted. His response struck me in the stomach. Still, I took a step backward. *Not my monkey, not my circus.* Or, rather, not my *wolf,* not my *pack.*

Tank and Ryder were animals to turn a stupid joke into a life-or-death altercation. Why, when I told myself that, did I not believe my own words?

No matter how hard I strained, I could barely see through the darkness. But I could smell the fury. Hear the thuds of impact. This time I advanced forward. Toward the roiling mass of fur and fangs. If I shifted, Tank and I could stand together. Surely Ryder would back down then....

But before I could do more than grab the bottom of my shirt in preparation for disrobing, movement caught my eye. A cabin door had been flung open. Harper padded out, pale PJs glowing.

And my hand dropped. My sister understood I was a werewolf, but she couldn't see this. Couldn't see blood on my fangs and hear my growls. Tank would have to take care of himself.

Another pang in my stomach, even though I was pretty sure the yelp had come from Ryder this time.

Harper couldn't see this fight...so I'd have to end it the sure way. The way that turned me into a hypocrite but would save Tank's hide without traumatizing my little sister.

Because the tried-and-true method of dealing with battling werewolves was to call on their alpha. Or their temporary alpha, as the case may be.

I sucked in a deep breath, then I hollered "Lupe!" at the top of my lungs.

Chapter 20

A second cabin door slammed opened, but it didn't disgorge the female I'd been hoping for. Instead, Butch emerged, took one look at the scene, then shifted as he fell forward onto four rangy lupine paws.

The singlemindedness of Butch's advance backed up my gut reaction that this fight wasn't a fun tussle. It was deadly serious. The eruption of smoldering resentments from alpha males forced to spend too long in close proximity. No way would it end easily or well.

The thought alone pulled fur out of my human skin. I needed to protect Tank....

No, I needed to protect *Harper.* Swallowing down my wolf with every ounce of willpower I could muster, I peered out into the night with simple human eyes.

Tank and Ryder were too fast and it was too dark to tell who was winning. But I smelled blood. This fight was nearing its climax....

Time, which had slowed to the speed of molasses, sped back up. The final seconds between attack and dismemberment had run out.

Then Lupe was on her porch. I felt her rather than saw her. Like a weighted blanket dropping over my head, bearing me to the ground.

Her words struck a millisecond later. "*Stand down.*" The command was simple, yet I found myself unable to breathe. The air in my lungs had turned to ice.

"Athena!" Flip-flops slapped against the ground as my sister raced toward me. Of course she'd run to help when she saw me collapsing. She'd never before been privy to the dark side of werewolves. She wouldn't understand how dangerous it was for a mere human to step into this mess....

I struggled against Lupe's invisible compulsion, the gesture doing absolutely nothing. Then my ears popped and the thousand-pound weight lifted off me.

I gasped an inhale. Waved an arm at Harper as I struggled upright. "I'm fine," I whispered, knowing she couldn't hear from forty feet distant.

Lupe was closer. "Take care of your sister."

Not an order. A reprieve.

And even though my inner wolf growled in fury, I took it. Didn't glance back to make sure Tank was okay as I speedwalked across the campground to meet Harper. Ignored the empty hole in my stomach that said I needed to tend to his wounds, needed to make sure his temporary alpha understood Ryder had been the instigator.

Because I was a lone wolf with a human family. No matter what my inner beast told me, Tank wasn't my problem.

Harper was.

***

My sister's eyes darted wildly. Just like when she'd been little and had woken as I brought her father home from yet another bar, his legs unsteady, mine nearly folding beneath his weight. If we were lucky, Nick would be sedated enough that the two of us could roll him into bed. If we weren't lucky, he would be verbally abusive, yelling after Harper as I shoved her out of the room.

Now, as then, her voice quavered.

"What's going on?"

Then, as now, I lied to protect her tender heart. "It's no big deal. The guys were wrestling."

Because Tank, Ryder, and Butch had been flung back into humanity by Lupe's order. I'd seen that much during the fleeting glance I'd allowed myself before returning to my true priority.

"They were wolves," Harper countered. "They were fighting. Are they going to be alright?"

I turned her around and started her back toward the cabin where another human slept. One who'd never even heard of werewolves. One who, I hoped, had never dealt with a drunk father either.

"This was a bad idea." The words

tripped off my tongue before I had time to consider them. Although, bringing Harper and Clara here *was* a bad idea. The question became—where else could my sister spend her break?

Definitely not with Nick.

"Don't make us leave." Harper's feet were no longer moving. She'd stopped stock still, within easy eyeshot of the wolf-tussle aftermath that I had a sinking suspicion was going to get worse before it got better. "Clara and Kira are having fun."

"And you? Are *you* having fun?" I hated the fact that Harper wasn't able to relax into this camp experience for her own sake. Hated the fact that I'd dragged her into yet another mess when all she'd wanted was a little simple human fun.

"Of course I am."

The scent of my sister's lie gutted me. But her continuation held the aroma of truth.

"Well, I *was* having fun. The marshmallows. The pillow fight."

Harper peered at me out of the corner of her eye. As if I cared whether her bedding maintained its structural integrity. Her shoulders, I noted, were straighter than usual. When she stood up for herself a second time, her voice was firm.

"Please let us stay."

I expected her to bargain with me. But she didn't...and I liked that. I liked the hints of backbone I saw growing in her after less than a day spent in Kira and Tank's company. I liked thinking of my sister enjoying herself.

So I nodded, deciding on the hard route, the route that would require more doing. "Then you'll stay here for the rest of break," I promised.

For my sister, I would make difficult work.

***

"A moment, Athena."

Lupe's voice caught me as I stepped back out into the darkness after tucking Harper in. Well, not literally tucking her in. After all, my sister was sixteen. Way too old for that.

But she'd let me straighten her comforter. Had smiled when I told her I had a sewing kit and would show her how to mend the tear in one side of her pillow tomorrow. She'd almost looked like a normal kid when she asked whether she and her friends could take the canoe out onto the lake the next afternoon.

I'd said yes. I always said yes if Harper's request wasn't a safety risk. Whether I had to mortgage more of my soul to gain access to the canoe would be a problem to be dealt with at a later date.

Not tonight. Because, right now, Lupe was too grim to be asked about canoe borrowing. Her anger curled around me before I'd taken two steps off

Harper's porch. Like an unfriendly python, it slithered cold and scaly against my skin.

"I'd planned this for next week," Lupe continued, speaking at a normal human tone even though I was still forty feet away. "But apparently we'll be moving up our timeline. Because we can't be a pack, but we must be a *team*."

Her words slapped me as I stepped into the circle of shifters, sliding between Lupe and Tank. His nose, I noted, was bleeding. Ryder, across from us, looked similarly battered. No wonder Lupe was pissed.

Only, her anger didn't strike the males who'd engaged in fisticuffs. It lashed out like a striking snake and bit me.

"Athena is a professional thief. She's stolen millions of dollars worth of art to line her own pockets."

Lupe's blunt assertion of my darkest secret rocked me back on my heels. My fists, I found, were clenched. Fur tickled the back of my throat.

"A mercenary." Butch's reaction was exactly what I'd expected, but it hit me harder after the day we'd spent together. He was the only one present who appeared civilized, which gave his words additional weight. "Can we trust a team mate who's in it for the money?"

Beside me, Tank growled so softly I hoped I was the only one to hear him. For my own part, I was glad the night was dark enough to hide the heat in my cheeks.

And, I mean, how could I argue? I *was* here for the money. The money...and the safe passage through Rowan's territory while I figured something else out.

Swallowing down anger, I kept my tone level as I responded to Lupe rather than Butch. "Do you intend to air everyone's dirty laundry?"

Our boss's arms crossed as she waited out our various reactions. The night had settled back into silence by the time she replied. "Yes, that's exactly what I intend to do. Secrets are a faster pathway to bonding than falling backwards into your team mates' arms and hoping they won't drop you."

Okay, I could see her point. Tank, apparently could as well.

"I'll tell my own secret then." His voice seemed to stroke across my skin, never mind that he hadn't looked at me since I entered the circle. I somehow knew that he'd volunteered in order to move the spotlight off of me.

"Is this about your face?" Ryder's voice was grittier than it had been. As if he'd lost his sense of humor during the preceding battle. "Because that's not a secret. It looks like the inside of a horse's asshole."

Tank didn't take advantage of the obvious opening. Didn't ask when Ryder had last spent time inside a horse's asshole. Instead, he shrugged. "Yes. My secret is that I did the damage myself."

I wasn't the only one who gasped. I had so many questions...and I certainly wasn't going to ask them in front of the others. Especially not in front of Ryder.

So I was grateful when Lupe interjected a secret of her own. "I was raised in a puppy mill. Sometimes, dealing with the stupidity of werewolves, I wish I was back there."

A puppy mill? As in, she'd actually been a wolf pup locked in a cage for her entire childhood?

Ryder gave us no time to digest Lupe's secret. He shrugged in a gesture that looked uncannily like Tank's, voice gruffer than usual as he admitted: "I stabbed my alpha in the back. Literally."

The night pressed in around us. So much darkness, and I didn't mean the lack of moonlight either.

All eyes turned to Butch, waiting for his secret. And...he shook his head.

"You don't want them to know?" Lupe asked. *She*, it appeared, was familiar with all of our dark spots.

"They haven't earned that knowledge," Butch answered. His tailored bathrobe spun out around him as he turned on his heel and stalked back toward his cabin, secret carried with him.

Which left me wondering, later when I was tucked in my own bed peering up through a grimy skylight, what could possibly be worse than stabbing your alpha in the back?

Chapter 21

By the time the alarm on my cell phone went off, I was the furthest thing from well rested. I'd tossed and turned for half the night, replaying my mistakes and my team mates' secrets. Revisiting Tank's use of the M word and his reaction to Ryder's presence. It all added up to more trouble than I could handle. My feet itched with the impulse to cut my losses and run.

But Harper wanted to stay. I needed Lupe to stand up for me so I wouldn't lose safe passage to my sister's boarding school before I found a long-term solution. And some small part of me wanted to learn more about this thing buzzing between me and Tank. To continue working toward the greater good.

Plus, my wolf was adamant. *Good pack,* she murmured. Which made no sense given the fact that the Samhain Shifters very much weren't a pack.

Still, I accepted her decision. Showered and dressed and headed out in search of breakfast. Or, that's what I intended to do. Instead, I literally stumbled across a pair of ankle-high boots on my doorstep.

Boots and braces. The same ones

I'd left behind in Butch's convertible. Something to keep my ankle from twinging, even though the injured joint felt a thousand times better than it had last night.

I crouched down, smelling the faintest residual aroma of wolf. Slid off my shoes and replaced them with Tank's offerings. The fabric cupped my injured ankle like a healing touch.

That, unfortunately, was the brightest spot of the morning. It went seriously downhill from there.

In fact, by the time we assembled at 7 am, the air stunk of sullen werewolves. Ryder looked hungover. Tank sported a black eye. And Butch was so intent upon meditating that he didn't greet any of us.

For her part, Lupe showed up late and rumpled, as if she hadn't slept any better than I had. She scowled then barked out an order. "Warmup for today is a run around the lake. Whoever finishes first can choose our exercise option tomorrow."

My ankle twinged. The lake's size ballooned the more I peered at it.

But this was what I'd signed up for. I just needed to find the path.

I'd taken a step toward what I suspected was the lakeside trail when Tank stopped all of us. *"No."* His denial was electric, raising hairs up and down my arms.

Ryder snorted, muttering something I couldn't quite make out but which I could guess wasn't complimentary. Lupe stilled him with a glance. Hands on her hips, she raised one eyebrow. "No?"

"Athena's ankle isn't cleared for running," Tank rumbled, not meeting my gaze.

"I can run," I countered. Weakness, I'd gathered from last night's tussle, wasn't the way to survive the next five days of temporary packishness.

To my surprise, Lupe was the one who shook her head. "Tank's right. Paying attention to others' needs"—she speared us all with a piercing gaze that made my inner wolf's ears pin—"is the best way to support the team."

"Unbelievable," Ryder muttered. Although there may have been an expletive or two thrown in between the "un" and the "believable" parts.

"Did you have something you wanted to share?" Lupe demanded.

A moment of silence. Then a grunted "No, ma'am."

"Then strip. To your underwear only, Ryder. There are kids around." Lupe's flash of smile was all sharp teeth and a complete lack of humor. "Same plan, different method of locomotion. First one to *swim* around the lake will be in charge of tomorrow's exercise choice."

***

Butch dove off the dock and sliced through the water like a dolphin released from captivity. "Holy shit," Ryder muttered, thigh deep in the same water. "This is as cold as a witch's tits."

"Can you swim?" I asked, taking in the way he patted at the surface as if it was a dog about to bite his crotch.

"Of course I can swim," Ryder grumbled. But his face was gradually fading to white.

Tank hesitated on the dock, peering back and forth between me and Ryder. His anger at Ryder, I could tell, was diffused by the latter's insecurity. Plus, I got the impression he didn't want to leave the two of us alone.

But I could take care of myself...and could handle one tattooed non-swimmer. "Go," I told Tank. "If you don't catch up to

Butch, we'll probably have to spend tomorrow morning learning to meditate."

Tank's lips twitched up ever so slightly. The air, cold one moment ago, warmed slightly. Despite his black eye and swollen nose, I had a hard time taking my gaze off his face.

Then he was gone, hitting the lake like a killer whale on a mission. "So you're a butt girl," Ryder observed, following my sight line. "I've got a butt."

He started to swivel around and show me. "Get all the way in the water," I demanded.

To my surprise, Ryder took a step forward. "Yes, ma'am," he grumbled. Still, it took us ten minutes to fully submerge.

At which point I learned that,

although I wasn't a pro at swimming, Ryder was awful. He appeared to know only one stroke—the doggy paddle.

"That's how wolves swim," he grumbled. "*Doggy* paddle. Get it?"

"As long as you're moving," I agreed easily. He was doing pretty well for someone who appeared inclined to sink rather than float.

We tried that for a while, moving about twenty yards in twenty minutes. "You might try bigger arm movements," I suggested eventually.

His resulting efforts nearly capsized us both.

So, we'd doggy paddle around the lake. It wasn't so bad, really, not after I got over the loss of feeling in my extremities. Although, strangely, my body warmed the more I focused on Ryder. As if his gasped jokes impacted the temperature of the frigid water.

The sun had risen above the trees by the time Ryder panted out an observation. "Professional thief, huh?"

"Alpha backstabber," I countered. "If you're tired, you could roll onto your back."

Ryder tried it, swallowing about a gallon of lake water in the process. He swore as he spat, and I angled myself closer in case he needed assistance.

But he bobbed back to the surface before I'd fully decided he was drowning. "Hey, it works!" He sounded childishly proud of learning to float.

And...I was proud to have taught him. The sun was warmer now and my tongue only hurt a little after endless biting to prevent myself from ribbing the sensitive masculine ego. I smiled and swiveled to take in the landscape—beautiful from this level—then jolted as I caught sight of the populated shore.

Not that this area shouldn't be populated. We were halfway around the lake now, level with a public dock. In addition to boat-mooring stations, there was a cafe present with small round tables out front.

So, yeah, multiple people milled about, eating and visiting. Only one of them, however, caught my eye.

"What is it?" Ryder was more alert

than I'd thought he was. His gaze followed mine. "Huh. That was fast."

What was fast about Marina showing up only a mile away from our campground was beyond me. *Ominous* was the adjective I would have chosen instead.

Because she wasn't there by chance. Of course she wasn't. Marina shaded her eyes with one hand, her gaze latching onto mine despite the distance. Then she beckoned me with one crooked finger.

"I've got to..." I waved my arm vaguely in Marina's direction. "Can you swim the rest of the way by yourself?"

I hated leaving him. Wasn't so sure he'd make it. But finding a way to sever my connection to Marina gracefully was important for the sake of Harper's safety. The memory of the horse and the honeysuckle niggled like fleas.

"Hey, I'm good." Ryder's heavy hand hit my shoulder, nearly submerging me. "Don't do anything I wouldn't do."

He treaded water and leered, more like himself than he'd been since setting foot in the water. A relief to my overprotective instincts, even though his admonition was nonsensical.

"If you get in trouble, yell," I added, not quite willing to let him go. "I'll hear you."

But Ryder was already swimming away from me, continuing his journey back to our campground. His splashing was louder than it should have been, but it was also rhythmic and unflustered.

Marina's foot, I noted, was tapping ten times faster than Ryder's arm strokes.

She didn't like to be kept waiting. And I was trying to stay on her good side.

I turned away from my team mate and toward my sister's teacher. Ryder would have to take care of himself.

Chapter 22

Marina peered down at me from the dock I clung to. "You stink of swamp muck."

"Well, hello to you too." I heaved myself up onto the wooden structure. And, okay, so maybe I didn't try very hard to keep residual lake water from splashing her. Maybe I enjoyed the way she skittered backwards like a cat unamused by drips from a watering can.

I wasn't just being spiteful, however. While Marina's equanimity was shaken, I demanded: "How'd you track me down?"

Because she shouldn't have been able to find me. And I didn't like the fact that Harper—who considered this woman a trusted teacher—was no more than a mile or two away.

Marina merely shrugged. "Secrets are a woman's prerogative." She dropped a towel at my feet. "Dry off. Meet me at the cafe."

"This isn't a social visit," I called after her. But she was already sliding through the crowd, leaving me alone to drip and fume.

I could either obey or dive back into the lake and catch up with Ryder, who seemed to be plowing through the water with renewed ferocity. Shrugging, I picked

up the towel. Removed the swamp muck
—what little there was of it—and followed
the trace of lemon-meringue-pie aroma
that Marina had left behind.

She didn't remark upon the way I
squelched when I took my seat, towel too
thin to fully dry me. Instead, she gestured
with her chin toward the two jumbo
muffins on the table between us. "Take
your pick."

I could taste the sugar just looking at
them. Two beautiful baked goods, tops
shiny with sweetness. I hadn't managed
to find breakfast before meeting up with
Lupe this morning. No wonder my
stomach responded to the sight of my
favorite flavor—blueberry—with an
adamant growl.

On the other hand...hadn't I read in a fairy tale—once upon a time—about the dangers of eating fae foodstuff?

No, that was Persephone, consuming pomegranate seeds in the underworld. Still, I chose the cranberry muffin—my least favorite flavor—and picked at the wrapper rather than stuffing any pastry into my mouth.

Only then did I return to the point. "You didn't show up last night."

Marina leaned in closer, her scent sticking to the insides of my throat as I inhaled. "And you don't care much about your sister, do you?"

***

"My sister?" I leaned in closer. Threats would come next, and I'd find a way to defuse them for Harper's sake....

Only, Marina didn't threaten. Instead, she delved into Harper's obvious weakness. "The child craves friendship. The only choices you've given her to sate that craving are within a werewolf vigilante squad."

"They're not...." I cut myself off, shaking my head to clear it. This was about Harper, not Tank and Ryder and Butch and Lupe.

Marina's voice was smug as she continued to focus on my sister. "I could help Harper build more appropriate social connections. Boost her self-esteem. Enhance her charisma. Her life could be easier than yours has been."

If Marina's goal was to knock me off balance, she'd succeeded. Were there really shortcuts that would make my sister's future rosy?

Didn't matter. "Harper's learning to make friends the hard way." Or at least I hoped she was. I hoped Harper wasn't just going along with whatever Clara and Kira wanted, desperate to be part of the human equivalent of a pack.

Marina shook her head slightly. Not a negation. More a sign of pity. "The fae can solve thorny problems with the snap of a finger."

"The fae?" Suddenly, Harper wasn't the only thing I cared about. If Marina was admitting what I thought she was admitting, then there was more at stake here than I'd thought. "You are one?"

My companion snorted very delicately. "Fae don't arrive until Samhain. I thought the old she-wolf would have told you that."

Lupe wasn't old. She might have passed forty, but she was at the peak of her fitness, both physically and mentally. I barely prevented myself from bristling while speaking just as plainly as Marina had done. "So you're a Sleeper," I suggested, referring to the human allies of the fae that Lupe had mentioned during our first meeting.

"Something like that." Marina picked up her paper cup and sipped at the steaming liquid. I noticed she hadn't offered me a beverage, even though something warm would have been much appreciated right about then. Perhaps safer, too, than solid food?

"Then we're enemies."

"Are we?" Marina's pause did just what she'd intended it to—it reminded me that I was a lone wolf. Out for no one except myself and my sister. "The way I see it," she continued after a long moment, "we each have something the other wants."

I shook my head, letting the towel slip loose from where I'd wrapped it around my torso. I wasn't here to do anything other than dredge up a promise of safety for my sister.

To that end, I let my wolf speak

through me. "I want you out of Harper's life."

"Done."

That was too easy. Still, I found myself settling back down at the table. "Done?"

Marina blew on her beverage and took another sip before replying. "If you don't care about friendship for your sister, perhaps you'd prefer a gift for the big male you're so attached to. His face...is unfortunate. That, however, can be fixed."

I should have left already. I had what I'd come for. Still...my entire torso bent forward. As if Marina was a tornado sucking me into her vortex.

My words, however, remained level. "With cosmetic surgery. If he wanted that, he would have done it already."

"Not cosmetic surgery. Magic." Marina wiggled her fingers and flower petals slid out of the air to fall onto the grungy plastic tabletop.

Everything else Marina had done could be explained away as slight of hand. But not this. The petals had come out of nowhere.

Magic. Marina really was affiliated with the fae.

***

And something clicked inside me. A pack bond? Not likely. But Lupe had helped me. Tank had helped me. Even Butch and Ryder, each in their own way, had helped me.

Now I had the opportunity to return the favor. I had an in with a Sleeper. Perhaps, rather than severing this connection, I should maintain it for the greater good.

"Just think what his life would be like if his outsides were as pretty as his insides," Marina continued.

I shook my head. I might be willing to nurture Marina's interest so I could keep tabs on her, but I wasn't throwing anyone I cared about under the bus. Instead, I offered up myself as sacrifice, broaching the problem I hadn't thought Marina could fix...until I saw flower petals flutter through the air.

"What I need is for the local alpha to

stop hassling me."

"The local alpha." Her lips curled up. "What a coincidence."

That didn't sound good. I wavered, pushing back my chair with a screech against the concrete...and Marina reeled me right back in.

"It would be a simple matter to increase your wolf's dominance," she murmured. "If you were as powerful as the alpha hounding you, he'd have no alternative other than to let you be."

I used the table to draw myself closer. This was supposed to be a ploy...yet I was interested. "You can do that?"

"The fae can. They would offer a boon if you do us a small favor."

Favor. The word was so minor. Innocuous really.

"My sister has no part in this," I reminded her. "And I'm not double-crossing my team."

"Are they a team?" The perfect eyebrow raised again. "Never mind. No, I won't ask you to double-cross your *team.* And your sister will not be impacted by my actions."

"What then?" Nervous energy had me picking up a crumb of muffin. I only realized when it touched my lips that I'd gone into robot mode and almost eaten a bite of the forbidden fruit.

Dropping my hands to my lap, I tried to tell myself it was a chill breeze that raised goosebumps up and down my forearms. That or the fact that I seemed to be playing right into Marina's hands.

She hummed, then shrugged. "I need another item. From a rich guy you don't like very much."

That sounded too easy. The sticking point being.... "Who?"

"Rowan McCallister."

I shivered. Had she known what I intended to ask before I asked it?

That said, I had no compunction against stealing from Rowan. "What do you want me to take?"

"First, we'll see if you can infiltrate." Marina rose, the flower petals on the table swirling around her in a way that didn't match normal air-flow patterns. Could a Sleeper really be capable of this?

I sat, ceding the high ground as Marina continued. "Find a way into Rowan's pack and I'll be in touch once you're situated. Then, if you're successful, you'll earn a boon from the fae."

Chapter 23

The water felt twice as cold when I slipped back into it a second time. Meanwhile, my mind whirled with questions.

Would I be helping my team or hindering them if I followed Marina's orders? Was Marina really just a Sleeper? Or did those flower petals point at something deeper and darker—a bona fide member of the fae?

Big-picture, those issues were important. Still, my primary concern was for Harper.

"Your sister will not be impacted by my actions," Marina had told me. But her words were open to interpretation.

And Harper would trust her teacher implicitly. Marina could have gotten here by car much faster than my best swimming strokes carried me....

So I was annoyed rather than glad when the figure waiting for me at Lupe's dock materialized into Tank. He held out a huge, fluffy towel as I splashed ashore. "You need a shower."

Why did everyone think I stunk today?

"Your lips," he continued, "are blue."

Oh. Tank was responding to the chill that seemed to have sunk into my bones.

I pulled the towel around me, basking in its warmth. "Thanks. But I've got to check on Harper...."

I turned away, but Tank was faster. "Is there a problem?" He was in front of me again, but not looking at me. Instead, he tapped at his cell phone for a few seconds before adding: "Kira says they're together. Harper and Clara are both fine."

"You're sure?" Air finally filled my lungs. The lightness in my head receded.

Tank cocked his head. "Positive. Is there a problem?"

"Maybe. Where are they? I need to talk to her."

"Hold on." Tank's hands came down on my shoulders when I started to step around him a second time. "I'll ask Kira to keep her eyes open. But you need a hot shower. And to eat. Training starts back up in forty-five minutes."

There was a grocery bag on the ground, I noted. One that smelled enticingly savory, like garlic and cheese and something I couldn't quite put my finger on.

Tank hadn't only brought me a towel. He'd collected a lunch for me also. That additional scent might have been joy.

Perhaps that's why I pushed back the decision about Marina's job to be made later. Chose to trust Kira with my sister's safety, even though I'd never outsourced the critical task previously. Still, I had questions. "Do you think Kira could hold off a Sleeper? Salt worked for me last time...."

Tank's eyebrows rose. "Is there something you want to tell me?" But he was already thumb typing. Glancing at the screen, I saw that he was passing on my instructions, along with a note not to scare the younger girls.

"Yeah," I decided. My chest was tight, but I nodded. "There is something I want to tell you."

Because, if I was taking this job, not for my own sake but for the sake of the Samhain Shifters, then someone else on the team ought to know about it. And I was ready, finally, to spill my guts.

Only, Tank apparently wasn't ready. "Good. I'll warm up your lunch while you shower." He pushed me before him, away from the lake and toward my cabin. "Then we can talk."

***

I dried myself off in the bathroom while listening to the homey sounds of a man puttering around my cabin's tiny kitchen. To my surprise, the noise didn't impinge on my privacy. Not when the scent of hot soup filtered in through a crack in the door.

Still, I braced myself for chill when I slipped out of the steamy bathroom. Last night, I'd shivered beneath the comforter. Now, despite a hot shower, the lake's chill still lingered in my bones.

But Tank had figured out how to turn

on the heat, a feat I hadn't been capable of. As I exited the bathroom, I found myself shedding a layer rather than hunting down another one.

"There's no table, but I think we should eat inside anyway," Tank rumbled, gaze meeting mine without any of the hesitation he'd shown previously. In fact, his eyes were hot now, as if I wasn't the only one who'd been aware of my nakedness one thin wall away from his domestic activities. "You need more time to warm up."

As Tank spoke, he motioned toward a colorful cloth spread across a patch of floor that had been filthy this morning but was now as pristine as it was going to get without mopping. Atop the cloth sat a bowl of soup and a sandwich garnished with something frilly and green.

"This is perfect." And I was starving. So starving I managed to tear my eyes away from Tank's broad shoulders long enough to focus on the lunch he'd made.

Still, it took only three mouthfuls before the issue of Marina bubbled back up inside me. Harper's safety. The danger of a Sleeper so close to the Samhain Shifter's home base.

And yet...when I set down my spoon and swiveled slightly to face my companion, something entirely different came out of my mouth. "Will you tell me why you cut your face?"

"If you eat, I'll talk." Tank's eyes were smiling, even though his mouth was a straight line.

"Okay." I took a big bite of the sandwich, which involved chicken and cheese and pesto, the whole thing just shy of too hot to handle. It was the most delicious morsel I'd ever eaten. I somehow knew Tank had assembled it himself.

The story he told, however, made me lose my appetite.

The tragedy started with pack drama far worse than what I'd lived through. An old alpha was replaced by his son, the latter weak and foolish. "I was strong enough that I could have overthrown him and seized the role of pack leader," Tank rumbled. "But it would have been the wrong move."

"So you messed up your own face?" The solution made no sense to me.

"Eat your soup," Tank demanded. Only when I was once again filling my belly did he delve deeper into awfulness that thoroughly confirmed my distrust of packs. Three different alpha-leaning males had wanted Tank to mate with their daughters. They promised him support if he overthrew the new leader of the pack.

"It stank of civil war," Tank explained in his deep rumble. "No matter which daughter I chose, the other fathers would have torn us down. Plus, that wasn't the kind of mating I was prepared to take part in." He paused, watching to make sure I sipped soup, before adding: "Then our alpha found out."

The pack leader killed one of the traitorous fathers. Evicted the two others. "I was worth too much to evict," Tank said, tone flat rather than prideful. "Doctoring skills are in short supply among werewolves. Lawyer skills too. But our alpha couldn't risk me rising up against him. He gave me a choice."

Tank had walked through door B, the door that let him stay with his pack. He'd shifted into wolf form and excised the charisma he'd been born with, scratching at his own face to do so. The external damage was just window dressing, the real changes within himself.

He hadn't removed his power, the alpha side that Ryder had reacted to. But the enticing charm that drew pack females to him? When Tank was finished, every potential mate turned up her nose in disgust.

"But that doesn't make sense." Despite myself, my index finger rose to slide down across the bump on Tank's nose. "This"—I traced the scar under his eye next—"and this are so minor. Small blemishes don't change who you really are. I barely even see them."

"Because you're special."

I shook my head. "No. You don't understand your own appeal. You...."

I gave him no warning before my face inched forward to join my fingers. I was half in Tank's lap by the time my lips met his lips.

If I'd thought our first kiss was incendiary, this one was a supernova. Hands gliding over skin. My front pressed up against his hard muscles. My fingers found a zipper and pulled.

Then something started beeping. Loud and adamant.

I ignored it. Grabbed hold of his collar to draw myself closer. Our skin needed to touch. My body needed....

The beeping continued. "Shit." Air pooled between us as Tank dragged a cell phone out of his pocket. I winced at how easily he'd pushed me aside.

But his pupils were dilated when his gaze met mine. One broad hand cupped my chin and he feathered my lips with a final kiss so soft it was almost intangible.

"We're late. Lupe's pissed."

Oh. *Oh.* I glanced over his shoulder at the kitchen clock. It felt like mere minutes since we'd set foot in my cabin, but the elapsed time had actually been over an hour.

And I hadn't managed to warn Tank about Marina or beg a favor for the sake of my sister. "I have to tell you things and ask you things."

"We can walk and talk."

We did, Tank slowing after the first moment to match my shorter stride. Our fingers curled together while I relayed the bare bones of my meeting with Marina. "She's fae," I asserted.

Because Marina had danced around the issue of whether or not she was a Sleeper. And my gut suggested human allies of fae wouldn't have quite so many skills.

I expected denial. After all, Tank was a pack wolf and Lupe had said there were no fae present before Samhain.

Instead, Tank nodded. "You were there. I trust your judgment."

My throat tightened, not with disappointment but with something sweeter and fiercer. "She's Harper's history teacher. I'm worried..."

"That she'll do something to your sister." Tank finished my sentence, making the leap that had been obvious to me.

I nodded. "Harper needs to be somewhere safe. Somewhere Marina won't look for her. I was going to suggest your pack, but now that you've told me about your alpha...."

"The former alpha." Tank's body language radiated purpose. "I knew he wouldn't last, and he didn't. The new alpha is Kira's brother-in-law. A good wolf. Honorable. Our pack is thriving."

I could see the others waiting for us through the trees now. I needed to stick to the point. Still, my hand rose to feather across Tank's face a second time. "Was it worth it?"

His answer was immediate. "One hundred percent."

Then, before I could ask, he offered.

"My pack will be glad to keep an eye on Harper and Clara for the rest of their vacation. Kira's brought humans home before. It won't be a problem hiding lupine natures." His voice dropped to a growl. "No one would dare invade our land."

I swallowed down fear of pack and accepted that this was the exact solution I'd hoped for. "Thank you. I owe you."

He shook his head, curt and adamant. "You owe me nothing. We'll talk to Lupe, explain the situation, then the two of us will...."

Now I was the one shaking my head so hard that Tank fell silent. The heat of Lupe's gaze bored into us. We weren't just late, we were dawdling within plain sight.

Still, Tank focused on me alone. "Problem?"

Memories of Lupe's gun made me wince away from Tank's game plan. I barely knew the woman. Tank was the only one I trusted. "I'm not ready to share this with anyone other than you."

Tank's cheek twitched as if he disagreed with me. But he didn't argue. "Okay. Then we'll make an excuse for the two of us to be gone...."

"No." I shut him down again, knowing I was driving a wedge into this utterly sweet but oh-so-fragile thing germinating between us. "Marina might be spooked if you come with me. This is something I need to do alone."

I held my breath, expecting an explosion. Men, especially werewolf men, didn't deal well with disagreement. They hated being told that a mere woman was going to solve a problem on her lonesome.

But Tank only closed his eyes for one split second, exhaling slowly. And when he met my gaze again he nodded. "If that's what you need, I'll help make it happen. But call me. Please. If you need any help."

Chapter 24

"Have you decided to join us?" Lupe didn't give me and Tank time to answer before continuing with the spiel we'd so obviously delayed. "Then we can finally begin our lesson in swordcraft. I'll let Butch explain."

And he did. In excruciating detail while I struggled to focus on something other than Marina and Harper and Rowan.

It was useful information, actually, if Butch could have summed it up a bit more succinctly. Fae, he explained, were allergic to all metals other than copper. Which meant a steel sword thrust through their torsos was the most effective way of expelling them back to the Otherworld.

"Doesn't kill them?" Tank asked, jabbing the ground with one of the weapons that had been handed out to us. Someone had attached heavy weights to broom handles then wrapped padding around them, producing a so-called sword that wrenched my arm muscles whenever I tried to lift it but made Ryder laugh when he smacked himself in the face.

Lupe shook her head. "No. The fae aren't entirely of this world, so nothing you do here will kill them. They can, however, kill you. And while they can't handle steel the way we can, their copper swords are sharp enough to do the trick."

Ryder's nostrils flared. "All it takes to expel them is metal? So why don't we shoot their asses?"

I winced. Not at the language, but at the bloodthirstiness.

Unlike me, Lupe was unfazed by Ryder's tone. "Guns have a tendency to backfire around the fae, making them worse than useless. Something about the ability to twist air and fire to their will. Whatever the reason, blades are our safest choice."

I attempted to follow along as Lupe showed us a few basic maneuvers. It soon became apparent that there was no way any of us, except Lupe and Butch, were going to be up to speed by Samhain.

Kira, in contrast, turned out to be quite the swordswoman, as I learned when the girls descended upon us in a mass of giggles and chatter. "Ooh! I want to play!" the older girl said, pouncing upon the pile of spare weapons. She hefted three of them before choosing her favorite, then used the practice weapon to batter Butch to a standstill. "My sister taught me," she explained through a smile so wide it must have made her cheeks hurt.

And, to my surprise, Harper seemed to have a knack for swords also. She showed none of the tentativeness I'd grown accustomed to from her, snatching up a weapon without asking for permission. Then she managed to knock my practice sword out of my hand when the two of us squared off.

"Nice work," I praised her.

"Kira said if I want something, I have to take it," Harper answered, brushing a strand of sweaty hair off her forehead.

My heart warmed. This *was* the right move. Werewolves and fae aside, the environment was good for my sister. She was growing right in front of my eyes....

But Lupe's voice rose above the clatter of practice weapons, preventing me from praising Harper further. "Now you'll learn what battle feels like. Let's split into two teams. Harper, Tank,

Athena, and Kira against Butch, Ryder, Clara, and me. Let's make it real."

I opened my mouth to protest the girls being included in a werewolf challenge. But...Harper needed to be treated like an adult. And—

I shot a glance at Tank. He nodded, our communication fast and wordless. With both of us focused on the same agenda, the girls would stay safe.

Lupe ignored all undercurrents as she provided one final admonition. "Go for the torso," she started. "A solid hit counts as a killing blow."

"Chests," Kira said. "Got it."

But the torso had two sides. And Ryder, as I remembered a moment too late, had stabbed his alpha in the back.

He wasn't beyond metaphorical back stabbings either. Which is a long way of saying—while our attention was focused on Lupe, the tattooed shifter struck.

***

I should have realized that Kira would be his target. After all, she was the only one on our team with swordcraft skills.

She was also a distance away from the rest of us, picking through the practice swords in search of a better blade, when Lupe set us loose. "Go!" our leader barked, and padded swords rose and clashed in unison.

What I hadn't noticed until too late

was the way Ryder sidled away from his group while Lupe laid out the game plan. How he'd slid around the edges of the game field until he was inches away from Kira.

I'd thought he was choosing weapons just like she was. That they'd each grab a sword and trot over to join their compatriots.

That assumption proved incorrect.

Because the moment Lupe spoke, Ryder dropped his sword and attacked using weapons he was more familiar with. One hand clamped down over Kira's mouth. The other squeezed her sword hand until her fingers released.

Meanwhile, the thud of padded weapons all around suggested I was the only one who'd noticed. So I ran. Ran toward Ryder, the brute of a werewolf with a thrashing child in his grip.

She'd managed to wiggle free of the hand over her mouth by this point. But Ryder's meaty paw had drifted lower. To her throat, a hold I remembered far too well.

Still, the release of her mouth allowed Kira to speak. "Ow!" she managed. "Get off me!"

Ryder didn't. Instead, he growled out animal aggression turned vaguely human. "Do you surrender?"

"No!" She was furious. Scared but unwilling to bend. Her foot kicked out wildly. Ryder dodged, bearing down with his right hand until her words turned into a wheeze.

Then he latched onto the arm she was using to try to jab behind her. Twisted it upward.

I felt the pain in my own body as Kira shrieked.

***

I darted through a pool of air that smelled like blueberries. *Marina.* Was she responsible for this disaster? Was it possible that strange warmth while swimming with Ryder was a pack bond building between us? Could Marina have used that tenuous connection to manipulate the burly shifter into doing her will?

Or maybe Ryder really was an asshole. Either way, I needed to focus, not on the past, but on the present. Time to fix what could be fixed.

I'd dropped my own weapon in my initial shock, but Ryder's was there on the grass waiting for me. My mind was unbelievably clear now. I scooped up the discarded sword, letting my momentum carry me into a slide between Ryder's legs.

I was aiming for a literal low blow, but he deserved it...and Butch got there first.

I hadn't even realized the elegant shifter was following. But his arm came out of nowhere, so fast I barely saw it moving. A sharp crack of fist hitting flesh.

Ryder's chin snapped backward. Kira was flung away from her captor rather than released.

Meanwhile, Ryder whirled to face his new opponent, already roaring. "What the fuck, man? I'm on your team!"

"Stand down." Butch looked twice as large as he had previously, the stink of fur so strong that fluff seemed to line my nasal passages. Was *that* why he meditated all the time? To prevent himself from unleashing this inner beast?

I glanced sideways, checking on Kira. She was already surrounded by a huddle of teenagers. Tank stood between them and Ryder, his wolf rampant behind his eyes.

The girls were safe...but Clara would

have a heart attack if somebody shifted. Harper might too since she'd only seen me furry when I was friendly. From the fur rising on Butch and Ryder's arms, there was nothing friendly about their impending shift.

"How do you expect to win—?" Ryder started.

And I pressed between them. Ignored the way hairs rose on the back of my neck as the cold draft of alpha aggression bore down on me from both the right and left hand. I raised my padded not-really sword then struck with words instead.

"Kira is a *child*," I spat at Ryder, willing him to remember what he'd said about her around the campfire. I had little expectation that it would work. But, strangely, it did.

Because Ryder glanced at me, peering down as if he was ten feet taller than I was. Our height difference must have triggered some werewolf instinct because the wolf receded. He blinked three times in fast succession then dropped his head into his hands.

"Shit." Ryder's scent morphed from anger to remorse in an instant. Like rotten peaches, sweet enough to attract wasps.

Taking a step around me, he headed toward Kira. Not the same Kira he'd battled earlier though. She'd found her feet and picked up a branch in place of a sword.

Now, she stepped away from the other girls, evading Tank when he tried to stop her. "Stay where you are," the girl hissed at Ryder.

Not that she had any need to defend herself or her gaggle of friends. Butch and I were already moving back into position, ready to manhandle Ryder into submission. Tank was also striding into place, ready to fling himself between Kira and Ryder.

And none of that proved necessary, because Ryder had regained his humanity. "Right." He stopped walking, scrubbing his hands through close-cropped hair instead. "I'm a fucking idiot." He growled out a huff of frustration. "I made a mistake. I hope you'll let me make it up to you."

"If we had real swords, I would have skewered you." Kira's eyes were slits, her branch still at the ready. The tip was broken off at an angle and pointed directly at Ryder's heart.

"You sure would've," Ryder agreed, no humor in his voice. He dropped down to his knees, this big, tattooed guy bowing his head in front of a teenager. "You can skewer me now if you want to. Like I said, I deserve it."

I glanced toward Harper and Clara who were watching wide-eyed. This wasn't human behavior and I always tried to keep my sister clear of werewolves.

But this was Kira's decision and I wasn't about to steal her moment of triumph. I held my breath.

"Whatever." The teenager dropped her branch.

Chapter 25

Kira had stood up for herself quite admirably, but I couldn't count on her safety the next time. And Clara—would Marina go after the human teenager next?

Just because my sister was off limits didn't mean my fae employer had lost her leverage points. "Lupe," I started, not knowing how I'd explain my absence, just knowing I needed to get out of there fast.

But the older woman wasn't paying any attention. Instead, she'd pulled a key out of her pocket and tossed it to Kira. "For the boathouse," she explained. "If you girls want to get in a canoe trip, this is your window. We're shutting down camp in two hours."

"Shutting down camp?" Harper's face fell. She glanced my way, waiting for an explanation. But I had none to give. Had we failed so horrendously that Lupe planned to put a new team together? I shrugged at my sister as the older woman explained.

"Three-day vacation for the 'dults." Her eyes sparkled as she exchanged a grin with Kira. "Although I expect them to work on their swordplay while they're away."

"They need to," Kira agreed, as if

she and Lupe were co-captains. But she accepted the dismissal, heading over to Harper and Clara and leaving the "'dults" alone.

Which was Lupe's cue to return her attention to us. I braced myself for recriminations...but none came. Instead, our boss was all business.

"Grab two practice swords and two real swords apiece. I suspect you'll have no problem finding someone to spar with during your vacation."

Vacation? This felt far too easy. I needed a way to bow out of Samhain Shifter events for a day or two and Lupe gave us all a leave of absence?

Of course, there was still the issue of Harper to be dealt with. I glanced at the kids, who were whispering in a cluster rather than racing for the boathouse. Kira nodded and my sister smiled. A real grin, not the pinched-lip fake she usually treated everyone too. How would Harper look when I told her I was sending her away in order to do yet another job?

As if she'd sensed my thoughts, Harper's gaze met mine and her face fell. "Would it hurt your feelings...?" she started, before spluttering to a halt. Her head bowed and she scuffed her feet. Turning to Kira, she muttered. "I'd better not."

My gut clenched. This time, the ease of getting what I wanted could likely be attributed to Tank. He must have thumb-typed Kira while I wasn't looking and the older girl had invited my sister to return home with her just as we'd discussed.

Still, predictably, Harper felt guilty about abandoning me. "Hey." Ignoring the fact that Lupe wasn't quite done with us, I strode over to my sister and dropped down to peer into her face. "No, it wouldn't hurt my feelings if you and Clara go home with Kira. I'll find a way to see you before the end of break."

"Awesome!" Like a light switch, Harper's joy burst out of her. She wasn't just going along with the other girls now. She was leading the way as they raced for the boathouse. Acting like a kid. Why walk when you can run?

As for the 'dults, we waited until the creak of the boathouse door promised that young ears weren't listening. Then Lupe finally explained what was going on.

"You did a good job." She cut off Ryder before he could do more than mutter. "Even you. You quit. You apologized. You'll do better next time."

The tattooed shifter's head rose, his gaze finally meeting ours for the first time since he'd realized he was engaged in a no-holds-barred fight with a minor. "Yeah. I will," he promised, voice a deep growl.

Something strong and solid flew between him and Lupe, the air filling with an electricity that had nothing to do with alpha aggression or incipient shifting. This was pack forming, werewolf bonds that skittered across my skin in a way I'd never been privy to before.

And in its wake...a warmth. Rightness. Like I was being hugged ever so gently by someone who truly cared.

Lupe's mouth twisted. "And *that's* why you're going on vacation. We need to become a team, but we can't be a pack. Not if we don't want the fae exploiting our weakness. Go home. Practice. Forget about each other. Then come back Tuesday night ready to work."

"Yes, ma'am." I wasn't sure who spoke. One of us? All of us? We turned away as a unit to gather weapons, but Lupe's voice held me back.

"Athena, if you have a moment."

The happy haze of pack togetherness faded in an instant. I'd been singled out.

Lupe's eyes bored into mine. "Do you have something you want to tell me?"

Maybe it was our recent near-pack bonding. Or just the fact that this woman was tough and capable and kind all at once.

Whatever the reason, I hated the fact that I still wasn't ready to spill my guts to her. Wasn't ready to admit that I'd taken a side job with someone who was likely our enemy, even if my primary goal was the good of the Samhain Shifters. Wasn't willing to explain how tantalizing some of Marina's offers really were.

Probably because those two

purposes were mutually contradictory….

I must have hesitated too long because Lupe frowned. "About your territory issues?" She raised both eyebrows and enunciated clearly. "Do you need me to speak with Rowan McCallister about your right to return to your apartment until Tuesday?"

Oh, right. The old problem…the one I was solving in a very outside-the-box manner. I shook my head. "No. I'm good."

Lupe's dark brown eyes were sharp now. I'd piqued her curiosity, and she didn't seem like the type to let things slide. "Do…?" she started.

Then Tank was beside me. "Try these," he suggested, dropping two practice swords into arms that had risen automatically to receive them. "How do they feel?"

"Heavy?" Unlike Kira, I had no idea how to choose a weapon.

And Tank, I suspected, didn't either. But he'd distracted me at just the right moment, long enough for Lupe to dismiss my reaction and move on. "Butch!" she called. "We need to talk."

So the moment passed, and the rest of the afternoon passed also. The girls returned from the lake damp from splashing each other but wreathed in smiles. By the time Tank dropped me off outside my apartment, they were arguing over who would get to take the wheel of his SUV.

"Do you girls even have drivers'

licenses?" Tank demanded, trying to sound tough but the words coming out laced with amusement.

"Learner's permit," Clara piped up.

"Me too," Kira added. "Because *someone* won't take me to do the test."

Harper's voice wasn't quite as loud as everyone else's, but she admitted: "I have a license."

"Lucky!" Kira exclaimed while Harper glanced my way.

It wasn't luck that had spurred her fast licensure. I'd wanted my sister to have an emergency escape hatch from Nick's house as soon as possible, so we'd gone to the DMV together the day she turned sixteen. She'd used that skill to flee a dicey situation twice already.

It was almost as if Tank smelled the shift in mood because he threw my sister a bone that set her above her companions. "Then Harper can drive. Once we're off the highway."

"And you'll take me and Clara to get our licenses tomorrow," Kira prodded.

"Maybe," Tank answered, eyes on me as I dragged my suitcase and all four swords out of the car. His voice dropped. "Do you need a hand?"

"No, I'm good."

And, surprisingly, I was. Even though Harper was leaving with a man I'd known for only a few days, I trusted Tank to protect her.

The only flaw was that I couldn't ride away in the exact same car.

Chapter 26

Instead, I lugged my suitcase and swords over to my own vehicle and headed west. Ten years ago, I'd parked in a secluded spot within McCallister territory but past the boundary of their daily patrol runs. That time, I'd snuck in to speak with my father and snuck back out again with no one the wiser.

Tonight, I intended to repeat the trick.

First, though, I needed information from Marina. When I called to tell her I was heading in tonight, I'd been shunted straight to voice mail. Now, though, a text response chimed as my headlights illuminated the narrow pull-off of my destination.

"Send me a photo of Rowan's bedroom," Marina ordered.

His bedroom? I deleted the incriminating evidence and pursed my lips.

Marina wanted me to take Rowan up on his offer, not only the overt one of joining his pack but the insinuated one of becoming his mistress. That would certainly be one way to get her photo.

But I wasn't that desperate. Instead, I intended to use my own skillset. Scout out the lay of the land tonight. Then, tomorrow, make a plan for a fast in-and-out.

After all, stealing a photo wasn't that much different from planning a heist.

So I slid out of human clothing, shivering for one split second before warm fur clad a lupine body. It had been only a few days since my last shift, but exhilaration consumed me. I leapt over a fallen log as easily as if gravity had reduced to lunar levels. Then I followed my nose to a muddy slurry of half-rotten leaves.

This was just what I needed to cover up any residual human aromas. The damp leaf litter rustled as I rolled and scratched, paying most attention to my paw pads. As long as I didn't drink so much my bladder threatened, feet were the biggest threat to passing the sniff test.

So I worked rotten leaves into my paws then shook most of the debris away from me. Specks of mud splattered out to stain nearby tree trunks and I couldn't resist huffing out a laugh. I'd forgotten how much fun it was to inhabit my lupine skin in a wild environment where I could act like a real wolf.

But I wasn't here to play. I was here to work.

So, just as the moon rose, I got down to business. Racing upstream, I crested a hill and peered toward the McCallister home place. Their lights were barely visible in the distance, just where I'd expected them. Probably a dozen houses. Not such a big pack that I needed to be overly concerned.

I'd thought their settlement would have grown in the last decade, actually, but it hadn't. I, on the other hand, was older and considerably wiser. So rather than making a beeline for the lights the way I had last time, I ran in the opposite direction. Up the crest of the hill I was on, then swinging a sharp left onto a taller ridge.

Because I'd planned ahead before making the drive today, checking a map and plotting a more circuitous route. The result should have made my foray even less likely to catch the pack's attention. But I was only halfway through the planned loop when a howl rose off to the east. Another to the north. A third one between me and my vehicle.

Coincidence. It had to be. Rowan couldn't have known I was coming, had no way of guessing my plan to sneak into territory that didn't belong to me. Most likely, this was a Saturday night hunting party. Just my luck that I'd stumble into the center of a clan out chasing deer....

I flattened my body against the ground as I slunk closer to the lights of pack central. It was the only route open to me, but I was no longer engaged in a simple scouting mission. Instead, I intended to swerve around the settlement and run as far as I had to in order to escape the semi-circle of werewolves. Then I'd hightail it back to my car and regroup.

That was Plan B, Plan A having been ditched at the first eerie howl.

And...it looked like I'd be moving on to Plan C. Because the darkness in front of me *moved.* I'd thought there were only trees in my path, but now I caught the flick of ears, the sway of a wolf tail.

Then four sets of eyes glowed back at me out of the night.

*****

Did I say four? Four in front of me maybe, but there were dozens present. Dozens of wolves seething through my personal space as I spun in a tight circle seeking escape.

There was none. No way out and no way through. Instead, I froze as wolves padded closer. A damp nose made contact with my butt and I snapped at the personal-space intrusion. Someone else slammed into my shoulder, knocking me off my stride.

They darted in and out so fast I couldn't get a handle on their locations. And while I was trying, teeth closed around my neck.

I couldn't breathe. Was this what Kira felt like when Ryder grabbed her in a chokehold? It felt worse than when Rowan had squeezed my throat in human form. I tried to swallow, but the obstruction wouldn't budge.

It was madness to try to fight free,

but I couldn't help myself. I snapped into the darkness, making contact with nothing. Dropped to the ground, hoping that would dislodge my attacker.

Instead, I ended up at the bottom of a pile of fur and paws.

Surrender. My lupine nature clawed at me, begging me to roll over and show my belly. That might stop my attackers...or might make it easier for them to tear me apart.

Instead, I growled. These strangers weren't my pack. I couldn't afford to surrender to them.

While my human and lupine natures battled, my opponent's fangs dug in deeper. I not only couldn't breathe now, I was also bleeding. Salt stung the insides of my nostrils. Hot liquid slid down my chest.

I couldn't think inside my fur. Couldn't catch my breath. Couldn't wriggle free....

All I saw was Harper's face. If I died now, Nick would have no reason to keep sending my sister to boarding school. He'd probably demand a refund of the money I'd paid ahead, then drink up every penny of it before taking his daughter home to wait on him.

And while Harper was able to drive, she was also sixteen. Stuck in his household for another two years as far as the law was concerned. Without me, she'd have no reprieve.

I had to be there for my sister, so I

gambled on werewolf morals. Sucked in my fur and croaked out a plea with my human voice.

"Stop."

I hadn't expected words to come, actually. But the instant I regained humanity, the wolf who'd been chewing on my throat dropped me like a hot potato. Something cold and electric passed over me as an alpha compulsion pressed the pile of wolves aside.

The compulsion pressed me also, but in a different direction. Forced me onto my butt so I could peer upward....

Then human fingers were gripping my feet, inspecting the muddy soles. "You didn't run far," Rowan noted.

He sounded so urbane. So human.

But his eyes were wolf yellow and I was unable to move my body. The moon came out from behind a cloud and his gaze settled on my naked breasts.

"Where did you park?" he asked, speaking to my nipples. His fingers prodded at the arch of my foot, a touch which should have tickled but instead threatened my gag reflex.

I wanted to snarl a denial. To save my car for quick escape just the way I'd intended.

But Rowan was all that stood between me and sharp wolf teeth. And at least he was two-legged, even if he had yet to release my foot.

Plus, his alpha command was pressing at me. Pressing at my throat, at my lips, at my windpipe....

So I told him. Told him the location of my car and the key I'd stashed on top of a rear tire.

"Troy, get it." His command bit at everyone alike but only one wolf peeled off into the darkness.

"The rest of you," Rowan continued, "it's time to head back."

Chapter 27

Rowan's pack mates weren't thrilled to cut their hunt short. I smelled resentment, heard annoyance in the pounding footfalls that didn't even attempt to remain silent.

But no one shifted and complained. Instead, they followed me and Rowan—now lupine—as we speared straight down the hill toward pack central. A third of the shifters peeled off as we reached the first puddle of lamp light, the one that I'd thought housed the entirety of the

McCallister settlement. But the rest kept running until we hit...a rectangular hole in the ground?

Well, not really a hole. A cement tunnel. Still, it wasn't large enough to walk through upright if we'd been two-legged.

We weren't two-legged. Instead, wolves streamed into the opening without pausing. I was the only one who hesitated, unwilling to dive through this dark, subterranean door.

I hesitated...and Rowan left the stream of wolves, padding against the tide until he stood shoulder-to-shoulder beside me. Well, no, that makes our relative positions sound too companionable. Lupine, Rowan had nearly twice the mass I did. Standing beside me, he didn't show solidarity. He *loomed.*

We couldn't speak in our wolf forms and Rowan didn't bother barking out another alpha order. Still, he got the message across quite admirably. I was expected to enter the tunnel. Was expected to follow along like a good little wolf even though, for all I knew, this tiny orifice was the only way in or out of his domain.

I slid a glance sideways into the night. The last of the stream of wolves had entered the tunnel, leaving me and Rowan the only ones present. And while I couldn't take him in a head-on battle, I might be able to outrun him for a short distance. I'd have to be clever. Focus his attention elsewhere then sprint to get out of range of his alpha compulsions.

After that, I could cut across country. Shake my pursuers. Find a phone and call for help.

Then what? I wouldn't be able to return to my apartment, the same apartment Rowan had broken into once this week already. Wouldn't be able to reel in Marina or keep her away from those I cared about. The best I could come up with was hiding in the forest for three days waiting for Lupe to open camp back up.

I was a doer, not a waiter.

So I let Rowan think he'd intimidated me. Dropped my head to my chest and inched toward the tunnel entrance.

Then, swallowing down the scent of damp and mildew, I padded inside.

***

The subterranean corridor opened up to human-height fifty yards later. Bright lights forced my eyes to squint. My nails clicked against unpainted concrete.

Rowan's lupine scent had been crowding me all the way through, but now he shifted upward. Motioning toward the sound of flowing water, he prodded verbally: "This way."

Glancing back down the tunnel, I saw nothing but darkness. Not even the moon, suggesting the grinding noise I'd heard was a door closing behind us.

There was no easy way out, so I stayed lupine but otherwise obeyed Rowan. Sidled through a human doorway and entered a gym-style locker room.

There, Rowan nodded at someone while I took my bearings. Naked shifters sluiced mud off their bodies without bothering with modesty. I'd never seen so many naked butts in one place before in my life.

They weren't all men either. Six women chattered at one end of the room, equally naked and equally oblivious to human modesty. I headed in their direction, still lupine, but Rowan reached down and grabbed my ruff.

"No. Wouldn't want any mistakes

before November."

I had no idea what he meant, but the words sent a shiver through me anyway. Enough so that I let him steer me in the opposite direction. To a far corner where I could shower in semi-privacy.

Not that the space was truly private with a human Rowan stepping beneath the shower head beside me. His voice came out as an amused purr. "I wouldn't have thought you were shy."

A challenge. I pressed human skin out of lupine fur and met it head on. "I'm not."

Rowan must have smelled my lie because he huffed out laughter. But that was good. Shyness gave me an excuse to run my gaze around the shower room a second time. Now I wasn't looking at the inhabitants but rather at the space itself.

Three doors. The one I'd come through plus two others. As I watched, the six showering women left in a gaggle through one doorway. Two men sauntered out through the other door.

Coincidence, or were there male and female wings to Rowan's underground den?

Rowan had seemed busy scrubbing dirt off his fingers, but he must have been watching me also. Because he broke into my thoughts with words that would have sounded like a suggestion from a human. "You'll stay in my spare room, of course."

From Rowan, the sentence came out

as a command.

And I should have been thrilled. After all, that would put me close to the bedroom I was supposed to be photographing for Marina, even if I didn't currently have my cell phone handy.

But my eyes had continued wandering while Rowan spoke to me. Seeking familiar faces...or familiar bodies rather. I couldn't pick out the cat-chasers from outside my apartment. For all I knew, they were here and my face blindness made me skim right over them. But one male posture looked familiar, even if it had been a decade since I'd last seen him. After all, I noted hints of similar features in my mirror every day.

"Dad?"

I hadn't meant to speak aloud, but surprise pulled out the name Ace had never given me permission to use on him. No wonder the man in question tilted his head away from me. My father wasn't any more interested in talking now than he had been a decade before.

Not that it mattered. I was here on a scouting mission, not a misplaced genetic quest.

"Is that why you decided to join us?" Rowan shut off his shower then shook his entire body as if he was still lupine. Alpha-scented water sprayed away from him, striking my chin, throat, and chest.

Now I smelled like Rowan. It was all I could do not to scrub away the odor. I felt like I'd been marked.

"No," I answered. "I was curious." Which wasn't a lie, even if it also wasn't the entirety of the truth.

"You're welcome to assuage your *curiosity* while we're next door to each other." Rowan stood facing me with no water to obscure my view of his muscles. He flexed them, aware of my perusal.

So *that's* why he thought I'd come? The male ego was boundless.

And while the museum girls would have been impressed by the view, all I saw was a wolf with too much power. Plus, over his shoulder, a hint of movement.

My father's head shaking ever so subtly. He slapped his ear afterwards, as if he'd just been trying to knock water out of it.

But that hadn't been his original purpose. Ace didn't think I should stay in Rowan's spare room.

My father was a stranger I'd met once before, a stranger who hadn't even been willing to talk to me when I hunted him down as a newly orphaned teenager. Still, I trusted him more than the territorial alpha literally flexing his muscles in front of me.

"I don't think that would be appropriate, do you?" I countered. "I'd rather stay with my father instead."

"In the bachelor barracks?" Rowan frowned.

"If that's where my father lives."

For a moment, I thought Rowan

would refuse me. But then he shrugged and barked out an order. "Empty room three for our *guest*."

The emphasis was interesting. Male eyes fell away from me, sliding to an approaching woman instead. Her they considered hungrily...and Rowan didn't speak up in her defense. Just let them look.

I looked too, although not for the same reason. The woman's hair was wet, suggesting she'd been part of the showering gaggle. But she was dressed now, if you could call a sports bra and tiny shorts dressed. There was less fabric on her body than she carried in her arms.

"Alpha." Her eyes stayed on the floor as she extended the folded bundle toward Rowan. So the stack of towel and clothes were for him?

No. He thumbed through the fabric as if testing it. Whatever the reason, it must have passed muster because he graced the woman with another nod. This time, she offered me the clothing.

"Thanks...." I let my voice trail off, expecting an introduction. But her back was already to me, bare feet slapping on the ground in her haste to retreat.

The men were gone too. I got the impression they'd been lingering until the word *guest* was thrown out there. Now, the only person remaining was someone who appeared to be a guard, standing at the doorway that led back the way I'd come.

No, that wasn't true. Another male cut through the far end of the shower room, entering the side the women had disappeared into. Moments later, he stalked back out, a girl who looked like she was about Harper's age trailing behind.

She might be Harper's age, but she was nothing like Harper. Instead, this girl was dressed in a negligee, hair curled and lips pouty with applied color. The male stunk of sexual interest. The girl's scent was covered up by perfume.

"What...?" I started.

"Dress," Rowan interrupted, opening a full-length locker that was more of a closet. The perfectly pressed suit inside couldn't have been there long, not in this room full of splashing water and high humidity. Had someone been left behind just to fill lockers with clothing? I dried myself off hurriedly then shrugged on my own clothes—a skin-hugging dress that revealed more than it covered—while trying to understand this pack.

I'd thought werewolf clans hunted as a unit rather than leaving servants behind to wait on their alpha. But the younger girl's hair hadn't been wet. She hadn't showered with us, likely hadn't run with the pack either.

Meanwhile, my mother had told me that werewolf females had only two life choices—virginal pack princesses or oppressed mates. Neither had sounded particularly appetizing...but the third choice evident within Rowan's pack boasted an even more bitter taste.

They're a harem. It was the only conclusion that matched the data. Rowan separating me from the women in the shower room. Using the term "guest" so adamantly. Warning the other males that I was off limits...for now.

All of this ran through my head as I followed him down a maze of corridors. "Your room," Rowan said at last, waving me into what did look very much like part of a barracks. The walls were unpainted cinderblocks. Two bunks filled up most of the space.

A host would have asked me if I needed anything. A toothbrush. Pajamas.

If he'd asked, I would have tried to

wrangle my suitcase, the one with tools and electronics hidden in the lining. But Rowan didn't offer.

Instead, he stood silent, waiting for me to either make a scene or enter the space that looked more like a cell than a bedroom. No windows. No knick knacks. Only a thin, grunge-colored blanket folded on the end of each bed.

Unfortunately, there was no point in making a scene when every wolf in this compound answered to Rowan. So I stepped into the room as the door closed behind me. The door knob, when I tested it ten seconds later, was locked.

Chapter 28

The door was locked, but the corridor was busy. Footsteps passed, heavy booted ones then soft barefoot ones. The latter intrigued me, so even though I didn't expect to be answered I called out anyway.

"Hello?"

The footsteps paused. For a moment, I thought they'd continue away from me. Instead, I caught a whiff of sex and perfume as someone female pressed up against the outside of my door.

"The alpha said you weren't to be bothered."

"But I stopped you," I reassured her. "You didn't approach me." Then, before she could think up an argument, I attempted to tug at her sense of hospitality. "Could you possibly track down my luggage? I suspect Troy didn't know where to take my suitcase...."

The female voice turned regretful. "I'm afraid I'd need the alpha's permission to do that."

Frustrating but expected. I changed tacks. "Do you have a key to my room?"

"The alpha..."

She didn't have to finish her sentence. Didn't get to either, because the light went out above my head.

The woman squeaked and retreated, footsteps slapping frantically. While she fled, I fumbled in search of backup illumination.

But there was no switch by the door. No bedside lamp. Just one overhead bulb that was on then off.

Shedding my dress, I shifted to wolf form. I'd expected lupine eyes to make the expanse penetrable. But the room was still pitch dark. No light leaked in through cracks around the door.

So perhaps the entire compound had a mandatory bedtime? One that affected even the hallway lights? What if someone needed to get up and use the bathroom while the rest of us slept?

Sniffing through the pitch blackness,

I discovered the solution to that problem. A tiny half bath, not really big enough to be called a room, branched off the edge of my cell. Just a nook with a sink and toilet. No door. One towel rack.

The guys whose scent infused the space had left behind a bar of soap— used—and a grimy towel. Did they live out of suitcases to have been able to pack up so quickly? Get rotated through rooms without any say-so in the matter? I shivered but kept sniffing, hunting for something I could use to escape.

I found the one possible tool—a phone—by following converging scent trails. The beds, door, and bathroom had seen the most use, but one corner of the room was also frequented. Shifting to human form, I felt along the wall with my hands. Something fell when I touched it, banging painfully against my knee.

I only realized I'd been struck by the receiver of an old-fashioned telephone when a question emerged at knee-height. "What do you need?"

This was a female voice, but she sounded nothing like the submissive women I'd met so far within the McCallister compound. Instead, she seemed vaguely annoyed at being interrupted. I fumbled for the receiver. "Who is this?" I asked.

"Jasmine. And you're Athena. I don't have all night. Can we get to the point?"

Jasmine was a switch-board operator it seemed, even though I couldn't see why we needed one in this digital age. Especially not one who was borderline rude.

Still, I stated the obvious. "I want to make a call."

Jasmine's voice turned cagey. "Who do you wish to speak with?"

I rattled off the number I'd memorized from Tank's business card.

A pause. Then: "An outside number?"

"Let me guess. You have to ask your alpha."

And...she laughed at me. "No. I don't have to ask my *alpha*. I can tell you right now I won't connect you. Don't bother me again."

                                ***

Since the door was locked from the outside but could open at any moment, I shifted to wolf form and settled down against the barrier. And, thanks to my wolf, I slept, even though I was trapped in a tiny cinderblock room with no means of egress. Slept until the overhead light flicked on and my stomach started rumbling. Then I yawned, shifted, pulled on yesterday's dress....and my door opened without benefit of a knock.

A woman stood in the open doorway, a bundle of fabric in her arms. She could have been the woman who'd offered me clothes last night or someone entirely different. Still, I was pretty sure she wasn't Jasmine when she opened her mouth.

"The alpha requested you join him for breakfast."

She didn't offer her name, so I didn't ask for one. Instead, I took a step toward the door, noting as I did so that a good night's sleep had finally taken the twinge out of my ankle. "Perfect."

The route to semi-freedom was open, even though there was a male standing guard outside it. That was a step up from the previous night when my nose suggested there had been no one close enough to hear me if I yelled.

But I didn't make it to the hall after all. Because the woman sidestepped to block the exit, failing to budge as I advanced on her.

"You'll need to change first." As if on cue, the door closed, locking us back into the bedroom. "Here." She handed over a bundle of fabric that did, indeed, seem large enough to cover an entire person, unlike the sad excuse for a dress I currently had on.

But when I shook out the silky fabric, I winced. "Uh uh."

She leaned closer, peering at what I was holding. "What's wrong?" Her head cocked.

"This?" I held up fishnet stockings and a thong in one hand. "I'm not wearing this in public."

"There's a robe." The woman used long fingernails to pluck the rest of the fabric out of my arms. The silky garment that had made up most of the bundle turned out to be a coverup that was only borderline too sexy to be worn outside the boudoir. "No one will look at you in the halls anyway," she continued. "They know you're the alpha's property."

I most certainly wasn't the alpha's property. I was someone with two and a half days left to gather photographs and deal with Marina before returning to something that felt more important than a mere job. Regardless of my attachment to a group that was due to disassemble in half a week, I had no intention of staying put.

"I'll go to breakfast in what I have on." I kept my voice firm, taking one more step forward until I was just past the lupine comfort zone.

Up until this point, the woman had acted like a normal person, albeit a slightly dense one. But now her eyes fell to the floor, her tone turning into that of a submissive wolf being forced to stand up to someone stronger than herself. "I'm afraid that's not possible."

I felt like a bully. Still, I wasn't about to back down. "Then Rowan will have to do without the pleasure of my company."

We stood there for a solid moment before the woman risked a glance upward. Her face was pinched. "The alpha won't like that."

I hoped not liking my answer wouldn't blow back on her. But this was the woman's pack, not mine. I wasn't about to start playing by Rowan's rules.

"Too bad," I answered.

And something flashed in her eyes. Something I couldn't quite make sense of.

Then she shrugged and turned away from me. Knocked on the door and was let out by the guard, leaving without looking back.

***

Dolling myself up so I could eat with Rowan was, apparently, my only option for breakfast. Because the door remained closed after that for what must have been hours, until a woman—a different one, possibly?—showed up with another offer of clothes.

The selection this time was skimpier than the first time. There wasn't even a robe to cover it. Just underwear and frippery.

"No," I said simply, sending the clothes bearer away.

After that, I appeared to be forgotten. Even the corridor turned silent, no footsteps or voices for what felt like an eternity. Finally, a bustle of activity prompted me to press my ear against the door. This time, I intended to make a break for it. Surprise the clothes bearer as she came in, then use her as a hostage to get myself out.

But no one came. And after fifteen

minutes of activity, the hall went silent. Ten seconds later, the lights went out.

It had been a full day since I'd eaten, my wolf reminded me. No wonder she stole my body as the room plunged into darkness.

Our stomach clenched painfully. So I didn't argue when she snapped up a skittery insect, swallowing it down legs and all. She sniffed for a while after that without further success, then scrabbled at the faucet until the water streamed out.

She didn't drink though. I'd done that already in human form. Instead, she splattered liquid all over the floor.

Which made no sense...until it did. Spilled water attracted additional insects. I couldn't see what kind they were in the darkness, a fact for which I was profoundly grateful. But I couldn't block out the minutes during which my wolf hunted, listening for the tiny scritch of legs on concrete. We swallowed enough bugs to take the edge off our hunger, then we fell asleep once again pressed up against the door.

"It's Monday," I guessed when the lights came on a second time, my body human albeit clad in a dress that had been stretched out of proportion by a night spent four-legged. If the lights followed a usual day/night cycle, then I had multiple items on my agenda for the next few hours. I needed to call my bank and make sure Marina's zeroes had been accurate so the check I'd given the

Highlands secretary wouldn't bounce. Monday was also when my stepfather expected a cash infusion. And, tomorrow, Lupe expected us back at camp.

I pounded on the door rather than waiting for someone to show up with clothes I had no intention of wearing. Passing footsteps hesitated then kept on walking. I picked up the phone but no operator answered. There wasn't even a dial tone.

Within half an hour, silence enfolded the hallway just like it had done yesterday. The door didn't respond to my attempts to batter it open. There was no window to crawl through. Nothing with which to pick the lock.

In fact, this room seemed newer than

I'd realized on first inspection. The cinderblock walls boasted no loose mortar. There were no handy cracks to pry apart.

Soft footsteps intruded upon my consideration of the construction timeline. A woman with no guard behind her? I suspected I could take a lone woman without the element of surprise, so I didn't hide behind the door the way I'd intended to. Instead, I straightened my dress and pasted a smile on my face.

The woman who entered winced when she looked at me. Maybe my smile was more of a grimace? Or maybe it was the wildness of my hair and eyes.

Either way, she gestured for me to follow her out into the hallway. "No mandatory clothing change?" I asked, and she merely shook her head mutely. "Where are we going?" I prodded.

I almost thought she wasn't going to answer, which was fine. Because we were no longer down in the barracks area. We'd climbed a set of stairs and started down a hallway with actual paint on the walls rather than bare cinderblock.

But my guide did answer. Glancing at me sideways, she spoke very softly. "You have a visitor. Tall, dark"—her face twisted—"but *not* handsome."

The doors along this hall weren't metal fire doors, impervious to all but a battering ram. They were instead polished hardwood with fancy doorknobs. As old and stylish as the downstairs was ugly and new.

I barely paid attention, though. Because I knew who fit that description.

My guide opened a door into a sunlit study. After days cooped up in the dank basement, light streaming through the windows and colorful trees outside should have swallowed all of my attention.

Instead, I had eyes for only one person. The man lounging in a padded armchair. To me, he was beyond handsome. He was beautiful.

My cheeks stretched with the force of my gladness. "Tank."

Chapter 29

Vaguely, I noted that my guide had left and closed the door behind her. But I didn't bother to check whether I'd been locked in yet again. Instead, my entire body expanded as if it had been filled with helium. I crossed the intervening space like Harper racing for an ice-cream cone.

But Tank didn't look at me. Rowan did from behind a gleaming mahogany desk, a fleeting glance. Then he dismissed my presence and kept talking to Tank.

"Nodes don't move," the alpha growled, brows drawn together in what could have been annoyance or confusion.

Tank shrugged. "I didn't think so either. But Lupe's the boss and Lupe says the node is now here. In your territory. She recommends your entire pack vacate the premises until after Samhain...."

His reasoning was cut off by Rowan's hand gesture. "We're not *running away*."

"Have you forgotten what happened three years ago?"

I had no idea what had happened three years ago, but Rowan clearly did because the intensity of his gaze averted. A lapse in alpha dominance, one Tank could easily have pounced upon.

Instead, the scarred male glanced in my direction as if only now noticing I'd entered. The tilt of his head suggested vague interest in my presence, but—hidden from Rowan's view—his eyes told a very different story.

Irises flashed yellow. Wolf. Alert, focused.

My own inner animal responded, pushing me into his personal space. My hands rose without my permission, seeking contact....

And Tank's eyes shuttered. Rather than reciprocating, he twisted slightly so his hand could reach mine shielded by the back of the armchair. Something slid into my fingers, something I didn't twist my head to look at.

After all, Rowan was focused on us, interested in our moment. He couldn't know that Tank had just slipped me a phone.

"Whether you leave or not," Tank continued, eyes leaving mine as quickly as they'd made contact, "Lupe requests the return of our team mate." He was once again facing forward. Once again entirely focused on the alpha who owned the room.

"Well, of course Athena will be made available during working hours," Rowan agreed easily. Too easily. He leaned forward, chin resting on steepled fingers.

"In fact, I'll lend you a few of my wolves to keep her company."

"That won't be necessary." Tank stood, his size a shield I hadn't realized I needed. Taking advantage of the moment, I stuffed the phone into the only hiding place available to me. The dress pushed my breasts together so tightly they formed a pocket. I could only hope the illicit item would stay put.

"Not necessary?" I couldn't see Rowan around Tank's broad shoulders, but I could smell the pressure of his alpha dominance. "Of course it's necessary to send an honor guard along with Athena. After all, she's an unmated female. In high demand."

The alpha paused, then he angled

his body until I was once again speared in his sightline. Hairs rose on my arms and neck as Rowan acknowledged me with the tiniest hint of a smile. "And it would be appropriate that Athena spend her evenings here."

The cage I'd unwittingly walked into closed back around me. The last of Tank's uplifting helium pressed out of my lungs with an audible wheeze.

***

Spending another night in my cell wasn't happening. But Tank merely shrugged. "Lupe will be here within the hour. Perhaps Athena could take a few minutes to clean up?"

I skittered backwards, cheeks reddening. The mangled dress, the grime on paws that had transferred to fingers. I'd forgotten what I looked like, but Tank had noticed.

Rowan's eyes glinted with amusement. He liked seeing me thrown off balance. "Of course." He pushed a button on his desk and the door opened, revealing my guide. "Take Athena to the showers."

"Yes, alpha."

Tank didn't even look at me as I left.

But the phone was there, evidence that he hadn't come solely because of a node that may or may not have changed location. Tank had been the only one aware of my plan for our vacation. I refused to believe it was coincidence that I went silent and he showed up.

No, Tank had come here looking for me. I'd never had dependable backup before. The helium returned with a vengeance.

But I needed to focus. Because Tank clearly thought it was too dangerous to face down Rowan directly. Instead, he'd slipped me the cell phone...an object I needed to get rid of before I stripped to take advantage of the showers we'd returned to.

"Do you think you could find me clothes?" I asked the woman who'd led me there, wanting to get rid of her. "Something I can work in."

She looked dubious but nodded

anyway. "I'll see what I can do."

I waited until she disappeared down the women's corridor before assessing my options. I could try to flee down the tunnel I'd originally come in through...but I remembered the door grinding shut and suspected it would be neither fast nor easy to figure out how to open it. Instead, I pulled out the cell phone and powered it up.

There was no passcode, which seemed entirely unlike Tank. Or, rather, just like Tank if he'd expected to slip the phone to me surreptitiously. The screen woke straight onto a note app, which confirmed the guess.

"Your sister is fine, but she's not with my pack," Tank had written. *"Her father*

came this morning to collect her. Threatened to call the cops on us if we didn't let her go. Mentioned money he was owed. Harper seemed disappointed but not frightened. I sent two wolves trailing them to keep her safe." Then he included Harper's number, as if I didn't know it by heart.

I dialed the digits...and nothing happened. There were no bars here. The underground bunker was shielded from satellites, perhaps by design or perhaps just by encircling earth.

My guide wouldn't be gone for long, but I had to get through to my sister. I padded around the tiled shower room, hunting any hint of reception.

There. By the tunnel leading out.

One measly bar.

I glanced back over my shoulder, saw nothing, then crouched and crawled inside.

***

Halfway down the tunnel, the call went through. "Hello?" my sister said, voice uncertain.

I needed to get out of the tunnel and hide the cellphone fast, but my shoulders relaxed anyway. Harper might sound tense, but she wasn't hurt. "It's Athena," I greeted her. "Where are you?"

"Home." The single word sounded as bleak as the prison I'd spent the last thirty-six hours in. "Dad dropped Clara off at school. She won't answer my texts. She hates me."

"I doubt she hates you. She's probably disappointed." I hated the tremor that had entered my sister's voice, but the clock was ticking. And Harper was physically safe if thoroughly depressed.

So I stuck to the point. "Why did Nick take you home?"

"He said the school called about a check not working?" Harper's voice rose at the end, a question she was afraid to ask.

Marina's check. I'd meant to check on that transaction, but for obvious reasons I'd dropped the ball. "It will work tomorrow," I told my sister, hoping I wasn't lying. "But that has nothing to do with your dad."

I pressed the phone closer to my ear, catching the rumble of a sports announcer in the background. I could just see Nick, sacked out on the couch munching chips and ignoring his daughter. He'd taken Harper home to mess with me. And, as much as I hated it, I could do nothing about that fact right now.

Meanwhile, through my other ear, I caught the faintest click of a door closing. Was that my guide leaving whatever room she'd entered to hunt for work clothing? If so, I needed to wrap this conversation up fast.

But Harper wasn't done with her questions. "Dad said you owe him money too?" Her voice grew quieter and quieter. "That when you pay him, you can pick me up."

Her last four words came out as a plea. It was the same voice Harper had used to ask for a puppy four Christmases ago.

I'd had to deny her then, and I had to deny her now. "I can't, Harper."

Shoes clicked on concrete. If my guide was close enough for me to hear her footsteps, I was close enough for her to hear my voice.

And yet, Harper was still talking. "Please. I know I'm only your half sister, but...." Her voice dropped into a quaver at the same moment Nick called out an order.

"Get off your ass and bring me a beer."

He wasn't an alpha wolf, but Harper was his daughter. Stuck in his house all week unless I sprang her from prison.

But I couldn't. I needed to deal with Rowan and Marina and Lupe. Meanwhile, my sister was safe. I knew that. I trusted Tank to choose pack mates who would keep the fae far away from her.

Worst-case scenario, Nick would keep Harper on house arrest until I finished this job and wiggled out from under Rowan's thumb. The so-called vacation would be unpleasant, but my sister would survive it.

And footsteps were getting closer by the second. I wriggled out of my dress and started crawling back down the tunnel toward the showers.

At the same time, I gave my sister the only thing I could—an apology. Cupping my hands around the phone, I whispered just barely loud enough for human ears to pick up on.

"I'm sorry," I told Harper, not certain she even heard me before reception was lost.

Chapter 30

I was in the shower, phone hidden beneath my rumpled red dress, when my guide reappeared. Yet again, her arms were full of clothing, but these were awfully familiar. Even from a distance, I could recognize the outfit I'd shucked before shifting to wolf form two days before.

"Does this mean you found my suitcase?" I asked, swiping one last time at the dirt ingrained in my skin. I'd spent most of my wash time talking to my sister, and my guide was tapping her foot impatiently. So I accepted the towel she handed me then wriggled into jeans.

It had never felt so good to pull my scuffed leather jacket around my shoulders. Especially when I slid one finger along the inside seam and felt the bump I'd hoped was still present. It was all I could do not to smile despite my guide's disappointing response:

"I'm afraid not. I think the suitcase might have gotten lost in transit."

As if Rowan's pack was an international airport able to reroute my luggage onto a plane bound for the other side of the country. Still, I didn't press the issue. Shrugging, I scooped up the dress, palmed the cell phone, then followed my guide down the hall back to my room.

There, I paused as I took in a familiar figure. "Lupe?"

The older woman nodded curtly before turning back to face the shifter beside her. He might have been one of the males who'd guarded me during my imprisonment, but if so he certainly wasn't restricting Lupe's movement. Instead, the power dynamic flowed the opposite way.

"It's clear the door knob was inserted backwards," Lupe bit out. When the male just stared at her, she elaborated. "The locking mechanism is on the outside not the inside. I expect it fixed before I return."

He was already examining the door

when we turned away, following our guide back up to the ground floor and into a banquet hall full of shifters. There, Lupe was led in one direction and me in another. My wolf, seeing the food at the only empty seat, plopped us down without my permission. It was all I could do to use a fork and knife when my wolf wanted to grab up handfuls to stuff into our mouth.

It hasn't been that long, I chided her, trying to pay attention to the bigger picture. Hard when the warmth of nourishment in my belly tried to soothe me into complacency. Rather than letting it, I assessed the utility of nearby objects.

Salt shaker. Knife. Those would definitely come in handy. Knocking both into my lap, I stashed them one at a time in my jacket's voluminous pockets....

"Nice trick," observed the female shifter seated to my left.

***

It was Jasmine, the sarcastic phone operator. I knew by her voice, even though she looked like all the other twenty-something brunettes.

"Busted," I answered, drawing the knife back out and using it to saw at my steak.

"What are you going to use the salt for?" Jasmine asked, not seeming bothered that I'd kept the shaker. Did that mean I could have held onto the knife too? I decided not to risk a repeat of the weapon grab.

"Slugs give me the heebie-jeebies," I answered. Which wasn't a lie...although I hadn't pocketed the salt to counteract slugs.

Jasmine scrunched up her face in sympathy. "Yeah, the downstairs isn't sealed yet. I asked Rowan why we were in such a hurry, but he told me not to trouble my pretty little head about that."

Pretty, little head was spat out with such venom that I couldn't help smiling. There was so much of interest in her short statement. I chose to focus on the most telling slip. "You call him Rowan."

"It's his name." Jasmine paused, then she gave me the information I'd been angling for. "He's my little brother. Seems silly to address him as 'alpha' when I used to call him 'baby boy.'"

"It must be tough to have a younger brother as your leader."

I expected her to turn coy, but Jasmine snorted then elaborated. "Some days, I wish I could shake sense into him."

"Because of the way he treats women?"

"You mean his harem?" Jasmine shook her head, not as if she was disagreeing with me but rather as if she was disagreeing with the entire notion. "He'll grow out of it. Or they'll get sick of kowtowing. Either way, it won't last."

These words, though, weren't firm

like her earlier ones. And maybe that's why she turned away from me. Turned back to her neighbor, leaving me to chow down alone.

To chow down...and to return to my original task of assessing the room. It was a large banquet hall, rectangular tables crowded with dining shifters. Too loud to use voices to arrow in on Samhain Shifters. Still, after a moment I picked out Lupe, then an eyes-on-the-back-of-my-neck sensation drew my attention to Tank.

He met my gaze for one split second then turned away, almost as if he didn't want to acknowledge our connection. Or, no, as if he was pointing out Ryder without having to raise a finger.

Five tables down, the tattooed biker waggled his eyebrows at me. In reaction, the veins on the side of Tank's neck bulged for one split second. Ignoring their half-friendly and half-not interaction, I tried and failed to pick out Butch.

Odd. It wasn't as if a tall, elegant black guy would be easy to hide in a room full of folks with skin tones ranging from light peach to burnt ochre. So where was he?

I frowned but lost the thread of that thought as the room fell silent. "Our guests," Rowan said, his words no louder than if he'd been speaking to the person across the table, "will be shown the utmost courtesy."

Despite the levelness of their alpha's

voice, it felt like everyone around me held their breath in order to hear him better. Shifters who'd been eating dropped half-finished rolls and food-covered forks. Eating or not, every eye focused on Rowan.

Then, without being asked, eight shifters pushed back their chairs.

The pack bond. That had to be how Rowan was providing instructions. Because the eight split apart in perfect synchrony, two heading toward each of the Samhain Shifters in attendance.

"Are you coming?" Jasmine asked. She was one of the eight, as was a male who'd sidled past half a dozen diners to reach us. Without addressing him or waiting for an answer from me, my seat mate started in the opposite direction from where the others were heading.

Or, no, that wasn't quite right. We were *all* being taken in separate directions. Rowan was splitting us up. Making sure our team didn't have a moment to compare notes and make a plan.

Jasmine swiveled back to face me. "Athena? Don't you want to see the garden?"

I had a feeling it didn't matter what I wanted. That the garden was where I was going regardless.

And Lupe wasn't arguing. Tank and Ryder weren't throwing their weight around.

So I shrugged and made nice.

"Sure."

***

I saw my team mates occasionally over the course of the day, but we never came close enough to speak to each other. Instead, we passed by from a distance, the endless tour no less restraining than being locked in the barracks had been.

But at least there were snacks, which kept my wolf happy. Well, that's not quite true. When we walked in the door of the gymnasium at the same moment Tank walked out of it, my wolf nearly broke free of our civilized behavior and pushed me after him.

Smells like strength, she prodded. *Safety. Home.*

Quiet, I responded, even though she was right.

"So that's why you wouldn't dine with my brother," Jasmine observed, drawing me back to the present. I tensed, expecting a jibe at Tank's ugliness. Instead, she added: "I can see why."

"You think Tank's attractive?"

Jasmine raised her eyebrows. "Attractive? No. Powerful? Yes." Then, changing the subject with her usual facility, she led me over to a bay of workout equipment. "Pick your poison."

I opted to start on the only one I knew how to operate—a treadmill. My wolf, however, saw no purpose in running in place when we could be running after Tank. I had to remind her that hunts required stealth and patience. We'd barely reached a detente when Ryder entered through the furthest door.

"Time to go," Jasmine told me, hopping off the machine that had been guiding her into strange contortions.

My wolf was willing, but I wasn't. Instead, I wiped my face with a hand towel, giving myself a second to think.

Because the issue of guides-turned-guards had nagged me while I followed Jasmine around all day long. If Rowan never gave us a daylight moment alone then locked Tank, Butch, and Ryder away for the night, we'd be hamstrung. Left at Rowan's mercy in order to finish our job.

Lupe, I hoped, was powerful enough to force the issue of our shared door staying open. After all, she'd managed to wiggle me out of Rowan's grip previously. But I'd seen no evidence that the McCallister alpha would show equal restraint toward her underlings.

He certainly hadn't treated me with much respect.

Which left me and Lupe wandering the halls tonight, hoping to find our team mates. Chances were we'd end up bursting in on random strangers. It would turn into a sticky mess.

"Athena?" Jasmine called from the far door. "Are you coming?"

Across the room, Ryder raised shaggy eyebrows.

The guys needed their own way out of locked rooms and I now possessed that solution. Because the bulging seam of my jacket hid my ace in the hole—a pair of lock picks. It felt strange to pull them out and leave them behind in the used hand towel. Because...what if I needed them? What if I was giving up my only escape from another day of eating insects and prowling the confines of a tiny cell in lupine form?

Pack, my wolf murmured before I could shush her. *Help them.*

We weren't pack. We were simply team mates.

Still, when I glanced back as I followed Jasmine out the door, my belly warmed at the sight of Ryder pocketing my offering. Worst-case scenario, at least one team mate would have a way out of his cell tonight.

Chapter 31

The rest of the day passed in a blur of shackling politeness. Although I hadn't been able to speak to any of my team mates, my illicit cell phone vibrated repeatedly in my pocket. And when I begged for a bathroom break, I discovered I'd been added to a walkie-talkie-enabled group chat.

Lupe: Report in.

Ryder: Barracks room fifteen is a dump. I'll manage.

Tank: I'm your neighbor in fourteen.

Butch: My room has no number. Turn left from the dining room, take the first right, then walk to the end of the hall.

Tank: Athena?

A pause, then:

Lupe: My lock has been repositioned so I can't be penned in. Yours?

Butch: No lock.

Ryder: Got a lock...and lock picks. Thanks, A-bear!

Tank: No picks here. My roommates say they're locked in every night.

After another pause, he'd added:

Tank: Are you there, Athena?

Ryder: Maybe she doesn't want to talk to your ugly mug. Maybe she wants some of my sugar instead. After all, A-bear gave me a present.

Tank: Ryder.

Lupe: Enough. Athena, are you able to receive messages?

That text had come through only ten minutes ago. I touched the screen to pull up the keyboard...then Jasmine tapped on the bathroom door.

"Everything okay in there?"

I wasn't locked up...yet. But I certainly wasn't free to travel wherever I wanted. Rowan was taking no chances.

"Fine." I flushed, using the second of stolen leeway to tap out the tiniest reply imaginable.

Athena: Here.

Then I left the privacy of the bathroom and followed Jasmine down yet another hall.

                    ***

I'd thought she planned to return me
to my no-longer-prison. But we didn't
travel downstairs. Instead, we journeyed
up.

Up from quality to luxury. At the top
of the stairs, a door opened into a space
that could have been called a room...if
you were used to the scale of mansions.

Dark windows promised that night
had fallen while I was stuck inside.
Rowan lounged on a black leather sofa,
smoking robe half open and shot glass
cradled in one hand.

"You can go, Jasmine." The alpha
waved dismissal and air movement

promised his sister had obeyed him. I didn't take my eyes off his face, however. My wolf was completely and instantly alert.

Leave, she demanded. *Predator*, she added.

As if I wasn't aware of Rowan's eyes glowing hungrily in the near darkness. Still, I shook my head and took a single step inside.

Because I wasn't yet ready to burn the bridge Rowan represented. Despite the vibrating cell phone in my pocket, I couldn't afford to. Not when Harper's school was within McCallister territory. Not when the Samhain Shifters would disband by the middle of the week.

Instead, I evaded. "Maybe this can

wait until tomorrow? I'm tired."

"My bedroom is around the corner." Rowan was standing now, his scent of hungry wolf enfolding me. He advanced and I took a step backward, my spine coming to rest against the closed door.

"You're frightened."

"I'm not."

His finger rose, nearly but not quite touching my unprotected throat. "Your pulse beats like a bird battering itself against a window pane."

I shivered and he smiled. The door knob turned easily in my hand.

His teeth glinted as his lips widened. "No, you're not locked in. Not now. Although I *have* locked wolves away for much longer than your short training session. Weeks. Months. One I forgot about. No one fed him. He died and we gnawed on his bones."

Rowan's wolf was so close to the surface, I could see its shadow beneath his cheekbones. This wasn't normal behavior. Not even for a power-hungry alpha.

"What do you want?" I demanded.

"A signature on a contract. Two years will be plenty. I tire of playthings quickly. Then, when your sister graduates, you're free to go."

A contract? From the little I knew about the fae, that sounded far more like their MO than like a werewolf's.

Surreptitiously, I hunted in my pocket for the stolen salt shaker. It had spilled out a teaspoon of granules and I pinched some up between thumb and forefinger....

Flinging the salt at Rowan's throat, I waited for him to sizzle or at least retreat away from me. Instead, he advanced another step until our fronts touched.

His voice quaked with humor. "You're fighting me off with pocket lint?"

I shook my head. Rowan wasn't fae. He was just a wolf toying with my future as if I was a junebug on a string.

The phone hung heavy in my pocket. I could follow Rowan to his bedroom, take pictures for Marina, hope they were enough to get me out of this mess....

Or I could deny Rowan and hope a solution arose in the next two days. Well, make that one day and a half.

"I"—I swallowed—"I have to think about it."

For half a second, I thought Rowan would stop me. He reached forward and my gut clenched around a wolf who wanted to shift and bite our way to freedom....

"By all means," Rowan said. Instead of stopping me, his hand tapped the door above my head and pushed it open. "Until tomorrow. I await your pleasure."

***

I fled down the stairs, unable to slow my descent even though Rowan didn't appear to be following. The ground floor was silent. The route to the basement, I knew from the day's endless tour, was right around the bend.

Meanwhile, the front door beckoned. I could leave, collect my sister, take her somewhere far away from Rowan and Marina. Nick wouldn't try very hard to find us, not when he had the rest of the Samhain Shifters to deal with. And while Harper would hate being on the lam, dodging strange alphas, she trusted me. She'd go and she'd behave.

She'd *behave.* I hated that. Didn't want to squash the small hint of independence and playfulness Harper had recently grown into.

So I pulled out my phone and checked the group chat. They'd discussed the job more since I'd sent my one-word answer—it appeared the node really had moved into Rowan's territory. Ryder mentioned strange behavior from his guides that sounded an awful lot like the cat-chasers outside my apartment. Tank had left me an opening to insert my experience with Marina but hadn't shared what wasn't his to share.

Then:

Ryder: Could there be fae present now?

Lupe: Unlikely. I was in South America last Samhain, but Rogers reported an easy night in this zone. More likely a Sleeper has been working on this pack all year. Did you notice the basement is just under twelve months old?

Tank: I did.

A pause, then:

Butch: Turning in.

Ryder: Ditto.

Lupe: Good night, everyone.

Tank: Athena?

Ten minutes later:

Tank: Athena?

That message had been sent nine minutes ago. And, even as I started to type, the phone vibrated again.

Tank: Athena?

As I read, my feet carried me down the hall away from both obvious options. Not toward the basement or the front door, but past the banquet hall then curving left.

Because something had been

niggling at me ever since Butch didn't show up at dinner. His astonishing facility with swords and his knowledge of the fae's aversion to metal. His refusal to share his deepest secret. The gloves he wore the entire time he was ferrying me around then took off when we got to camp.

At camp, the doors were simple wooden latches. We'd eaten finger food with no need for utensils. The only metal was the grilling supplies Tank had handled.

Lupe was so certain there couldn't be fae here, but the available data added up to one obvious conclusion. *Butch isn't a werewolf,* I typed. *He's one of the fae. Or at least a Sleeper. I'm in his room. If you get this, I need help.*

I left the message on the screen but didn't tap the arrow to send it. Instead, I eased open the door of Butch's bedroom, unsurprised to find that he'd merited an abode with windows, curtains, a desk, a bed.

The shape beneath the covers appeared to be sleeping, but I held my breath anyway. Eased inside, using a hint of my wolf's ability in order to make my footfalls as silent as if we were in the forest hunting game.

Butch was facing the wall, everything but his head covered by a quilt embroidered with vines, birds, and flowers. Quite a contrast to the faded, grubby coverlet I'd been granted. Of course, a fae would have been able to manipulate Rowan's pack into giving him the best.

In one hand, my thumb hovered above the send arrow on my cell phone. My other hand gripped the salt shaker, ready for a repeat of the same test Rowan had just passed.

But I didn't have time to throw any salt around. Because Butch rolled over, the scent of sun-sweetened peaches rising in waves off him.

Or, rather, off *her*. Because this wasn't Butch. This was Marina.

"Little wolf. I wondered how long it would take you to guess."

Chapter 32

My thumb fell onto the touchscreen. I didn't toss the salt, however. Instead, I inched backwards, buying time for Tank to come to my assistance. "You aren't Butch." I shook my head, trying to make sense of inconsistencies. "That's not possible. I saw both of you at the same time."

"At Harper's school?" Marina swung her legs out from under the covers. Despite having ostensibly been sleeping, her pajamas were uncreased and perfect.

Silk and unisex, they would have looked as good on Butch as they did on her.

"Yes," I agreed.

The odor of peaches intensified. "Appearances can be deceiving."

As she spoke, the phone vibrated in my hand. I didn't glance down, but Marina's gaze flew to it anyway. Her eyes narrowed. "I told them to remove all of your electronics. Give me that."

If she wanted my phone, I wasn't handing it over. So much for a pleasant conversation. I straightened my shoulders, readying the salt shaker. "No."

And now I heard a soft but solid thud below me. Had Ryder found time to pick his lock and open Tank's door already? Were team mates other than Tank even awake to assist us? Or was Marina drawing Rowan's wolves toward us using the McCallister pack bond?

"Why did you want me in Rowan's bedroom?" I asked, trying to buy another minute. I had to trust that the sound in the basement pointed to pending assistance. Or, if it didn't, that Tank would find a way to overtake whoever was coming our way. "I'm guessing there's nothing here to steal."

Marina licked her lips, the gesture unconscious. As if she could taste the power of McCallister pack bonds. "Of course there's something here to steal. So *much* of it."

As she spoke, her hand lashed out like a snake, latching onto my shoulder. I had no idea how she'd gotten so close. One minute ago, she'd been on the other side of the room. The next, she had me in a superhuman grip.

Pain and surprise opened my fingers. The salt shaker struck the floor with a dull clatter. My cell phone landed six inches away.

I'd thought I was the one stalling, but Marina had been hunting this entire time. And she'd won.

Now I had no weapons beyond my wolf. My wolf and my hope that team mates could arrive before it was too late to save me.

I drew my inner beast upwards...

...then stopped as Tank's voice emerged from the open door.

"Butch. Drop her."

If I'd thought my wolf was close to the surface, Tank's was ten times closer. His voice rasped out halfway to a lupine growl. Despite being in the clutches of the fae, my shoulders relaxed away from my ears.

"Athena appears addled," Marina/Butch answered. It was disconcerting, hearing a masculine voice emerge from this person I knew was a woman. Even more disconcerting not to smell a lie in the words.

But I *was* addled. Addled by the fae's grip. By the fact that when I tried to speak, Marina's hand clenched down so hard my teeth bit into my tongue.

"Like the time I borrowed your car?" Tank's voice was wry and I could almost hear his head shake dismissively. Was that how he remembered the night of our first kiss? Me being *addled*? I winced.

Marina took in my reaction and her teeth bared in a smile. "Yes. Exactly like that."

The scents in the room sharpened one second before Tank bit out: "Wrong answer." So I was ready. Ready to slam my free elbow into Marina's midsection, to use my full weight to drag myself out of her grip....

Lupe's voice whipped across the room, proving Tank hadn't arrived solo.

"Rune Pelletier, *freeze*!"

The command would have worked on most werewolves. But, of course, Marina wasn't a werewolf. In fact, she laughed as if we were playing straight into her hands.

She laughed...and dropped her disguise. Or so I assumed from Ryder's ten-syllable string of expletives. Tank kept his response simple: "You're not Butch."

Marina's voice was now female. "You mean I'm not *Rune Pelletier.* Thank you for the true name. I'll use it wisely."

So names were powerful for the fae? Names...like my sister's, which Marina had known from the first time I spoke to her.

Harper's safety pulled at me like a

magnet, but the immediate issue was Marina. I crouched at her feet, forgotten for the moment. Dismissed as a pawn no longer useful on a crowded chessboard.

My glance skimmed around the room, hunting a better weapon. Finding none, I snatched up the salt shaker and unscrewed the top.

That was plan B, though. Instead of tossing granules at Marina, I followed Lupe's lead and dredged up a full name.

After all, Harper had called her history teacher *Ms. Rothschild*. It was at least worth a shot.

"Marina Rothschild, tell us where Butch is," I demanded.

A peach-scented foot came down on my fingers as she laughed.

***

"You think I'd hand over my true name? Amateur hour." Marina's words were light, but her heel ground into my bones. "That was an *impersonation*, little wolf. If you'd paid any attention to your sister, you would have realized I wasn't her teacher. Too bad you don't listen to her prattle."

Harper didn't prattle. But, yeah, sometimes she exploded into words that flowed over and around me. The fact I'd failed as a guardian stung as much as Marina's foot crushing my hand.

I tried to cling to what was important, but I couldn't. Couldn't hold tight to faith that I was a proper guardian to my sister. Couldn't hold onto the salt shaker either. Instead, it spun away from both of us, my final weapon lost.

My final weapon…but I had three allies behind me. I heard the faintest shuffling of werewolf footfalls, then silence as the sharp tip of a blade landed in front of my nose. "I wouldn't," Marina murmured. Not to me. To my allies.

And they didn't. There was nothing but silence from the others as Marina toyed with her prey—me.

"For a wolf, you're surprisingly blind," she mused, tilting my chin up with her sword. I'd hoped the weapon was an illusion, but she must have had a real sword hidden away in her pajamas.

Because even though she used the flat of the blade, the metal was cold and unyielding against my skin.

"Didn't you wonder how Rowan assembled a harem?" she continued. "Didn't you wonder how his pack became so skewed?"

"I thought that's just how alphas were," I admitted, fingers fumbling for the shaker while I strove to keep my chin steady. The salt was almost within reach. Almost….

I grasped at the glass container and it scooted an inch in the wrong direction. Away from me, away from Marina too.

"They *were* a little off from the start," Marina agreed, seeming not to notice the salt shaker as I fumbled for it a second time. Her sword relaxed away from me as she spoke. "That gave me a toehold. It was simple, really. Find the cracks and *push* into them. Once the harem formed, it became simpler yet."

The sword should have been my sole concern, but Lupe had provided words of wisdom during our short swordsmanship lesson. *"Focus on your offense. If you play defensively, you're sunk."*

So I eyed the salt shaker rather than the sharp blade now an inch away from me. The lid was off the former. Maybe....

I strained my shoulder reaching for it. But my fingers made contact. I couldn't grab hold, not at this distance. But I could push it. And as the glass cylinder swirled toward a darkened corner, the contents spewed out.

"An outcast sub-pack," Marina continued. "Their bonds taste so very good...."

Her smugness faded into a hiss. A few grains had touched her foot, an accident so minor I barely saw the salt strike.

Marina's reaction wasn't minor. She jumped backward as if the salt was a live wire. Her face contorted, for the first time looking something other than beautiful. Her sword was no longer at my throat.

And I scooped up salt with aching fingers. Reared back to fling the mound of granules at Marina...only to be slapped into stillness by Rowan's voice.

"Stop."

My arm wouldn't move but my head could. Could turn to face the doorway, where my three team mates were now outnumbered by dozens of McCallister wolves.

I say wolves because their eyes glowed hungry. But they were human, most of them. Human and ready to take my team mates down.

Human and ready to defend Marina. After all, she'd tapped into their pack bonds as she'd so smugly revealed.

I had allies also. But we were outmanned and inside enemy territory.

Still, Lupe, it turned out, was the more dominant alpha of the two. Her rebuttal vibrated through my bones as she countered Rowan. *"Athena, what you do next is your own decision."*

My decision. To lose the goodwill of the alpha who would decide whether I was allowed to spend another hour in my sister's company. To cling to the tenuous possibility of connection I'd built with the Samhain Shifters, hoping they'd protect me from Rowan's inevitable backlash. Could I really trust that someone other than me would watch my back?

Between me and Rowan, Tank nodded. As if he could hear my thoughts and was making me a promise. He didn't dip his chin to hide his face either. Just stared straight into my eyes.

"Don't do something you'll regret," Rowan snarled. "I've offered you an easy two years, but I could instead force you into the harem. Do you want to be pawed by a different stranger every night or will you..."

Whatever he intended to offer, I didn't listen. Instead, I flung the salt into Marina's face.

Chapter 33

Marina screamed and Rowan roared. The air reeked of fur. From us. From them. I blinked against the awfulness and found Lupe and Tank four-legged, holding the doorway against an unbeatable tide of wolves.

"Give me anything you want to keep, A-bear," Ryder suggested, voice surprisingly calm as he brushed past me in human form. He grabbed a chair and slammed it against a window. When that didn't work, he grunted and hoisted up the small but solid desk to repeat the move.

Ryder was right. The windows were our only way out. And Marina was already rising, with no puddle of salt left to throw at her....

So I joined my team mates. Tossed my jacket to Ryder then shifted. Dove at the fae with teeth bared.

Marina tasted foul. Like rotten fruit writhing with maggots. And I didn't get the impression the chunk I'd taken out of her thigh really harmed her either. Instead, I barely dodged the hand that lashed out, grabbing for my muzzle....

I sidestepped, kicking with my hind feet. Not at Marina, at the ground. The sandy scatter of salt granules sprayed upward, not enough to injure but enough to push her back.

One step. Two. Enough, barely.

Because delay was all Ryder needed. The window shattered. "Move it!" he roared.

He was still human. Weighed down by various shed possessions plus a wooden chair leg. He used the latter like a club as a McCallister wolf tried to enter the room from outside the window. His furry foe yelped while Ryder roared a second time: "Any day now would be nice."

Obeying, though, meant leaving Rowan's horde of wolves to tear at our hindquarters. Lupe and Tank backed toward me. I joined them, shoulder to shoulder. A rush of air, then the desk landed between us and our foes.

We spun and ran, three abreast as if our muscles were wired in synchrony. Leapt through the space where window glass had recently blocked our egress. Sprinted after Ryder, who seemed to know where he was headed.

Before we got there, Marina's voice spiraled upward, the scent of maggoty peaches flying off her. "You are *mine*, Athena D'Argent. Stop where you are."

Rot choked me. Pushed into my lungs. Swiveled my body backwards....

Then Tank was pressing me forward with the mass of his furry body. The maggots in my lungs wriggled once then receded.

A car door opened. I leapt inside.

***

Ryder navigated our retreat like a race-car driver on crystal meth. And, as distance yawned between me and Marina, I finally found myself able to catch my breath.

To catch my breath and shift, looking frantically for a cell phone. I hadn't toed Marina's line, so she'd go after my sister....

Tank was ahead of me. "Code red," he barked into his phone. That must have been what he asked Ryder to carry for him. He'd chosen his phone and I'd chosen my leather jacket, a gift from my mother that even now lay crumpled on the floor at my feet.

And why was I thinking about phones and leather jackets when my sister was in danger? "Harper?" I asked, not wanting to intrude, but needing confirmation.

Tank nodded, gaze distant as he pressed the phone closer to his head.

"*On it,*" an unfamiliar male voice crackled through the speaker. "*We'll report if there's any problem. I don't expect one. She's right in front of us.*"

The call ended and the car swerved, pushing my naked shoulder into Tank's equally naked chest. Then his arm was around me, holding me safe and still as he swiveled to peer backwards.

"Three cars," he told Ryder.

From the front passenger seat, Lupe's voice was calm as she interjected: "Take a left."

Tires squealed, but this time my torso didn't move. Just my stomach, sloshing in the direction the car had been going before settling into our new trajectory.

Tank's phone rang. The instant he accepted the call, I grabbed it out of his hands. How could I not when I'd heard Harper's voice?

"No, I won't!"

"Give her the phone," I demanded, hoping Tank's friend would obey me. And he did, without question. Another crackle, then my sister's refusal echoed in my ear.

"I don't know you!"

"Harper." When she didn't answer, I yelled it. "Harper!"

"Athena?" The sounds of struggle faded. *"There are strange men...."*

"They're friends. I need you to go with them."

"Get on the highway," Lupe said from the front seat. But Ryder didn't signal and change lanes. Instead, he waited for the last possible instant before spinning across oncoming traffic. Tank's arm was all that prevented me from flying into the window.

And...all of that was irrelevant. Because my sister, for once, wasn't willing to heed my advice.

"I don't want to leave! Clara knows

where I am. When she stops being mad, she'll call me. And my phone is inside the house."

I considered sending her in to get it. But Tank's head shook. There wasn't time. Plus, if Nick got involved....

"Listen to me," I said instead. "It's important you go with these men right now. If you do, I'll give you a"—I paused, trying to think what Harper wanted—"a *puppy.*" Which would mean I'd be the one with a puppy when she went back to school in less than a week. But I'd manage.

Only—"*I'm not twelve.*" From the tone of Harper's voice, I was losing her. Losing my ability to manage the situation.

"They have a sedative," Tank

murmured in my ear. "If necessary, they'll use it."

No. That wasn't happening. My sister wasn't going to wake up woozy, kidnapped by strangers....

Instead, I promised what I knew Harper wanted far more than a puppy. What she wanted, but I had no idea how to give.

"I know you hate vacations with your father," I told her. "If you go with Tank's friends now, I'll find a way to make sure you won't have to do that again. You and I will be a normal family. We'll have a house where you won't be ashamed to bring friends over. I promise. I'll find a way to make it work."

Harper caved. I could tell she didn't really believe me. But the dream was enough to tempt her to give in and leave with her bodyguards. The dream...which I had no idea how to turn into a reality.

"We'll figure something out," Tank assured me. As if he'd read my mind. Or, more likely, given the way I was still tucked beneath his arm, he'd read the tightening of my muscles.

"I hope so," I answered. But there was no time to deal with it now, not with Rowan's wolves following us so closely.

We shook them, though. Or, rather, Ryder shook them. Wound in and out of traffic until no one followed. At which point, Lupe ordered us in an unexpected direction—

"Back to camp."

Tank's eyebrows rose. "Don't you think that's the first place Marina will look for us?"

"That may be. But camp is where Butch intended to spend his vacation."

And Butch hadn't been at the McCallister compound. Marina had taken his place there. Which meant our team mate was in danger...or worse.

"There are swords in the trunk," Lupe continued. "From this moment on, your weapon needs to be your most cherished possession. Eat with it. Sleep with it. If you see fae, it's your only real defense."

"Slide over," Tank murmured. My

cheeks reddened as I realized I was still pretty much on his lap.

"Sorry." I scooted away, the loss of his heat almost physically painful.

But Tank drew me closer instead. "No, not that way. Half the seat flips down...."

Then I was completely on his lap, his muscles pressing into my skin like the most enticing sort of massage chair. The evidence of his own approval hardened against my butt and....

"Could we save that for later?" Ryder grumbled. "Some of us are trying to drive."

Tank, to my surprise, merely chuckled. Whatever rivalry he and Ryder had engaged in was over. Between fighting against each other and fighting beside each other, what could have been a jibe turned into more of a brotherly tease.

I was the only one whose face burned.

"Can you reach the swords?" Lupe demanded, breaking the moment. Her voice was curt, reminding us that pack togetherness was a hazard.

"Just a sec...." I slid my arm into the darkness of the trunk and fumbled around until I drew out a bundle of scabbarded weapons. One for each of us...plus one.

For Butch.

The car fell silent after that, nothing but darkness outside and inside. Tank and I kept our eyes peeled for ambushes, but no one stopped us. And, at last, we turned up the familiar gravel drive near the lake.

Camp was empty. The air, when we rolled down our window, smelled like fallen leaves and dew.

No sign of wolves, past or present. Still, the rest of us raised our swords and eyed shadows while Lupe strode directly toward Butch's cabin. The door opened. The light flicked on.

Around the silhouette of Lupe's back, I caught sight of our final team mate. He *was* here. Seated, meditating on the bare floorboards.

No, not meditating. A sword had been thrust through his back.

Chapter 34

My heart twisted. That's the only explanation I can give for the pain in my chest, the difficulty of forcing oxygen down my windpipe. I was frozen. We were all frozen.

No, that's not true. Tank pushed past us, pressing his fingers against Butch's jugular. For a long moment, we held our breath. Then Tank shook his head.

"Alright." Lupe's voice was firm. "Now we know. Time to get out of here."

"We can't leave him like that." I'd

thought the words, but they came out of Ryder's mouth. As unlikely as it seemed, our most uncouth member and I were united in wanting to show Butch's body respect.

Lupe shook her head. "No time. We need to regroup. Samhain is Wednesday."

My brow furrowed. "But Marina's already crossed over."

"And if she has free rein, she'll open the node so wide that half of her friends and neighbors can enter. This job is more important than ever." Lupe's eyes narrowed. "And she thinks you're an asset to her. Why is that?"

Busted. The information I'd never shared solidified in the air between us.

For half a second, I stood frozen. Then Tank's hand settled against the small of my back.

That warmth, his silent support, gave me the strength to speak. "When we were staying here, I saw her at the boat dock," I started, only to be interrupted by Ryder's gruff negation.

"No. We saw Tank there."

"You thought that was Tank?" No wonder Ryder had teased me. If I'd trusted my team mate enough to ask for more information at the time, I would have realized Marina possessed fae glamour. None of us would be in this mess.

My gaze slid to Butch, his torso somehow as erect in death as it had been in life. His loss was inconceivable. This werewolf who'd been the voice of reason among us during Ryder and Tank's battle. The one who'd uncomplainingly ferried me around during a full day of errands. Who'd supported us all even though he didn't trust us to accept him for who and what he was.

I swallowed. And this time I told Lupe the entire story. Stealing for Marina. The crazy huge check she'd given me in exchange. My weakness—wanting to make life better for my sister—hung out like butt cheeks in an ultra-mini skirt.

And...Lupe shook her head. "That's not enough for her to have a hold over you. You'd have to give her something. A gift with no payback."

A gift. Was that what the wolf bracer had turned into? "Can I see your phone?" I asked Tank.

He raised his eyebrows but passed it over. Logging onto my bank account's website, I winced at the negative balance.

"Marina's checks bounced." I'd forgotten the financial element in the midst of the other awfulness. My inability to pay for Harper's boarding school, to buy off my stepfather, tightened like a noose around my neck.

"That would do it," Lupe agreed, not noticing my reaction. "If the check was only glamour, you technically gave her the bracer for nothing. A gift. The perfect way for her to get a hold over you."

Ryder winced, suggesting Lupe had explained this issue in more detail before I became part of the team. Beside me, Tank's fingers found mine and squeezed.

Lupe, though, was the one who continued speaking. "You're a liability to us. We need you far away from the node on Samhain. I appreciate your past assistance, but as of tonight you're off the case."

***

"No. If she goes, I go."

Tank's voice came from behind me, but I felt it rumbling through my skin. When had he pulled me back against his body? The warmth felt good, and yet....

I stepped sideways so I could look up at him. "Tank. This is important."

His hand landed on my hip. As if creating empty air space between us was inconceivable. "I agree. This is important."

"We don't have time for hormones," Lupe interrupted. "The node's location is unidentified. Butch called to say it had moved, but now I don't know if that was Marina or Butch on the phone."

Ryder erupted into a cascade of cursing that brought the faintest smile to my lips. Then I frowned as something occurred to me. Butch's knowledge of the node. Lupe's use of his full name in an attempt to freeze Marina. His unwillingness to share his darkest secret....

"Butch really is fae?"

"Part fae. Part werewolf," Lupe said absently. She'd pulled out her phone. Hunting for a replacement for me and Tank? It was inconceivable to think she could face down Marina and the entire McCallister pack with only Ryder by her side.

"So, shouldn't a sword through his body cast him back into the fae world rather than killing him?" Plus, if he was dead, why would Marina have sounded so pleased about learning his true name?

Lupe's finger stilled. "Butch clearly doesn't have that much fae blood in him. But perhaps...."

The sword sticking through Butch's

body now looked like an opportunity rather than a horror. Two hands—mine and another's—landed on the sword hilt at the exact same moment. And, to my surprise, Lupe lowered her eyes and stepped aside.

"You do it."

Pull the sword out of Butch's back and hope he would gasp back to life rather than collapse into a puddle of decaying meat? I took a deep breath and...

"Wait." Now it was Tank beside me. Tank, who pulled Butch's shirt away from his skin with one hand then used his own sword to sever the fabric in one ripping stroke.

When I cocked my head, not

understanding, Tank explained: "I don't want him to heal into it."

As if he expected Butch to not only survive days with a sword impaling his lungs, but to bounce back within seconds. I liked the way Tank thought even though such a recovery felt impossible. Butch's skin, when I accidentally brushed it, was stone cold.

"Now," Tank murmured.

The single word gave me the strength to yank the sword backwards. Ignoring the churning in my gut, I kept pulling. Metal rasped against bone. Shreds of skin scattered onto the ground.

There was no blood. Shouldn't there have been blood if Butch was still living? Instead, our team mate collapsed as if the sword was all that had been holding him upright.

Collapsed into the arms of Tank and Ryder, who eased him onto the floor boards. Butch was dead, I was sure of it.

Ryder was equally certain. His expletives seared with the heat of an oven.

But Tank wasn't ready to give up. He pressed two fingers into the indentation of Butch's throat a second time then smiled. "He's alive."

***

Butch was alive, but he wasn't conscious. Definitely wasn't about to hop to his feet and swing a sword.

"I'll take care of this," Lupe told us. "Ryder, feel free to take one of the Jeeps by the boat shed. You're off duty until Wednesday morning."

She didn't even glance at me and Tank. We were dismissed. Off the team. No longer relevant.

Or, no, that wasn't true. "Athena," Lupe called as I turned away. "You'll still be paid. Tomorrow morning, I'll cut you a check."

And...I was furious. Yes, cash had been one of my incentives for joining the Samhain Shifters in the first place. But Lupe's reassurance made me sound like Nick, being paid off to let Harper continue boarding school. "I don't..." I started, knowing even as I spoke that there was no way to argue the point with someone who could overpower me with a single word.

But Tank spoke over my refusal. "Fae. Can they feed on mate bonds or just pack bonds?"

Mate bonds? I twitched even as Lupe's lips pursed. For a moment I thought she wasn't going to answer. Then, reluctantly:

"Pack bonds only, as best we can tell. Yes, you'll be helping rather than hindering if you go along to guard Athena's back."

"Good."

Tank's hand on my spine pushed me out of the cabin. And I went, even though I hated it. Went because he was twice as strong as I was, his physical ability to overpower just as much a given as Lupe's ability to force compliance with an alpha order.

I went...but I vibrated with anger. Tank thought he could force me to mate with him and use that bond to protect me. This was why I'd steered clear of packs and alphas for the last decade. This was why I'd done everything I could think of to achieve independence from other werewolves.

So why was the worst part seeing the trauma Marina had inflicted on Rowan's pack and knowing the same could strike Kira and her family? Why was the worst part being forced out of the Samhain Shifters' strike?

"Wait here," Tank told me. We'd reached the boathouse, the dark shape towering above us. This was the weedy backside that I'd never had time to explore previously. Multiple Jeeps waited, old and dilapidated. Fallen leaves slicked their interiors.

But when Tank entered the boathouse and emerged with a key, the engine of the one he tried sprang to life.

There was no top, but Tank rustled up two knitted caps, one for each of us. Mine physically warmed me, but did nothing to soothe the fury whipping through my veins.

This was bullshit. I wasn't going to be taken away like my sixteen-year-old sister, locked in a room for my own safety until Halloween was past.

If I'd spoken, my words would have cut like daggers. So it was probably a good thing that the fabric and the wind made it impossible to speak.

Impossible to do anything, really, other than dwell on my failure. Yes, Butch was alive, but only barely. And I was drawing Tank away from the battle, forcing him into the role of bodyguard to the Samhain Shifters' weakest link.

Marina would win, and it would be my fault. Well, my fault plus Lupe's and Tank's for being idiots....

As if he could feel my thoughts rising to a boil, Tank pulled over. Shut off the engine.

The silence was as dark as the night.

"You need to go back..." I started just as Tank said:

"What do you know about...?"

We both stopped, waiting for the other to continue. And even though I wanted to slap him, I swallowed down my anger and ceded the floor. "You first."

I expected Tank to tell me where I was being taken, why this was all for the best. Instead, he rumbled out a question. "What do you know about the McCallister pack?"

His eyes reflected moonlight. Not lupine. Entirely human.

I cocked my head. "Why?"

Tank coughed out the faintest hint of a laugh. "I got the impression you weren't ready to be done with this."

He was making no sense. "And I got the impression you were willing to let the fae cross over in order to protect me."

"I am. I will. If that's what you want."

But...it wasn't. Of course it wasn't. "No," I shook my head. "I want to win this."

And Tank smiled, all twisted scars and glinting wolf teeth. He was big and scary and completely magnificent.

"Alright then. What do you know about the McCallister pack?"

Chapter 35

What I knew was that their compound was a fortress. Rowan ruled with an iron fist and most of his pack obeyed without question. Still, my time there had uncovered a single weak link.

I waited to make the call until we were ensconced in a railway sleeper car. A safe haven that kept us moving and out of Marina's reach while providing a little breathing space.

By this point, it was long past midnight. But my contact answered on the first ring anyway.

"McCallister residence. How may I help you?"

As I'd suspected, Jasmine was in charge of the landline listed in the phone book in addition to monitoring internal phone calls. Now, the question was, had I misread her annoyance with her brother's management of the clan?

"Jasmine. This is Athena."

Beside me, Tank waited in absolute silence. He hadn't argued for or against this tactic. Had merely bowed his head when I suggested it and swung into Walmart in search of a burner phone.

A burner phone...that could still give away our location if Jasmine possessed the know-how to trace satellite linkages.

Sure, we were currently an hour's drive from Rowan's center of operations. But we were still within pack territory. For all I knew, he had wolves stationed this far out.

Ten seconds ticked by. Twenty. I pulled the phone away from my ear, preparing to hang up and cut my losses....

"No, I'm afraid we didn't plan a delivery for today," Jasmine said at last.

"Someone can hear you," I observed. "But they can't hear me?"

"Yes, exactly." Her voice was as warm as I remembered it. And, this time, it vibrated with mischief.

So I took the chance. "You can't be happy with what's going on in your pack."

"I'm not happy with it." Jasmine's initial words were fierce before she scaled them back for the benefit of her eavesdroppers. "But that's acceptable. I can work with that."

"It's going to get much worse Wednesday night," I warned her. "Tank and I want to make it better. But we need your help."

Another pause, during which I wondered how I'd ever thought myself able to talk this woman around during a five-minute phone conversation. I was asking her to betray her pack and her brother. Of course she'd turn me down flat.

Instead, she hit me with a question. "What are you suggesting?"

"I'm suggesting that you help Tank enter your compound. If we have eyes inside, we might be able to end this before Samhain. Shut down the harem. Turn your clan into a cohesive pack."

Could werewolves smell truth over the phone? I held my breath, hoping my earnestness had transmitted.

And, whatever the reason, Jasmine agreed with me. "I can pick up the package tomorrow. Just tell me the time and place."

***

The seats in our sleeper compartment folded down into a bed. One bed. Barely large enough for two, if you liked each other very much.

There was no couch to retreat to this time. So I shouldn't have been surprised when Tank slipped back into the shoes he'd unlaced the moment we entered our compartment. "I'll be in the dining car."

That would have been the safe route. The smart route.

But I was feeling neither safe nor smart.

Instead, I reached up and grabbed his lapels, halting his forward momentum. "Wait."

His eyes struck mine like a physical blow. My breath caught in my throat.

"I'm not that much of a gentleman," Tank growled. "Last time, you were exhausted and wounded. This time, if you ask me to stay...."

"I'm not asking. I'm telling."

The words carried us all the way to the bed.

Once there, I expected him to pounce, to push, to hurry us forward. After all, Tank's eyes were full of wolf. His skin smelled wild.

Instead, he trailed broad fingers down my chin, my neck, pausing when he reached the barrier of my clothing. His voice was even deeper than usual, desire rolling over me, as he growled: "I've wanted to undress you ever since you sent those girls hunting for naked statues."

"You knew?" I wasn't sure which was more seductive. Tank's hands sliding down to my belly, barely grazing the skin as he suited actions to words, peeling away my clothing. Or the fact he'd been familiar enough with the museum to understand my art-history joke.

He hummed an affirmative, reaching behind me. I expected his hand to cup me somewhere interesting, but it didn't. So I twisted sideways, saw what he was aiming for.

My fingers landed on top of his fingers, bringing us chest to chest. I breathed my admonition into his collarbone. "No."

"You don't want the light off?"

"If you're shy," I told him, "you'll have to get over it. I want to see my prize."

"Your prize?" His face twisted into a

smile that sent a tremor through me. Not a tremor of fear, though. A tremor of heat.

Then his hands were cupping those more interesting places. Light and color and emotion cascaded over and through me.

There was nothing cold and static about Tank now. He was the opposite of the statues I'd sent those teenagers hunting. Fire and motion. Seduction and heat.

"A masterpiece," I murmured.

"You are," he agreed. "*We* are."

It was the last word either of us managed before we lost ourselves in the creation of something more tangible than art.

***

Hours later, I woke to find Tank's index finger stroking my bare shoulder. Remembered heat suffused me. Tingles slid all the way down to my toes.

But Tank didn't take it up a notch. Not this time. Instead, he breathed into my ear. "Tell me about your family."

"My family?" I pulled back a few inches so I could peer into his face.

The train clacked past a lone streetlight. The glow flickered across his scars, one streak then gone. Despite my best intentions to keep my fingers to myself, they rose to trace the uniqueness of Tank.

He didn't flinch back the way he had

the first time I touched him there. Instead, he leaned into my hand while replying. "I want to understand all of you. Where you came from. Where you're going."

It had been days since Tank had admitted to ripping apart his own face for the sake of his pack. During that time, I'd shared the barest of tidbits about my own heritage. And yet, Tank hadn't asked until he thought I was ready.

Patience—another asset to add to his long list of appealing traits.

And he was right. My defenses had been ripped away along with my clothing. So I told him. The good parts, most of which centered around a single mom who took me to art museums. Who berated security guards for trying to shoo me into the children's section. *"My daughter knows how to behave,"* Mom had promised as I peered up at a Vermeer, nose inches from the painted canvas. The implication, not voiced but heard by all involved: *"I'm not so sure I can say the same about you."*

"Your mother sounds like a firecracker."

Over Tank's shoulder, the first hint of dawn softened the horizon. Soon, it would be morning and this perfect interlude would be over. Soon, I'd be sending Tank into battle without me. My stomach lurched.

"And your father?" Tank continued, drawing me back to our shared moment.

This part I was less proud of. But he

deserved to hear it. So I took a deep breath and went on.

"When Mom died, I tracked down my dad to ask for his help with Harper. I didn't expect much. I mean, I was conceived during a one-night stand. Ace had no intention of becoming a parent. Still, I'd hoped he'd accept responsibility on paper at least."

Tank's hand slid over my skin, warm, supportive. I closed my eyes and finished the story.

"Ace wouldn't even speak with me when I went to find him. His alpha— Rowan—had laid down the law."

Tank's jaw muscles clenched beneath my fingers. The hand on my spine tensed. "Your father's an asshole," he rumbled. "You're better off without him."

"He's a pack wolf," I corrected, even though I didn't entirely believe that. Had seen inklings that there might be different ways of being part of a pack.

"We're not all like that," Tank promised, his huge hand rising to cradle my skull.

He drew me closer, his breath fluttering across my forehead. "When all of this is over," he promised, "I'm bringing you back to meet my alpha. You'll like him. You'll like everyone in my clan."

There was no question there, but I answered anyway. "That sounds good," I murmured. Then I leaned the rest of the way in for what felt like our first and last kiss.

***

We waited for Jasmine in a crowded food court. A neutral location, close enough to the car we'd rented so we could make a run for it if she ratted us out to her brother. Plenty public so she wouldn't worry we'd take her hostage and use her as a pawn.

But the flaw in my plan became apparent as people whirled around us. A quarter of them were the right age and gender to be Jasmine...and I didn't know her well enough to recognize her in a crowd.

Tank, to my dismay, didn't recall

meeting her. Of course not—she'd been a limpet stuck to my side during the few hours he'd been in residence. Tank and I, in contrast, had been kept far apart by our minders. I was about to suggest we give up when a voice rose above the clatter of plastic food trays.

"Athena."

I turned to the woman whose face was unfamiliar but whose voice was unforgettable. "Jasmine."

She nodded, all business. Ignored Tank's extended hand and continued to speak to me. "There's no time for pleasantries. They expect me back in two hours."

And we were over a hundred miles away from the McCallister compound. I nodded, expecting her to turn on her heel and lead Tank out of my life. Instead, she continued gazing at me, wolf alert behind her eyes.

"I want your promise you won't injure my brother."

Could I promise that? *Should* I promise that?

"Our purpose is defanging the fae," I told her truthfully. "As best I can tell, your brother is an honest victim. But if he allies with them...."

"Then he's an idiot who deserves what's coming to him." Jasmine nodded. "If he doesn't, though, I want everyone off McCallister land by noon on November first. I'm not stabbing my clan in the back. I'm *helping* them."

"You are."

"Alright then." Now she did turn on her heel, swiveling away from me.

And it hit me fully what I was setting up. Yes, a strike that might win the day...but also a nearly impossible situation for Tank to tiptoe through. My own experience within the McCallister compound hadn't been good, but Rowan had kept me alive because he'd wanted something from me.

He wanted nothing from Tank.

"Be safe," I murmured, hating the way my voice caught on the final word.

Tank heard, though. Heard and understood. Rather than following his guide, he pulled me into a bear hug. Wolf hug. Whatever. His bulk and scent enfolded me.

And, like I'd done with Harper, he made a promise we both knew was out of his power to keep.

"I'll be fine."

Chapter 36

I waited all day for Tank to contact me. Paced in my hotel room until management called to request I cool it. Bit my fingernails to the quick.

Or, rather, my wolf did. She wanted out. She wanted to follow Tank. She wanted. She wanted. She *wanted.*

"I want too," I growled, swallowing down fur that tried to creep up my throat every time I inhaled too deeply. "I want to go back in time and fix the holes in our plan. Go in beside him. Go in *instead* of him. But we can't. We can only move forward."

Forward. Yes. Rescue. Now.

My fingernails, I realized, had thickened into claws while I wasn't looking. I clenched my fists. Bit back the wolf. Calmed her with the rational, human understanding we both needed to nurture if we intended to help Tank.

"We have to wait."

How long?

Her demand or mine? I couldn't tell.

Wherever the thought came from, it had definite merit. Tank should have contacted us long before now. His silence said it all.

Still, I forced us to pause and consider what might have gone wrong.

When taken at face value, the proposed timeline had been simple. Jasmine would smuggle Tank into the McCallister compound, sword and all. He'd find a way to send Marina back to the fae Otherworld. Then Jasmine would get him out of the compound and he'd give me a call for pickup.

Only, Tank hadn't called. Not that evening. Not overnight. Not by dawn on Samhain itself.

No more waiting. Rescue, my wolf repeated.

"We can't rescue him alone," I rebutted. The wolf stilled long enough for me to reassemble the few belongings I'd scattered around the hotel room. The whole time, my mind whirled with options, not all of which terminated in dead ends.

Tank and I had agreed that I wouldn't return to Rowan's compound alongside him. It was too dangerous when the gifted bracer meant Marina knew where I was at all times.

But even if I couldn't batter down Rowan's doors personally, I could do *something.* I just needed allies. Powerful allies.

"The question is—how much will it cost?"

Doesn't matter. Do it.

My wolf's strength prompted me to dial one of the numbers I'd memorized. Tank's friends. Harper's keepers. The phone rang half a dozen times before anyone answered, long enough to raise a niggle of worry. The fact the speaker was out of breath when he finally picked up didn't ease my concern.

"Who is this?" he demanded.

"Athena. Harper's sister."

A rustling as if the phone was being transferred. Then the same voice, more muffled as if from a distance. "Say something."

Harper's voice when she obeyed was clearer than his had been...and more feral. "You're just trying to make me lose."

Lose? "What are you losing at?"

"Athena?" Harper's voice softened. "I'm *winning* at arm wrestling. Kira and I both are."

A hoot in the background confirmed her assertion. Then a grumble emerged from the male as he took back the phone. "They're cheating."

Given what I knew about Kira, I wouldn't be at all surprised by that fact. But I sidestepped the issue. "You believe I'm Harper's sister?"

"Yes."

"Then will you give me your alpha's phone number?"

"Sure. Would have given you Gunner's digits anyway. All you had to do was ask."

He rattled off a series of numbers while I tried to work my head around the fact he hadn't called his pack leader "alpha." Still, I managed to commit them to memory. "Thanks," I offered.

His answer was muffled as if he was

speaking to someone away from the microphone. "I saw that!"

This time, the peals of laughter came in the unmistakable tones of my sister. I smiled as I hung up the phone.

***

My smile didn't last long. Going to an alpha for help was the last thing I'd ever thought I'd be doing. There would be strings attached when I made my request. No, not strings. Make that ropes. Huge, thigh-thick ropes like the ones I'd seen dangling from the sides of ocean-going ships.

But the emptiness in my gut forced me to grasp at any possibility of assistance for Tank. My inner wolf was adamant about the fact.

Still, I put off the unsavory task until I'd checked out of the hotel then driven aimlessly in my rental car to ensure Marina hadn't sent someone to follow me. I was far enough from her current location that I hoped she'd ignore my movements. That did appear to be the case.

Finally, though, I couldn't put off the call any longer. I pulled into a grocery-store parking lot, eying shoppers through the windshield until I was certain none were shifters. Then I took a deep breath and dialed the number I'd been given.

This time I rushed out my greeting as soon as the line connected. "You don't know me, but I'm Athena," I started.

Only to be interrupted by a voice just as gruff and growly as the one I craved to hear again. "You're Tank's…"

And Gunner, in turn, was interrupted by a female. "Hush!" she hissed.

I blinked, trying to understand who this was with the temerity to silence an alpha. And, more relevantly, what she held over him to force him to obey.

Because he *was* obeying. Gunner had hushed, giving me leeway to elaborate. I cleared my throat and dove in.

"Yes, I'm Tank's team mate in the Samhain Shifters. The thing is, I need your help."

The woman's demand for silence

was forgotten as Gunner pounced upon my statement. "Lupe already called us," he acknowledged. His voice was frustrated. I was pretty sure the tapping I heard was fingers drumming on a tabletop. "But there's nothing we can do. Everyone here is Tank's pack mate. Lupe swore he wouldn't be present, but I begged to differ. Tank doesn't stop halfway. He'll be there for the showdown, and if I come our bond will place him in danger."

If *he* came? The alpha himself?

Of course, that's what I was about to ask for, in a manner of speaking. For Gunner to put himself on the line...just not in person.

"Your instincts are good," I agreed,

speaking carefully. "Tank's at the node already." Now, how to broach the massive favor I'd dreamed up while sitting by my silent phone all night?

Only, I didn't have to. Gunner bit out a curse. "He's there? And you're calling." His voice hardened. "In that case, you need alphas from other packs."

"I'd hoped for *anyone* from other packs. Or, rather, one from each pack. Preferably people who can handle swords. People who can get there before sunset tonight."

Because that's when the node would open. When it would be too late to send Marina back and halt the invasion.

When it would be too late to disentangle Tank from whatever swamp he'd gotten mired in. The emptiness in my stomach intensified.

Gunner's response confirmed my suspicion—he was capable of delivering assistance if he was willing to expend social capital in order to do so. "Lupe said she hadn't had much luck interesting other packs. I could call in favors, but it would take serious arm twisting."

"I know." I hated this part. The promise I'd have to make. Hated it...but was entirely ready to take the hit to ensure Tank's safety. "I'll owe you anything you want if you do this for me. Anything that won't injure my sister. But I, personally, will..."

In the background, the other woman laughed. This was Kira's sister, Mai. I somehow knew that. Well, not somehow. Knew because who but Gunner's mate could have silenced an alpha so powerful I could feel the chill of his presence over the phone?

"There *is* something we want," Mai called, knowing I'd hear her even though it was clear her mouth wasn't close to the microphone. "When everything is said and done, you'll come here. I want to meet you."

"Good bargain," Gunner agreed, his voice suddenly so warm it felt like the sun had broken through the clouds above me. I peered up at the sky, but there was no sign of our planet's personal star. The day was still just as gloomy as it had been a minute before.

"With or without Tank," Gunner continued in a tone that almost sounded teasing. Then, returning to business. "I can promise you at least half a dozen sword wielders from different packs. More maybe. Where do you want them to meet?"

I rattled off an address, feeling shell shocked. Hung up the phone. Then dialed the final person on my list.

***

I'd expected stonewalling from Gunner and gotten sunshine. Lupe, however, bit back even harder than I'd suspected she would.

"You realize Marina probably has

him." The leader of the Samhain Shifters was furious, but she kept her voice level. "You haven't helped matters. You've made everything ten times worse."

If we'd been face to face, my wolf would have forced me to cower. As it was, I held my ground. "It was a valid risk to take. And I'm fixing it."

"Oh, you are?" she scoffed. "How exactly?"

Between her words, the memory of my withheld information flowed between us. I hadn't been a team player then, but I was being one now.

"I have the promise of at least six sword-wielding shifters," I told her, expecting at any moment to be interrupted. The line stayed silent, though, as I elaborated. "They'll all tie red bandannas around their left arms so you can recognize them. I just need to know where the node is. Has Butch improved enough to track that down?"

More silence, and when Lupe responded she didn't answer my question. Instead, she did one better. She acknowledged that I'd succeeded where she'd failed. "I'm...impressed. And I apologize. I thought Butch was right and you were in this for the money."

My wolf sharpened my answer. "I was then. I'm not now. About the node...."

I half expected Lupe to spout out something about *need-to-know basis*. Instead, her voice turned businesslike, almost as if I was back on the team. "As of now, Butch still believes it will materialize at the McCallister compound. We won't know exactly where until later this afternoon. In the meantime, we'll meet you and your backup. Where and when?"

I shared the gathering location I'd agreed upon with Gunner. And I was about to hang up when Lupe supplied information I wouldn't have thought to ask for.

"Your connection to Marina—she owes you a favor."

"*She* owes *me*?" Simple solutions leapt to the fore. I could ask Marina to hop back through the node and take all other fae along with her. I could ask….

"Something commensurate with what

you provided. The museum job took only a couple hours of your time, so your boon would have to be similarly minor."

"I can't just ask her to end this?"

I could hear the rustle as Lupe's head shook. "No. But you should consider what you might ask for. In a pinch, the boon might be turned to our advantage. You'd have to get the words just right though. She'll be hoping you leave a loophole of inequality to let her reel you back in."

That was the only warning she provided. Lupe didn't remind me that Marina would know the moment I headed in her direction. Didn't warn me a second time that my presence could be worse than my absence.

Instead, she accepted the fact that I'd be joining the strike force when we assembled an hour before sunset. She trusted me to make it work.

Chapter 37

I'd expected Gunner's promised half dozen sword-wielding alphas, but cars kept pulling into the Walmart parking lot for the better part of an hour. Despite the danger of leaving them unattended, I rushed inside to buy bandannas and one other item. And when I came back out, thirty men and women milled around with wolves behind their eyes and swords belted at their hips.

They were wild and dangerous and I assumed the driver of the ride-share van

I'd booked would refuse to allow us inside once he set eyes on us. Instead, he greeted us with a big grin and a thumbs up. "Nice costumes! Let me guess—Lord of the Rings?"

"Right," I told him, glad he didn't have the lie-sniffing abilities of a werewolf. "Exactly. We're going to a house party...."

Someone behind me snickered. Someone else rumbled out a growl at an accidental invasion of his personal space. The air grew so electric it seemed as if fur would fly.

I glanced at Lupe, expecting her to take over. But she didn't. Just shrugged and let the alphas be alphas. My heart was in my throat as I stuffed them into far too few seats, knowing full well that territorial werewolves only got ornerier in close proximity. By the time our driver returned his attention to the road and his music, their ire felt like ants running all over my skin.

A sword grated against its sheath and I spun, expecting battle to erupt right there in the cramped confines of the vehicle. But Lupe's hand on my shoulder stopped me. The intensity of her gaze suggested it was better to leave the alphas alone.

"Ryder and Butch will meet us there," she informed me.

I blinked, trying to focus despite the reek of fur so intense I could barely breathe. "Good. Great."

Now someone was snarling. He wanted to open a window. Predictably, three other voices disagreed.

And I couldn't help myself. Lupe was keeping out of the mess because it was suicide to dive in the middle of such powerful werewolves. But if they couldn't ride together in a van without arguing, how were they going to unite long enough to vanquish the fae? And free Tank?

So I whirled, facing them directly. My gaze met alpha eyes, every single one amber with incipient wolf.

"Is there going to be a problem?" I bit out, imagining the alphas were teenagers. I straightened my spine and glared, pretending they'd forgotten to turn in their homework. Had made up some half-assed excuse about a nonexistent dog.

And, to my surprise, they responded just like Harper would have.

"No, ma'am."

"You lead and we'll follow."

"We know what we're here for."

And while the electricity in the air didn't lessen, every sword stayed in its sheathe for the remainder of the ride.

***

Grumbling faded as we disembarked from the van at the far end of Rowan's driveway. Now the alphas were alert to pending battle, their wolves visible behind their eyes for a different reason. One sniffed the air and pointed toward the forest.

"There."

Sure enough, McCallister shifters slid out from between tree trunks. All were men, the women apparently not being allowed out of the harem. There was still diversity though. Some were lupine. Some human. The latter boasted swords as menacing as our own.

But men and wolves all waited, standing in an unbroachable line for one long moment until Rowan emerged from their midst. His teeth were sharp as he scanned the alphas, even sharper when his gaze settled on me.

"This is private property. My territory

is closed to your kin."

The implication shook me. "My sister..." I started, the words torn out without my permission. My fingers slid to the cell phone in my pocket. Could Rowan have found Harper and...?

Now Lupe did step forward, speaking over me. "We're here on Samhain Shifters business. As you know, that provides free passage anywhere we wish to go."

Rowan didn't even answer this time. Instead, he drew his sword.

Metal rasped against metal all around me. If I'd needed any additional proof that Rowan was in Marina's pocket, here it was. In the past, Rowan's offensives had tended toward fangs and fur.

Still, if his side was using swords, ours would also. I yanked out my weapon, wishing I'd found time to do more than learn two parries and a single attack. I'd hoped we wouldn't be using our swords until fae materialized. I'd hoped...and I'd been wrong.

Because the time for speaking was apparently over. I opened my mouth to try to talk Rowan around....and our forces crashed together. Grunts, roars, and growls. A blow swung toward my midsection and I barely dodged.

We were outnumbered, but the alphas Gunner had assembled were masters. Better than Rowan's underlings and ten times better than me.

I did my best to hold my spot in line anyway, but I almost dropped my sword the third time someone came at me with a berserker's fury. "Behind me." The gruff growl emerged from a female alpha sporting a red armband. Rather than waiting for me to comply, she grabbed me with her free arm and pushed me where she wanted me to go.

Then I was being pressed backwards over and over. Away from the fighting. Away from danger. I stumbled as my feet landed back on the road.

Stumbled...and took in two final allies arriving with dramatically disparate modes of transportation. Ryder's was what I would have expected, actually, if I'd taken time to think about it. His legs gripped the broad barrel of a motorcycle, and he whooped as he swerved toward the enemy line then back in my direction.

Butch, in contrast, appeared atop what at first appeared to be the most beautiful horse I'd ever seen, in real life or on television. It gleamed. Purple, blue, and black, the colors intermingling from hooves to nostrils.

But, no, it wasn't a horse. An enormous silver horn emerged from its forehead.

"A unicorn," I breathed. Then I blinked and Butch was walking toward me, stride hitching as his injury slowed him. Maybe I'd imagined the unicorn? Regardless, I wasn't the only one who noted Butch's struggle to walk.

"Here." Ryder was gruff as he patted the back of his idling motorcycle. "My hog can take two. He glanced at me. "Three, I guess. You're skinny."

I struggled onto the far back, behind both Ryder and Butch. Then, before the former could steer us to the frontlines, I provided alternative instructions. "We have to find the node."

"To your left," Butch murmured, voice quiet. His body, before mine, was bowed.

Ryder's wasn't. He was ready for any adventure. Revving the engine, he roared so loud my ears rung. Then we were off.

****

It should have been exhilarating, riding a motorcycle to the rescue. Instead, all I could think about was Tank. Where was he? He would have found a way to join this battle if he was in control of his own movements. Was he even still alive?

Shaking my head against my own thoughts, I refocused. *Marina*. I was here to find the node and the woman who'd been toying with us. I was here to protect werewolves Tank cared about from the dangers of fae invasion.

To that end, I clutched Butch's waist, steadying him as much as hanging on while we skirted the margins of the battle. The directions he gave us, though, didn't let us steer clear of the fighting entirely.

Then Rowan's forces swung out to meet us, slowing our forward progress. It wasn't long before the motorcycle stalled.

"Crap," Ryder growled, kicking the ignition then revving the engine. "Hang on. This is going to get rough."

"Wait," I countered, something off to our right catching my attention. It was one of the alphas Gunner had assembled greeting an enemy as if he was an ally. "Nice sword, Clifford," the alpha called to the advancing man whose raised sword was ready to skewer him. "Do they need me out front?"

But that wasn't Clifford. Not that I knew who Clifford was. But I knew this guy was one of Rowan's underlings. I recognized him by his long, curly hair and his extreme lankiness. This was the shifter who Lupe had ordered to change her lock.

I slithered down off the side of the motorcycle and dove between the two shifters. By chance, the situation suited one of my two practiced parries and I managed to catch our enemy's sword before it skewered my ally's gut.

Still, the reverberation juddered up my shoulder. My fingers buzzed painfully. The chances of me halting a second blow were zero.

Then Ryder was there, driving between us with all the finesse of a stampeding bull. "What the fuck?" He roared. "Dude's got a red bandanna."

Not-Clifford had no red bandanna.

He was dressed in jeans and a hoody, nothing tied around his arm at all.

But he grinned at Ryder's words, breaking away from my so-called defense and swirling back toward his compatriots. Now he knew what we were using to recognize each other....

"Glamour," I explained tersely. "Get the bandannas off everyone. Figure out an alternative marker. And don't trust what you see!"

Ryder, to my dismay, didn't move. "I can do that," he growled, "or I can drive you to the node."

Not both. Obviously.

I closed my eyes for one split second, understanding at last why Lupe always looked vaguely dyspeptic. It made my stomach ache to guess the proper course of action. To send friends into danger without me.

But there was only one solution. Ryder was the obvious choice to brute force our allies into understanding the danger of this new glamour. And...

"We're close enough so I can walk," Butch agreed before I even had to state my case. Joining me on the ground, he swayed only a little. I steadied him with a surreptitious hand around his elbow.

"Go," I told Ryder, the emptiness in my stomach lessening. And he went. Roared back into the battle, stopping at intervals to fire off short verbal bursts at our allies.

Convinced he'd get the job done, I

turned away. Back to the darkness beyond the battlefield. Back to the one ally I had left. "We're close?"

Butch nodded, all the while walking a curving path that started large then spiraled inward. Minutes later, he stopped in what appeared to be an empty patch of lawn.

"It's here," he murmured, prodding at the soil with one boot toe.

"You're sure?"

I'd expected a fairy ring of mushrooms. An earthen burial mound. *Something* to suggest this wasn't just a patch of lawn no different than the others.

I'd also expected Marina. But she was absent, her presence only visible in the glamour that continued to trip up our allies.

"I'm certain," Butch confirmed.

The confusion on our side was worsening, I noted. For a minute or two, ditching our armbands might have helped us. But our enemies seemed to have caught on to that already. In the distance, I saw one of my own allies turn away from Rowan as if expecting a friend to guard his back.

This time, I was too distant to warn him. Could only watch in horror as the nameless alpha was mown down.

The fae trickiness would all end at sunset, however, and the light was already dimming. Sunset would mean Marina's friends coming through the node, but there were enough of us left to stop them. We'd stop the fae and break whatever hold Marina had over Rowan....

The sun dipped below the horizon.

Swords clanged all around me.

Nothing happened at the portal site.

Chapter 38

Which is when I realized where the node was. Not here, *at* my feet. Here *below* my feet. Down in the subterranean living quarters I'd spent days locked within.

Now I was the one swearing, using Ryder's words to warm the hollow pit of my belly. Butch and I alone couldn't storm the walls of Rowan's compound. It was doubtful if all of our allies together could do so, not with the defenses I'd seen during my tour.

But a single thief might make it past those defenses. If she was subtle. And skilled.

"I need a distraction."

I expected Butch to push for more information. Instead, he half-bowed, the gesture almost toppling him. "Any particular location or duration?"

"Away from the compound. As long as you can last."

Then I fell back on my strongest skill —innocuousness. Sheathing my sword and dropping my gaze, I prepared to make a break for it.

Something exploded behind me and I ran. Past McCallister shifters, who were shouting and panicking. Whatever Butch was doing, it had certainly attracted their attention.

And I was a lone female. Apparently unarmed and overtly submissive. The macho McCallisters were hardwired to let me past.

I made it to the treeline before dropping the act. Heard battle rematerializing behind me and winced as I imagined Butch crumpling during his distraction's grand finale.

Because he wouldn't have given up so soon unless he'd run out of energy. Or unless someone had forced him to stop.

Had Ryder backtracked to help him? Had Lupe come to his assistance? I wouldn't be able to tell at this distance, so I didn't even look.

Instead, I curved through the woods

until I reached the back face of Rowan's mansion. The whole thing had been security alarmed up the wazoo, from what I remembered during the day Jasmine walked me through it. But I suspected they hadn't had time yet to fix the window Ryder had broken during our escape....

Sure enough, an expanse of plywood met my fingers as I pushed through the final line of shrubbery and straightened. Tensing, I waited for motion-activated lights to come on. For sirens to blare. For the guards Rowan must have left behind to arrow in on my hiding place.

But nothing happened. I'd gotten lucky. This location had no external security. And the internal security, I hoped, had been disabled during our hurried retreat.

Now, finally, the weight in my pocket came in handy. I drew out the battery-powered drill I'd bought before meeting with the alphas. Made short work of a dozen screws.

The plywood fell to the ground as I attempted to lower it. Splinters bit into my palms. But I was smiling.

Or maybe my wolf was smiling. When I ran my tongue across my teeth, they were remarkably sharp.

And it was a good thing my inner wolf was present. Because lupine eyes saw the movement inside the darkened room before human eyes would have.

As suspected, Rowan hadn't taken all of his fighters with him. Someone left behind had heard my drill and come to investigate.

I shoved myself through the windowless cavity, tackling my enemy to the ground.

***

The other shifter didn't struggle. Instead, she lay there beneath me, scent heavy with annoyance. After a moment, she put that emotion into words.

"If you'll let me up, we can deal with the problem in the harem."

"Jasmine?" I recognized her voice. Still, she'd been the one who led Tank into what appeared to have been a trap. So I rolled sideways but kept my hand clamped down on her wrist. "Where's Tank?"

"Is that really relevant given the bigger picture?" She was blustering. I could tell because her shoulders slumped when I squeezed her wrist bones together.

"Where," I repeated, "is Tank?"

"He's fine," she assured me. "I hid him in the harem yesterday just like he asked me to. But one of the younger girls saw him and shrieked so loud half the pack showed up. If it wasn't for those scars...."

My own patience was fleeing quickly. I shook Jasmine, or rather my wolf shook her. So this was why alphas turned so brutal. If I'd been in wolf form, I might have given her a little nip to speed the story along.

The shake, luckily, was effective at getting Jasmine back on track. "Rowan locked him in the barracks," she explained before my wolf could entirely take over. "I don't have the key and we lack the time to look for it. The sounds from the harem are getting stranger...."

That was where the node was. I knew in my gut.

Still when I released Jasmine and sprinted down the stairs, I didn't head toward the harem. Instead, I retraced the far more familiar path to the room I'd been locked within.

***

Tank wasn't in the exact same room that had caged me, as Jasmine explained when she caught up. My guide was annoyed by the side trip, but she led me to the proper door anyway. Stood beside me and tapped her foot as I pulled out my lock picks.

"There isn't time for this. Can't you hear the fighting?"

I could. And the fact I could hear it through several yards of soil and concrete was a bad sign indeed.

Still, I was more concerned with whether Marina was aware of my proximity. Maybe, if I was lucky, she couldn't tell the difference between me being here and up above on the battlefield. Or, more likely, she simply wasn't interested while opening the node.

Either way, there was no hurrying the lock. No hurrying the slow search for the proper tumblers. *Ah, there.* I grinned as I heard the sound I'd been waiting for. The click of an obstruction drawing back.

The door swung inward so fast I lost my balance and fell forward. Onto Tank. Into Tank. He smelled like home and I wanted nothing more than to snuggle up against his skin.

Instead, I drew back, cocking my head. There was dried blood on his face, as if Marina had tried and failed to force him to do her bidding. His shoulders weren't stooped, though. And he'd taken advantage of his time in solitary confinement to assemble an armful of something I couldn't quite make sense of.

"What are those?"

"Slats from the cot. Metal." His eyes smiled even if his lips didn't. "Do we know where the node is?"

"Yes, if you'll let me *take* you there," Jasmine huffed, grabbing a slat and turning back down the passage we'd come in through. *She* was ready to fight, even if she didn't know anything about the danger we were facing.

Jasmine was clearly coming with us, so I provided the bare minimum of information. "Metal through a fae's chest will send them back to the other side," I called after her, even as the fingers of Tank's free hand slid between mine. His sturdiness was grounding, making up for lack of sleep and far too high stakes.

And even though we should have followed Jasmine immediately, Tank used our joined hands to draw me in closer. Then he kissed me. Or I kissed him. Whoever did the kissing, it was fast and fierce. More like the meeting of wolves than the affection of a man.

My wolf and I responded, curling around our partner. Hot, intense, the rest of the world faded....

Until, abruptly air separated us, all except our interlocked fingers. I'd pushed Tank away at the same moment he'd ended our embrace. Jasmine was still in sight, fifteen feet distant.

"There's no time..." I started just as Tank promised:

"Later."

Together, we raced to catch up with Jasmine. The heat between us would have to wait until we closed the node. We were ready to dive into battle first.

Well, not quite ready. I fumbled to exchange weapons without unlocking our intertwined fingers.

"Are you sure?" Tank's eyebrows rose as I offered him the sword I'd chosen out of Lupe's stash back at the campground.

"I'll do just as well with a stake," I promised, taking the bundle of slats he still held in his hand. "There are a lot of these. Did you expect me to bring an army?"

"From the sound of it, it seems you did."

This time he did smile, an expression that should have been horrifying with the new streaks of red joining old scars and twisting his face into a Halloween mask. Instead, a burst of joy hastened my footsteps. And Tank sped up to match me until we ran in perfect synchrony. Ran like pack wolves on a hunt.

Ran into air that sweetened ominously. Papaya, then pineapple. By the time the three of us passed through the shower room and turned into a passage I'd never traversed before—the one, I assumed, leading to the harem—it felt like I was racing through a human-sized bowl of fruit.

A bowl of fruit that was already rotting. Rotting into words just loud enough to hear over our pounding footsteps.

"If I help you through, you'll be indebted," Marina warned, her voice even more beautiful than it had been previously. Her bell-like tones rang down the corridor, carrying floral odors along for the ride.

"Understood." The chorus came in at least half a dozen voices. All were equally beautiful, but their combination was so dissonant it set my teeth on edge.

"For one year, you will remain indentured," Marina continued. "At the end of that time...."

I never learned what would happen on the next Samhain because Jasmine burst through the doorway ahead of us. She wasn't waiting for backup. Wasn't waiting for the right moment. Instead, she was bound and determined to squash the danger to her pack.

Tank and I could do no less.

Chapter 39

Inside, the harem was so pink I had to close my eyes for one split second. Pink walls. Pink furniture. Pink-clad women standing in a circle with joined hands.

Between us and them, Marina guided the portal opening like an orchestra conductor. The junction between earth and the Otherworld was a black hole that made the surrounding pink pinker. A looming pit of danger that, I suspected, was responsible for the stench I'd recently waded through.

And yet, the harem girls didn't struggle against its opening. Instead, they closed their eyes and swayed to inaudible music. They tilted their chins toward the awfulness as if soaking up the sun.

They were in league with Marina, or at least appeared to be. Were we really going to have to take down all the McCallister females in order to save their pack?

Moralities, however, slipped away from me as Marina spun to face us. She was outside the circle of pink-clad women but she moved in time with them. Meanwhile, behind her back and within the portal's darkness, shapes coalesced.

Shimmering. Gleaming. Like clouds of floral-scented smoke.

The fae were through, but they weren't yet solid....

Then a harem girl fell to her knees and the circle broke. Fae began materializing. There weren't half a dozen, the way I'd assumed from their voices. There were hundreds. Far too many to count.

And Tank didn't hesitate. He flung himself at the clouds of half-solid enemies, swinging his sword in broad arcs that whipped through a handful of fae with each stroke. The ones he cut down dissipated into nothing, but there were so many left.

There were hundreds of fae to

fight...and every minute more emerged into solidity. The newcomers were feeding, I realized as the harem girls' swaying turned boneless, on the shifters' connections to their own subpack.

"Jasmine! You have to get them out of here!" I yelled, pressing toward the pink-clad women.

"Tell your mother how to suck eggs, why don't you?" Jasmine shot back, wading into the spinning haze of fae. Her slat was raised, but defensively rather than offensively. "Ladies," she said. "Follow me."

They didn't, of course. If they'd been in their right minds, they wouldn't have assisted Marina's portal-opening in the first place. Instead, they stood there, more bobbing than swaying at this point. The few open eyes were glazed and faint smiles curved each woman's lips.

And the fae swirled between us and them. Every time I tried to take a step forward, two fae pushed me backward. They weren't solid enough—yet—to do real damage, but I still ended up being buffeted like a boat in stormy seas.

Jasmine was doing no better. The bed slats, unlike Tank's sword, weren't sharp enough to cause serious damage. The metal protected us, but that was it.

Still, I did have an awful lot of slats on hand....

So I did the only thing I could think of. I remembered the way Harper had gained assertiveness after spending just a few hours among werewolves. She'd been buoyed up by pack and had risen to the challenge. Was that all Rowan's harem needed? To be shown their own strength?

Slipping the bundle of slats between my knees, I drew one out and flung it. Another. Another. Tossing them through the air.

Weapons whipped across the haze of fae, who ducked rather than trying to catch them. I tossed seven slats into the cloud of fae and harem girls, keeping only one for myself.

Metal spun through the air, seeming to catch sunlight even though that was impossible down here in the basement. A slat cut through one immaterial fae's shoulder and he bared smoky yet still sharp teeth that were far too large to be human. I couldn't tell if the gesture was a laugh or a scream.

Probably the former, since he twisted his smoke tighter and began drifting toward me. Randomly flung slats wasn't the way to expel our enemies back to the Otherworld. Plus, seven slats was nothing in this battle against hundreds of ethereal beings.

But I wasn't trying to kill the fae. I was trying to wake the harem girls. Give them a weapon. Prove they weren't helpless to impact their own fates.

The first slat hit a harem girl on the forehead. She stumbled backwards, sinking to the ground. I winced. My ploy wasn't working.

But Jasmine caught on and ran with it. Her voice turned fierce as she dove for the fallen slat and sent it spinning back upwards. "You're *wolves,"* she growled, sounding for all the world like Ryder at his surliest. "Act like it!"

This time, the slat was grabbed out of the air by a girl Harper's age. The next slat I'd thrown thudded into the fist of a mature woman. Four, five, six, seven. One after another, the rest were caught.

"Now *fight!*" Jasmine ordered, suiting actions to words by slicing at encircling fae.

Maybe the burst of command was what did it. Or maybe the harem girls were boosted simply because the handlocked circle had broken. Either way, glazed eyes cleared. Smiles turned into frowns.

"Slice through their chests!" Jasmine called, repeating my instructions.

And they did. Slats caught the air, caught fae not yet materialized. The harem girls were more successful than Jasmine and I had been. Perhaps because they were at the center of the portal? Because their energy had been used to open the node wider? Whatever the reason, hazy fae poofed into nothing beneath their onslaught. The room was growing less crowded rather than more so.

But the solidified fae weren't so easily vanquished. One grabbed the hair of a teenager who fell, shrieking. Another swept an older woman off her feet.

The members of the harem weren't trained in swordcraft. Like me, they had little chance of standing up in the face of outright battle....

Before I could speak, though, Jasmine was on it. "Lillian, grab Catherine's legs," she barked. "Minta, take her feet. You and you, help McKenzie up."

The fallen woman was lifted. The teenager scrambled upright with the help of her compatriots. The harem girl I'd accidentally struck in the head was also on her feet.

Those with weapons formed a bristling circle protecting the unarmed from damage. Slowly but surely, they inched backwards. Away from the portal. Away from danger. Tank and I were the only ones in the midst of the fae now. I turned to help him...

...And found Marina in front of me. She smiled, the chill of her regard raising goosebumps all over my skin.

***

She was glad to see me. That couldn't be good.

I jabbed out with my slat, ignoring the tremors of *wrongness* sliding through my body. Marina had no weapon and made no move to stop me, so this should have been easy.

It wasn't. I felt like I was trying to push a needle through a bar of iron. My arm moved a mere millimeter before freezing into place.

Marina smiled then, the fruity scent of her breath seductively awful. She raised one perfectly arched eyebrow. "Are you ready to discuss your boon?"

Behind me, the slap of bare feet against pavement promised that Jasmine and the other women were fleeing the harem. I was glad. They were safer gone. Still, I swallowed as I realized Tank and I were the only ones left to deal with the fae.

"My boon?" I asked, risking a glance sideways. Tank's sword had been remarkably effective. There were less than a dozen fae left now, although the ones who remained were sucking up the remnants of the others. As if each fae sent back to the Otherworld left all of their energy behind.

"Yes." Marina took a step closer, whipping my attention back to her. Her voice sweetened and I tasted elderberry syrup, as if I was an ailing child being dosed by her mother. "So many opportunities for you to consider."

I tried to ignore her words and stab her torso just like I'd told Jasmine to do. But my arm wasn't moving. Instead, something forced me to consider what Marina had to say.

Ideas I'd dismissed swirled around me like yellow jackets above rotting fruit in an abandoned orchard. Harper's social network. Tank's charisma. My place in the werewolf world.

Marina took another step forward, the buzz of yellow jackets turning into words of seduction. "Do you really want to depend on the goodwill of an alpha to keep yourself and your sister safe?"

I flinched, my bed slat drooping between us. In the midst of everything, I'd let myself forget about the future. About the fact the Samhain Shifters would disband in a matter of hours, leaving me bound by Rowan's whims.

Rowan's whims weren't likely to be very friendly, either. Not after I'd led an invasion onto his home turf.

Alternatively, if I accepted the veiled

offer Tank had provided, I'd become bound by the whims of another alpha. An alpha I'd never met in person. Sure, Gunner had seemed like a nice guy over the telephone. He'd called in favors to build an army of reinforcements.

But that was for Tank's sake. Not for mine.

"Or perhaps you want to work within the system. Win a debt of gratitude from your mate. If he owed you, he'd protect you."

I'd been stung by a yellow jacket once as a child. The wound hurt, but the terrifying part was the swelling in my throat. The way it became difficult to breathe.

I could barely breathe now. Had

enough air left in my lungs for one word, if I was lucky.

Out of the corner of one eye, I caught the flicker of motion as a fae scratched a long streak across Tank's face. The cut was deep. The beginning of another scar?

"He'll be even more hideous after this battle," Marina mused. She almost looked like a yellow jacket. Her waist was slender, her eyes large. "But I can fix that for you...."

Pack, my wolf whispered, a thread of longing.

So I said it. The only thing I *could* say. Croaked out his name. "Tank."

Marina smiled, the facial twitch thoroughly inhuman. The scent of rotting fruit was so strong now that it choked me. She thought I was making the choice she'd boxed me into. She thought she'd won.

But I wasn't talking *about* Tank. I was talking *to* him. And he'd been listening, waiting for my cue.

The instant I spoke, he spun away from the fae. Toward Marina....

If fae had been wolves, at least one of the newcomers would have called out a warning to his mistress. The woman they were indebted to. The one who'd brought them over from the faery world.

But fae weren't wolves. Instead, they watched, beautiful lips curving into beautiful smiles, ready for their debts to be zeroed out the easy way.

Meanwhile, Tank's eyes met mine, a question. Did I want this? Was I ready to trust my fate and Harper's fate to a pack with no fae-created safety net?

There was no question about it. I nodded.

And, like Ryder had admitted doing to his alpha, Tank stabbed Marina in the back.

Chapter 40

She collapsed around the blade, her body beginning to dissipate immediately. But I wasn't done yet. I caught her, my hands on her shoulders, lowering her to the ground while I hissed into her ear.

"You owe me a boon."

"Yes...." Her voice was a breath only. The scent, strangely, had sweetened, losing the rot it had held a moment earlier.

Ignoring the sweetness, I continued. "I want Butch's true name left here when you return to the Otherworld. You'll tell no one. Will forget it yourself."

Marina's body lightened in my grip with each breath she exhaled. Now, she seemed to weigh as little as Harper had when our mother died. There were mere seconds left to seal this bargain. Still, I kept talking, intent upon leaving no loophole.

"But do this only if you agree that it's an equal trade for the gift I gave you. I want nothing left between us. Do you understand me?"

Marina nodded. "Ru—" she started.

I slapped my fingers over her mouth, not wanting the other fae to hear her. *"Rune Pelletier,"* she breathed against my fingers. *"I release your true name."*

And then she was truly gone.

With the dissipation came a gust of wind so intense it knocked me forward. Tank's blade only barely missed me as I was flung against his chest.

His sword and my bed slat clattered to the ground as his arms encircled me, cushioning me as we plummeted. The floor was hard beneath my back now. I could barely see curtains and papers and fae spinning around us, the roar of wind whipping everything toward the node.

Everything other than Tank...and me within his arms.

As we huddled there together, the wind's roar grew distant. Not softer—air still slashed against every patch of exposed skin. Scarves and fae and feathers fluttered past us.

Instead, it was as if I'd driven up a mountain too quickly for my ears to equalize. The pressure grew unbearable, turning distant sound into a ringing awfulness.

Then, with a pop, the portal closed.

We lay there for a split second, regaining our breath. Me underneath, protected by Tank's body. My face was tucked into the nook of his shoulder. Then...it wasn't.

Cold air wedged between us as Tank was ripped upward. One moment he was my rock. The next, he was reeling backwards, something sharp menacing his throat....

Time seemed to freeze, the world

coming back into total focus. Half of the final fae were gone, sucked back into the Otherworld along with Marina. But five had grabbed onto chairs and tables and draperies, resisting the pull.

Now, without the wind to contend with, four were retreating. Running for the open door Jasmine and her friends had left through moments earlier.

The fifth had chosen attack over retreat.

I couldn't tell whether the being was a man or a woman. Maybe it was both, or neither. And that didn't matter. Because its hands ended in claws as long as a grizzly bear's. They raked at Tank's exposed neck, barely missing. It wouldn't miss a second time.

Rather than fighting back, Tank roared: "Athena! Don't let them get away!"

As if I'd chase four fae who were currently harming no one and let this bear slay my partner.

The sword was too far away for me to reach. On the ground past the bear being. My bed slat was closer, but still four feet distant. No way I could scoop it up then rise fast enough to push the blade through the fae's chest.

But my pockets were full of salt. The not-really weapon that had slowed Marina down for one split second. I grabbed a fistful and flung it....

The particles struck Tank as well as the fae. There'd been no time to warn him. He coughed out a curse as salt hit open wounds and uncovered eyes....

The bear being, though, was more hindered. It staggered backwards, clawed hands waving wildly. One struck Tank's shoulder, sliding through his shirt. Blood blossomed....

But I was ready. I was on my knees, grabbing the bed slat. "Tank!"

He glanced down as the slender piece of metal flew upwards. Grabbed it out of the air as if he'd known it was coming. Thrust the metal through the bear being's chest.

***

The bear fae collapsed then

disappeared, just like Marina had done. Only without the sucking wind, presumably because the node had already closed.

Which left four fae loose amid over a hundred werewolves. They could slide into the gap Marina had left in the power structure. Could turn the battle above us ten times worse.

Because the fighting hadn't ended. I could hear it. Swords clanged above us. Screams of rage or pain or both erupted. Perhaps it was my imagination, but I could have sworn I could even smell the blood.

Tank and I didn't have to speak. We grabbed our weapons and we ran.

The floral scent in the fae's wake

was much weaker than Marina's had been. As if these new fae hadn't possessed sufficient time to marshal their energy. Which was a good thing...except for the fact it made them nearly impossible to track.

Not that we travelled far along their scent trail. Instead, when we pushed our way out of Rowan's house, we were greeted by a wolf. She snarled once then shimmered upwards into humanity.

"My brother refuses to end this." Jasmine sounded furious. From the sounds and smells behind her, I could understand why.

Rowan might have been in Marina's pocket to some extent. But the instigating fae was gone and the McCallister alpha had turned no less belligerent. The fighting wasn't over yet.

"Your pack would stop if their alpha told them to." Tank's rejoinder was a non-answer...or at least I thought so at first.

Then I saw what he saw. Jasmine, facing him down. Staring directly into his eyes the way Ryder had done. The same Jasmine who'd known how to activate the harem girls, who'd been able to *command* them. She wasn't acting like a wilting wallflower, shrieking at the sight of Tank's grotesqueness. Instead, she resembled just what she was—an alpha werewolf.

The breeze shifted and the reek of blood was replaced by a hint of honeysuckle. The fae weren't entirely gone yet. It was time to divide and conquer.

"I can handle this," I promised Tank. And he didn't argue. Merely nodded and turned toward the honeysuckle. Sniffed once, then broke into a run.

"This is the thanks I get for helping you?" Jasmine demanded when I turned back to face her. "You send away our only support?"

"No, *this* is the help you get," I countered. Then, raising my voice, I called to the alphas who had obeyed me in the ride-share van. "Alphas! Gather! It's time to make a treaty with the true leader of this pack."

***

It turned out that the McCallisters were willing to follow a woman if she came with powerful allies. Especially since the battle had been trending against them. Several of his own underlings leapt upon Rowan, taking him down in a pile of werewolves. Soon, every sword was dropped.

There would be growing pains, of course. One of those pains being Rowan himself, who Jasmine was intent upon rehabilitating. Another being the harem girls, who gathered dropped weapons and seemed keen to use them against their own pack mates. The new McCallister alpha had a lot on her plate.

Still, that was a problem for later. For

now, pack bonds sizzled through the night as McCallister shifter after McCallister shifter bowed to their former leader's sister. The connections flared bright for one split second. And in that moment, I learned how a pack leader was born.

The exhilaration faded in the face of Tank's lack of success though. I sent Ryder and Lupe after him as soon as swords returned to scabbards, but they found only one of the four runners. The other three were gone, scattered to the winds where they could slowly gather their strength and power over the course of the upcoming year.

"I'll hunt them," Lupe assured us as a McCallister healer triaged the grievously wounded from both sides of the battle. In my opinion, Butch was among the dangerously injured, his legs barely holding him upright. But he'd waved away Ryder's efforts to bring him over to the medical station. He wanted to be part of this conversation.

And his experience made that effort worthwhile. "It takes newly arrived fae weeks or months to start causing trouble," Butch assured us. "We have time to hunt for them."

"*I* have time." Lupe's correction of Butch's pronoun struck me in the stomach. Her continuation turned that pain into ice. "You've all served well and I'll commend you to your alphas. Thank you for being a Samhain Shifter. Your job is complete."

To no one's surprise, Ryder was the one who reacted. "Oh, hell no," he growled. "They're still out there. We're not finished."

And as if that was all it took to formalize our connections, light sparked between us just like it had between the McCallisters and Jasmine. Pack bonds kindled. My stomach warmed for one split second then chilled back down as Lupe slapped us with a cold dose of reality.

"If you want to hunt fae, you can't do this." She waved her hand at the tendrils of light dancing in the air between us. "Pack bonds are a liability."

As we'd seen with Rowan. Marina had found a way into his pack and used his harem's bonds against them. She'd used *me* as a locational beacon and would have done much worse if I'd had pack bonds to feed off....

I shivered, but none of the glowing tendrils winked out. Not even mine.

"How long will it take for the bonds to regress?" Tank asked. He sounded like the lawyer he was, seeking loopholes.

Lupe shook her head, shrugging uncertainty. "A month? Two months?"

"Then we'll hunt solo for the rest of the year," Tank decided. "Keep contact to a minimum. Then reconvene once you consider it safe."

But his voice trailed off as if he'd just now remembered that my experience with pack was rocky and tortured. He cocked his head at me, clearly prepared to backpedal if I bowed out of the upcoming venture.

And I could, I realized with a jolt. While I still needed to dig up sufficient cash to fund Harper's schooling, the territory issue was no longer pressing. I had a feeling Jasmine wouldn't threaten us the way her brother had. After all, I'd helped her become alpha. She was a better person than Rowan on his best day and her worst.

So, no, I had no real reason to stick to this hunt. I had no pack to be endangered by the fae. No personal stake at all in this struggle.

And yet....

When we'd first met, I thought every

one of these Samhain Shifters was a threat to me. Now, the bigger threat felt like it came from letting them go.

So I let my wolf speak through me. "I'm in," we said together. "Let's find those fae."

Chapter 41

Unfortunately, flashing red and blue lights put a kibosh on further fae hunting. A cop car rolled up the driveway with sirens blaring, which was handy since it gave us time to shuffle the most severely wounded out of sight.

The most severely wounded...and the dead. Two alphas wouldn't be going home to their packs tonight, and four McCallisters hadn't lived to see their clan's regime change. If the officers produced a search warrant....

But it turned out blood and mayhem weren't the reason the police had come.

"That's my sister!" Harper was out of the car before it fully stopped, running toward me the way she had before she grew into her teenage self possession. I grabbed her shoulders, pulling her in so hard that her elbow bit into my stomach. Neither of us cared about smears of dirt and blood.

I just hoped the police officers didn't possess werewolf eyesight. Or that they assumed we were in the midst of costumed Halloween revelry. It was hard to focus on the bigger picture when my sister was so distressed.

"Are you okay?" I murmured into her hair. "What happened?"

Her answer came out in a rush of words that made little sense. "I didn't mean to. I texted Dad to say I was okay and he asked me where I was and...." Her voice broke.

Then a flashlight blinded me. Harper hiccuped a sob as she was wrested out of my grip by what smelled like a female human. "Ma'am, please step away from the child." The woman's voice grew muffled, as if she was speaking into a mic. "Is this the one who absconded with your daughter?"

Daughter? Was Nick here? The reason for Harper's crying?

Beneath my shirt, fur rose on the back of my neck. Of all the times for my wolf to try to claw free of my humanity....

Then Tank's voice soothed as it passed me. "This is a misunderstanding. I represent Athena D'Argent."

I blinked as the flashlight lowered. Saw through blurry eyes as Tank passed over his card to the second officer, a man.

Behind the cops a car door slammed. Then Nick himself was tromping toward us. He'd waited for the police to squash all signs of danger before emerging, despite the fact his daughter had already raced ahead into the night.

At that realization, my wolf tried to make another break for it. But this time I was ready for her. *Words will win this.*

She growled then subsided. The two

of us were starting to learn each others' strengths and weaknesses. This moment was mine.

My relief at regaining control of our shared body was short-lived. Because Nick met my gaze, his face smug. "Athena had no legal right to take my daughter out of my custody," he asserted. "She didn't even consult with me before doing so. I consider that a kidnapping attempt."

By human law, he was right. I couldn't explain why Tank had sent werewolves to protect Harper. Concerns about fae glamour were unlikely to hold up in court.

Only...Tank turned toward Harper and raised his eyebrows. My sister nodded, dropping into a crouch so she could dig through her backpack.

"But you're not my father." Harper's voice was clear as she rose back to her feet. She was almost as tall as Nick, I noticed for the first time. And despite boasting his red hair and his slender frame, Harper had a very different sort of heart.

Because Nick drank to drown his cowardice, but Harper was the furthest thing from a coward. She was standing up to her own father, risking everything she currently possessed in hope of a better future.

"Not your father?" Nick snorted. His gaze dropped to the single sheet of paper my sister was clutching. "What do you think you have there?"

Rather than handing the paper to Nick, Harper passed it over to the female police officer. Tank was closer than me, and I could tell the moment he read whatever was written on it. Because he broke out into the truest, most beautiful smile imaginable. My gut lurched as my wolf turned a stomach flip.

One millisecond later, Tank's hand rose to shield his face. An attempt not to scare the humans. And his voice was even as he inserted himself into the disagreement yet again. "In my professional opinion, this birth certificate appears to be genuine."

Birth certificate? My mother wasn't the type to cheat on her partner and she and Nick had been together for years before Harper was born, even if they weren't legally married. So I didn't see how Harper's birth certificate could help matters.

The male officer apparently agreed. "Still doesn't solve the issue of custody. If this man isn't the father, Harper has no parent in attendance. We'll have to call a social worker."

Harper flinched and the female cop noticed. "It's going to be okay, honey," she soothed. "Foster parents are nice. We'll sort this out."

The woman was trying to be kind, but Harper was already crying. Foster care wasn't what I'd promised her. I'd promised her a real home and a real family. I intended to make that promise stick.

To that end, I shouldered my way into the huddle. The cop had moved her flashlight away from the paper but I pulled upon my wolf until I could read the dark squiggles on the birth certificate.

There was Harper's name, the date, the location. Mom's name and....

Now my smile was as wide as Tank's had been. "How about we let Harper's father decide?"

***

The last time Ace had been called upon to act like a parent, he'd dropped the ball so fast it might as well have been greased and lit on fire. This time, though, he had an alpha pushing him toward us rather than away from us.

Or so I gathered by the way Ace fell all over himself to make things right.

"Of course this is my daughter," he lied, causing every werewolf in the vicinity to wrinkle our noses at the stench of his assertion. Why my mom had listed him on the birth certificate was beyond me since he clearly wasn't Harper's father....

Although, considering the contrast as Ace's strength faced off against Nick's weakness, I wasn't so surprised after all. Mom hadn't felt able to leave Nick, but she'd wanted a better life for her children. And that was what we were about to ensure.

Unfortunately, the cops remained dubious. It wasn't lost on them that Harper had run to me but hadn't even recognized Ace until he started speaking. Luckily, my biological father appeared to be cannier than I would have expected.

"I wasn't able to take care of Harper the way I wanted to, so I gave my older daughter custody." He nodded his head at me, and Tank slid into the conversational gap.

"We have financial records to back this up. Athena has been paying for her sister's schooling for some time now. Harper has spent breaks with her sister. Ms. D'Argent has clearly been acting in loco parentis."

The male cop wavered. "A judge will have to make that determination."

"Of course," Tank agreed. "But until that time, doesn't it seem like the best-case scenario to remand Harper into the custody of the person she clearly wants to spend time with? Her sister? The one her father has chosen to keep her safe?"

If Nick had been a werewolf, his teeth would have sharpened. He was losing the battle, but he wasn't quite ready to concede defeat yet. "Perhaps you should let us discuss this between ourselves," he suggested. I could almost see the dollar bills reflected in his pupils.

And the female cop nodded. "If the family is able to come to a consensus, that would be in the best interests of the child. Come on, Harper. Let's give the adults a few minutes to talk."

***

"How much?" Tank asked the moment the officers were too far away to hear us. Then, being a lawyer, he clarified his question. "How much to testify in court that Harper is not your daughter?"

"She's very important to me." Nick's voice was oily. And I should have flinched.

Because "very important" meant six figures at least. Maybe seven figures. And I had negative dollars in my bank account at the present moment.

Meanwhile, Tank glanced at me. A question. Was I willing to cede this financial responsibility? For a second, I found it hard to meet his gaze.

After all, I'd lost so much independence when I accepted Rowan's money years ago. Had gotten swallowed up in a different sort of lopsided financial relationship with my stepfather, one he summed up with the farcical: *"Family gives and family takes."*

From Nick, the statement had been a joke. But sometime in the past twenty-four hours I'd stopped worrying about being in debt to Tank. Money, I gathered, was easy for him. So was lawyering. And members of a pack took what was easily and willingly offered while giving from their own strength in return.

Tank was my pack and my family. I'd decided that. I trusted him not to hold this over my head.

So I lifted my chin and nodded. And rather than debt, heat flared between us. Tank was pleased by my willingness. Not so pleased, however, that he let Nick off the hook.

"I'll be assuming responsibility for Harper's tuition, of course," Tank continued. "You will be expected to bow out of that facet of her life as well as all others."

Tank's voice was level, but for one split second his wolf rose huge and ferocious behind his eyes. The old scars and new wounds turned his face into a monster's mask....

And Nick backpedalled so quickly he literally stumbled over himself. "I... You...."

My stepfather turned away from Tank to glare at me, his face red and his eyes furious. Of course Nick knew I was a werewolf. It was one more reason for him to resent me. But I'd always tried to keep my furry side under wraps around him. Perhaps that decision had been a mistake.

Because, after one split second, his glare turned into a cringe. No wonder when my inner wolf had risen to face him. When I didn't even try to stop her as she sharpened my teeth and brightened my eyes.

Nick's gaze dropped to the ground and stuck there. He wasn't trying to prove his dominance over me at this point. He was just trying to protect his skinny neck.

First the stick...then the carrot. "Is this sufficient?" Tank tapped a number into his phone and held the device out to Nick. The gesture changed the mood instantly. My stepfather's ratty little head nodded up and down so quickly he once again lost his balance.

"You'll receive one third now," Tank continued, as if he brokered deals with greedy fathers every day of the week. "The remaining two-thirds will come when you sign the final custody paperwork."

"Of course." Nick's voice sweetened. Now he sounded like he was toadying up to rich parents at Highlands.

I turned away, disgusted that I'd let myself lose sleep over such a small, small man.

Then Harper was sidling back under my arm, her cop minders left behind for the moment. Her words, when they emerged, were mouse-like. "I don't have to go to Highlands if it's too expensive...."

I winced. Harper had seen what I'd been hoping to shield her from. If her father was willing to sell her to the highest bidder, of course she'd consider her place with anyone else threatened by thin ice.

But there was no ice beneath her feet when it came to me. And the assurance of continuing at Highlands, at least, I could offer her.

Or, rather, Tank could offer it to her. I risked a single glance in his direction, my head cocked in question. He rolled his eyes as if to say, *Didn't I already make that clear?*

Smiling, I hugged Harper a little closer. Then I told her: "You can go wherever you want to go. You're my *sister.*"

Harper's body tensed rather than relaxing. "Half sister," she whispered, low enough so the police officers couldn't hear her. "Tank gave me the idea to hunt for the birth certificate, but I'm pretty sure Nick's my father."

I was too...and that made exactly zero difference. "You're my *sister*," I repeated. "And I would do anything to give you what you want. I can talk to Clara if that's the hangup...."

"Naw, she already texted." Harper shrugged, but this time her cheeks bunched up into a half-squashed smile. "We're going to ask to room together again next year. If you can afford it, I want to go back."

I swallowed against the lump in my throat. Soon, Harper wouldn't need me. She was already starting to fight her own battles.

So instead of asking more questions, I hugged her closer. For this instant, at least, my sister was all mine.

Epilogue

Seven weeks later....

Frosty leaves crunched beneath my paws. The red fox in front of me—Kira—turned her head to glare backwards. Then she gestured with her chin toward Harper, who had managed to stay completely silent despite walking beside us in clunky human form.

I rolled my eyes at the two of them. Yes, I got it. I was a slow learner. I hadn't spent much of my life four-legged, so there was plenty left to pick up on.

Still, it wasn't as if we were in any danger. We were out for a solstice stroll on Gunner's land, a prelude to the wild and crazy party I'd heard would take place that evening. I inhaled a deep breath of cold forest and trotted after Kira's receding tail tip, trying a little harder to keep quiet.

Harper didn't try so hard. She giggled at our exchange, and neither Kira nor I glared at her. Instead, I grinned and the scent drifting off Kira suggested she did as well.

This was what it had been like ever since we arrived for my sister's winter break. Tank had broached the topic during one of our ill-fated fae-hunting trips, and as soon as my sister heard about the offer to spend winter break among werewolves she'd insisted I accept. Her instincts had been good. The gruff, growly alpha I'd spoken to on the phone turned out to be a cuddly teddy bear. Mai, his mate, was a font of knowledge about raising a teenaged sister. And the rest of the pack fell all over themselves to make us both feel at home.

Only Tank remained strangely standoffish. That first day, he'd shown me and Harper to a two-bedroom house in the middle of the pack village, one that appeared to have been emptied out just for our use. He dutifully checked on us once a day. Otherwise, though, he left us to our own devices. He'd even taken to dipping his chin around me, as if he was afraid of being judged for his new scars.

Which was why Kira had decided we were going Tank hunting. "I watched him yesterday," she'd told me and Harper over breakfast. "He heads out into the woods every morning. Doesn't come back until after sunset. We should follow him. See what he's up to."

I'd agreed because of the way Harper's eyes lit up at the prospect of hunting. But also because a few hours alone in the forest sounded blissful. Gunner's pack was almost too welcoming. I hadn't enjoyed a moment to myself since we'd arrived.

And I wasn't fated to enjoy a moment to myself now either. Kira, despite her chiding over my loud footsteps, wasn't able to restrain her mischievous nature. As Harper and I rounded a boulder, my sister shrieked as a fox landed atop her head.

They spun in a tight circle, my sister lunging at Kira and Kira dancing from head to shoulders and back again. Add in teenage emoting and the result sounded like a massacre.

No wonder Tank came running. A flannel shirt hung half off his lupine body as he barreled toward us four-legged....

Of course, there'd been no need to run. Because Harper had grown into herself over the last seven weeks. No longer did she default to her friends' wisdom. Now she made one final grab, this time connecting with the ruff of the fox's neck. Then she shook Kira just hard enough to get her attention before dropping the smaller creature to the ground.

"Shift back. Now." Harper's furrowed brows made her look an awful lot like the pack's alpha during one of his rare growly moments. And, despite her lack of shifter blood, the effort worked.

A two-legged Kira peered up at us from where she'd landed, buck naked atop the frozen leaves. She didn't exactly look contrite, but she *did* look adorable. "Aw, come on. I was just having fun."

Harper wasn't so easily swayed. She'd already removed her backpack and now she dropped layers of fabric onto Kira's head and shoulders. "Clothes. Shoes. Get dressed. It's time to leave the love birds alone."

Love birds? Okay, they had a point.

Tank and I had both turned human while my sister was dealing with her friend. His flannel shirt had made its way around my shoulders, his right arm settling around my waist.

My left arm followed suit, cupping naked muscles. No wonder the cold of the day abruptly warmed.

"Scat," Tank growled, pretending to be mad at the teenagers.

Kira hissed at him, even though she was now fully human. "Whatever. Didn't want to see your naked butt anyway."

"Yeah, I've seen way too many of those lately," Harper agreed. She graced us both with an attitude-enhanced wave, then she and Kira scampered back the way they'd come.

***

Alone, the ease with which my body had pressed up against Tank faltered. During the last seven weeks when we'd been living separately, he and I had carved out date nights and filled entire days with joint projects. The shared hours had melted in my mouth like rich chocolate. Still, it felt strangely different to be here with him amid his pack.

Perhaps that's why I took a step backwards, regretting it the moment his arm fell away from me. The absence of warmth reminded me that Tank was completely naked. "You must be frozen."

"Colder now." His eyes crinkled and

then, yes, his chin dipped.

"What's with that?" I tilted his face back level with one finger. Asked the question I'd been wondering about ever since I'd made my decision to use Marina's boon for Butch's sake. "Do you wish I'd asked Marina to take away your scars?"

Maddeningly, he answered my question with a question. "Do the scars bother you?"

My wolf was the one who growled out our answer. "You know they don't."

And...Tank smiled. Didn't dip his chin at all as he answered. "Then, no. I wouldn't change a thing about the past."

For one long moment we stood there, separated by air and unasked questions. His eyes were all I saw, deep wells of kindness and understanding.

Then he rumbled out what sounded like an invitation. "I'd wanted to wait until tonight to show you. Put in a few finishing touches. But we can go now if you want."

Show me what? Rather than asking, I cocked my head then nodded. And...my hand was in his, Tank's forward momentum pulling me deeper into the forest.

All the while, I had the most stunning view imaginable. Tank's naked butt.

I was so intent on the shifting musculature, in fact, that I didn't realize what he'd led me to. Not until he tilted my chin upwards just like I'd done to him a moment earlier. My cheeks reddened as my jaw dropped.

Because there was a tiny house in front of us. Like the witch's gingerbread cottage out of Hansel and Gretel. Small but so carefully constructed it was a thing of beauty. I itched to pull out my sketchbook and capture the way the structure perched beside an icy waterfall.

"What do you think?" Tank sounded shy now. Which made no sense.

"It's stunning. What is it?"

"A retreat. For when the pack gets to be too packish. A place to paint maybe. Or to draw."

I frowned. Tank was many things, but I hadn't realized he was an artist. "You draw?"

"*You* draw," he corrected. Then he

opened the door and led me inside.

There was a fire in a pint-sized wood stove, or so I assumed when I drew closer to the room's center and was hit by a cascade of warmth. Windows were placed just right to capture the sunlight, which in turn illuminated an easel. One side of the room opened into a miniature kitchen. Above us, a loft was filled with what appeared to be a queen-sized bed.

I raised my eyebrows. Felt my cheeks bunching up into a grin that felt like one of Kira's. "Tank Morales. Is this a love nest?"

I didn't realize what I was saying until the words emerged. *Love* nest. By silent yet mutual consent, Tank and I hadn't talked about this whatever-it-was growing between us. Hadn't tried to pin our emotions down into words.

And even though I wasn't very experienced with relationships, I had a feeling two months together might be too soon to throw around the L word. Once again, I'd put my foot into my mouth.

I started to backpedal and Tank spoke right over me. He straightened, looked me directly in the eyes as if he'd never dipped his chin once. "I want you to know that I would never use an alpha compulsion against you."

"An alpha compulsion?" I cocked my head, realizing that concern had never even occurred to me. And why should it? I trusted Tank. He'd never order me around the way Rowan had.

"Our partnership would be equal," he continued. "I want my mate to be happy."

His mate. The heat from the wood stove was blazing now. As if someone had thrown on ten extra logs...which clearly hadn't happened. I unbuttoned the top of my borrowed flannel, feeling Tank's eyes latch onto the triangle of bared skin as if I'd just stripped myself bare.

Well, why not? I undid another button. Another. "Is that a question?" I demanded.

"Would you like it to be?" He stepped forward, huge and imposing and wonderful. His hands helped me wriggle out of the arms of the shirt he'd lent me.

And I didn't flinch away from either his words or his fingers. Instead, I leaned into both of them.

"Yes," I told him. "Yes, I would."

I hope you enjoyed *Moon Glamour*! Butch's adventure is up next in *Charmed Wolf*. While you wait, you can enjoy a bonus scene through Tank's eyes and a tidbit about face blindness (along with two free werewolf novels) when you sign up for my email list at www.aimeeeasterling.com.

Meanwhile, if you haven't already checked out the Moon Marked series, you're in for a treat. The trilogy follows Mai and Gunner while allotting plenty of page time for Tank and Kira. The first book, *Wolf's Bane*, is free in ebook form on all retailers.

Thank you for reading. You are why I write.